SAPPHIRE

A Lt. Kate Gazzara Novel Book 3

BLAIR HOWARD

A Lt. Kate Gazzara Novel

By

Blair Howard

Dedication

This one is for Jo, as always

Chapter One

Tuesday, September 8, 1987

Bolton County, Ohio

Ohio State Trooper Dan Walker rolled his cruiser off the road onto the grass shoulder. Well, to call it grass would be something of an exaggeration. It was, in fact, a dry patch of dirt, deeply rutted and surrounded by tall weeds and grass-like undergrowth skirted by unfettered woodland: low-lying vegetation, small trees growing beneath large trees, dense and impenetrable...or was it?

Dan really didn't care. He needed to take a whiz in the worst way, and he knew this was as good a spot as any; he'd used it many times. A quick pee just inside the tree line where no one could see—then set up the radar and wait. *Yeah, sit and wait, that's what I'll do*, he thought dryly and chuckled, knowing full well a nap was in his near future. He turned off the engine, exited the cruiser, locked it, and then ambled off through the weeds.

He unzipped, tilted his head up, closed his eyes, and sighed deeply as he relieved himself. For maybe two minutes he stood there, enjoying the moment, then shook it vigorously. *Only three times,* he thought grinning—*any more than that is considered playing with yourself. Ahhh*—and then he zipped up.

He was about to turn and go back to his cruiser when he spotted something.

He squinted through the flickering sunbeams that filtered through the treetops. *Hmmm,* he thought. *I don't remember seeing that before.*

It was just off to one side, maybe fifteen feet away.

It's a box, a wooden box. What the hell?

He looked around. He didn't like leaving his cruiser unattended, but it wasn't as if this was the interstate. It was, in fact, nothing more than a rural two-lane roadway, little traveled and quiet.

He turned again and squinted at the object of interest.

Dumped. Rolled down the slope. Whatever it is, it's big. Okay, so let's go take a peek. Aw shit, my damn pants...and my friggin' leg.

His uniform pant leg had snagged on a bramble of some sort, tearing a triangular hole in the material and scratching his skin.

Damn, damn, damn! He almost turned back, but he didn't. Why he didn't, he wasn't sure. What he was sure of was the uncomfortable, itchy feeling at the back of his neck.

He stumbled through the underbrush until he finally reached his objective.

Yeah, it's a box. Solid. Well made. Good box. Why would anyone... He stared down at it, his stomach rising to his throat. He had a horrible feeling that he knew what it was. The box was maybe four feet long by twenty inches by twenty-four and made from three-quarter-inch plywood. He looked around, taking in every inch of the terrain.

If this is what I think it is... He kicked the side of the box. It moved slightly. *Hmmm, not heavy. Maybe not, then. Okay. Now what? Better call it in, I suppose. You never know.*

He turned and struggled through the vegetation, back up the slope, and out onto the dirt patch where his cruiser was parked.

He slid into the car and keyed his mike.

"11 to Post 44. Signal 3."

"44 to 11. Go ahead."

"Show me Signal 3 on a large wooden box off the road on Highway 52 Northbound, Milepost 333. No vehicles or persons nearby."

There was a pause, then:

"44 to 11, PC Allerton advises caution."

The post commander? Geez!

"Okay," Dan replied but waited for a moment, thought about what he wanted to say, then said, "11 to 44. The box is a large wooden container, sealed. There is no apparent name or label present. What do you advise?"

"44 to 11. Lieutenant Allerton is sending Sergeant Beavers to your location to assist. Do not attempt to open the container until he arrives."

"11 to 44, copy."

And so he waited, closing his eyes after turning off the radar, and he didn't open them again until Sergeant Billy Beavers arrived some thirty minutes later.

"Whatcha got, Dan?" his voice boomed through the open window of the cruiser, startling Dan awake. "Caughtcha nappin', did I?"

"Er, no. No! I was just restin' my eyes. Sun's bright today, Sarge."

"Restin' your eyes, my ass. You were asleep. I catch you again—an' I'll be watchin'—your ass will be grass. Understand?" He didn't wait for an answer. Instead, he asked, "So where's this box, then?"

Dan led him down the slope through the undergrowth to where it lay, just as he'd left it. Sergeant Beavers crouched down beside it, stared closely at it, leaned in close and sniffed at one corner. He stood and said, "No smell. It's what, four feet by two by two? Can't be anything much. You should have a pry bar in your unit. Go get it. Let's open this baby up."

He did, and they did, but neither one of them was prepared for what they found inside.

The top came off easily enough; just a few nails, bright and shiny in the sunbeams. Inside was what appeared to be bundles of old clothing wrapped in a colored blanket.

On their knees now, they leaned over the open box, heads almost together. Beavers reached tentatively over the edge and touched the blanket, poked it with a forefinger, then took hold of an edge between finger and thumb and pulled. The blanket moved easily enough; he dragged it back some more, revealing...

"Oh shit!" Beavers gasped, dropping the blanket and reeling back, landing on his butt. He could still see the empty eye sockets staring balefully back at him.

"Holy crap! Leave it alone," Beavers said, grabbing Walker's arm and scooting himself back away from the box. "Don't touch it, Dan."

"Don't worry. I ain't."

Together they stared, mesmerized, at the partially revealed skull. Then still staring into the box, Beavers said, "Go back to your unit and call the sheriff. Be careful how you walk; disturb the scene as little as possible. Have Milt get his crime scene team out here. When you've done that, call Allerton and let 'im know what we got. Then wait at the roadside. I'll stay here."

~

BACKUP ARRIVED QUICKLY, IN LESS THAN FIFTEEN
minutes. The first to arrive was Bolton County Sheriff
Milton "Milt" Grambling—known fondly to his deputies as
"Grumbling Milt." Grambling was quickly followed by the
crime scene "team," which consisted of Bolton County's
only forensic tech Deputy Rufus Watson. The next to
arrive was Deputy Gene Drake, one of the county's two
full-time detectives. The part-time coroner who was also the
full-time funeral director, Lawrence "Birdie" Cackleton,
arrived a few minutes later; he was driving his hearse. He
parked the vehicle on the shoulder, barely leaving enough
space for other vehicles to pass. Then he flipped his keys to
Dan Walker, still on the road by his cruiser, and joined the
others now standing in a wide circle around the box.

Cackleton, acting as coroner, stooped down beside the box
and stared at the partially uncovered skull, shook his head
thoughtfully, then said, "This one's been dead a long time…"

"No shit," Deputy Watson let slip.

Cackleton looked sharply up at him, opened his mouth to
speak, but changed his mind. He stared into the box,
thinking for a moment, walked slowly around it, his hands
in his pants pockets, and then shook his head before gently
moving aside the remaining coverings.

Slowly, carefully, he uncovered the rest of the skull, then
paused and leaned back so everyone else in the group
could see.

"Holy shit!" Deputy Drake said in an awed voice.

"No shit," Cackleton said, dryly, and then resumed stripping away the blanket and rolled-up items of clothing beneath it.

As he worked his way down from the head, because of the size of the box, he began to think he was dealing with what once had been a little person, a "dwarf," but it soon became evident that that wasn't the case. The legs had been severed at the knee and the lower leg portions, having then been wrapped, were placed neatly beside the hips.

Finally, the coroner stood, legs akimbo, hands stuffed deep inside his pants pockets, head bowed. He remained motionless, staring down at the skeletonized body.

"As I said, been dead a long time; completely dried out: everything—blanket, clothing, bones. What little tissue's left is like leather. Ain't no way to figure time of death; two... three years, maybe more, maybe even five or six. Has to be a homicide. Someone chopped off the damn legs; her fingers are missing too. But here's the thing: the box is clean—looks like it might have been made yesterday. It ain't been out here more'n a few hours, a day at most. See the grass under it?" He stooped, grabbed a corner of the box and lifted it a little; the grass underneath it was crushed flat, but fresh and green. "So where the hell has it been? Where did it come from?"

He lowered the box, stood up, stuck his hands back in his pockets. "We should probably get the bones to Doc Lewiston. He's done this kind of thing before. Maybe he can determine the cause of death," Cackleton said, looking at Sheriff Grambling. "Unless you want to turn it over to the BCI, that is?"

"The Bureau of Criminal Investigation?" Grambling tilted his head and stared at the coroner. "Hell no. No offense, Sergeant Beavers," he said to the state patrol officer.

Beavers rewarded him with a sloppy grin but said nothing.

"We can work it, right, Gene?"

Detective Gene Drake looked decidedly uncomfortable but nodded anyway.

"Yeah, course we can," Grambling said to no one in particular. "Okay! It's your case, Gene. I suggest you start by checking missing persons for the past six years... What?"

"Sheriff," Drake said. "We don't even know if it's a man or a woman. How'm I supposed to do a proper search without knowin' that?"

"How tall's the body, Birdie?"

"Hell, how should I know? It's in pieces, for Pete's sake." He paused and stared thoughtfully down into the box, his lips moving silently.

"At a guess, five-two, five-four."

"So a woman, then?" Grambling asked.

"Could be, could also be a kid, or a short guy."

"Damn it, Birdie. I need better'n that. What about the hair? It looks long, so a woman?"

"As I said," Cackleton said, "you need to get the bones over to Doc Lewiston. He'll be able to tell you for sure."

"Okay, do it, but wait until Rufus gets finished examining the scene," Grambling said. "Now, everybody else get outa here and let him get to it. Birdie, you wait up on the road until he's done, then take it all to Lewiston."

And that's what they did.

It was later determined by the local GP, Dr. Lewiston, to be the body of a young woman aged between twenty and thirty. He identified the cause of death was due to manual strangulation—the hyoid bone was broken—and estimated it had occurred sometime between three and six years earlier.

Detective Drake initiated a three-state search of missing person reports for the years 1980 through 1987, but to no avail. Eventually, the investigation stalled and, though he worked the case diligently for more than a year, the woman in the box remained unidentified. The case went cold and was eventually shelved and forgotten, until...

Chapter Two

❧

Thursday, May 7, 2015

Chattanooga, Tennessee

It was cold that Thursday afternoon back in May 2015 when Assistant Chief Henry Finkle walked into my office. The heating had been off for hours. Finkle's arrival, however, added a new chill to the surroundings: the never-ending unwanted attention I received from him was, even then, becoming almost unbearable. It finally came to a head... Oh, but that's a story for another time.

My name, by the way, is Lieutenant Catherine Gazzara, Kate to my friends. I've been a cop since 2002. Today, I work homicide in the Major Crimes Unit at the Chattanooga Police Department, have done so for more than ten years. Well, except for a stint with the Cold Case Squad back in 2015 when all this took place.

As usual, Finkle barged into my office without knocking, startling me...

Assistant Chief Henry "Tiny" Finkle. Tiny? Yeah, tiny in both stature and mind, but no one had the guts to call him that, at least not to his face. He was a diminutive little man: just five-eight and slim, maybe a hundred and forty pounds. Nobody knew how old he was—he kept it a closely guarded secret. I figured him to be in his early-to-mid forties; his brown hair had yet to show the first gray hair. His thin face, high cheekbones, thin nose, and beady black eyes all reminded me of a possum. Rat might have been a better description. Though his signature shit-eating grin made him a dead ringer for Disney's cat in Cinderella. He was also a bigot and a misogynist. I put up with his asinine remarks and pathetic attempts at flirting because I had to. If I could, I'd report him for harassment, but he was smart, didn't do it in public. Someday I'd figure out how to stop him...

"A-hah," he said, lightly. "Caught you napping, did I?"

I looked up at him, sighed, then said, "What do you want, Finkle?"

"What I want is a wild night between the sheets with you. How about it, Kate? How about we get out of here, rent a sleazy little motel room for a couple of hours, and I—"

"Give it up, Finkle," I interrupted him. "First, I'm sure a couple of minutes would be more than enough. Second, you're married. Third, I hate your guts and would rather die than let you within ten feet of me. But you knew all that, so what do you really want?"

He grinned the grin, seemingly unperturbed by the rejection. "The chief wants you and your partner in his office, now."

"What does he want?"

He leered at me, turned to go, hesitated, then looked back at me. "Nothing good, I hope."

I watched the door close behind him, pursed my lips and shook my head, exasperated.

I sat for a moment staring at the several piles of paperwork on my desk, gave a sigh, rose to my feet and headed out of my office, through the situation room toward the elevator. Chief Johnston's suite of offices was on the first floor at the far end of the building.

I threaded my way through the maze of jumbled desks to where my newly minted partner, Sergeant Lonnie Guest, was seated at his desk, his eyes mere inches from his computer screen, and tapped him on the shoulder.

"What?" he said, without looking away from the screen. "Can'tcha see I'm busy?"

"Busy doing what?" I asked, looking at the screen over his shoulder. "If that's porn..." I could see that it wasn't, but I'd already learned that Lonnie was quite addicted to the sad side of life. *He needs a good woman,* I thought as I looked down at him. *He's not a bad-looking guy. Maybe if he lost a little weight... Nah! A lot of weight.*

He rolled his seat away from the desk and looked up at me, smiling. "Not this time, LT. What's up?"

"The chief wants us. Let's go." I turned away, gesturing for him to follow me.

I always thought the long walk along the corridor to the chief's office must be something akin to the condemned man's last walk to the execution chamber. I'd been a cop for more than thirteen years, and I'd taken that walk many times; nothing good ever came of it.

So, it was with a feeling of deep trepidation that I walked into the great man's outer office that day. Cathy, his secretary, looked up and smiled at me, somewhat sympathetically, so I thought.

"You can go on in, Lieutenant. He's waiting for you."

I nodded and pushed through the heavy soundproof doors into Chief Wesley Johnston's inner sanctum.

Johnston was seated as he always was behind his desk, his back ramrod straight, bald head shining in the weak sunlight that shone in through the window. The shaft of sunlight had an almost ethereal effect. I wouldn't have been surprised to hear heavenly music playing softly in the background.

Johnston was—still is—a big man. Not overly tall but hefty, powerful. Probably from being ex-military. Marines, I think. His uniform was pressed, the creases sharp, perfect. A gold clip held his tie precisely in place. The gold stars on his collar glittered as he moved. His big head was round, shaved, and polished to a shine; the huge white eyebrows were a perfect match for the Hulk Hogan mustache. And he had an air of authority about him, not arrogance... Well, not exactly, but he was used to getting his own way, and he expected unquestioning obedience from his staff and the entire department.

Assistant Chief Henry Finkle was at the right side of the desk, his arms folded across his chest, the ever-present grin belied the narrow chips of ice that were his eyes. I looked from one to the other. Johnston had already adopted the pose: he was now leaning back in his chair, his elbows on the armrests, his hands curled into fists except for his fore-fingers which were steepled together at his lips, chin lowered almost to his chest. I'd seen it so many times before. Finkle? There was no way to know what was going on between his tiny ears but, from the way he looked me up and down, I could guess.

"Good afternoon, Lieutenant Gazzara," Johnston said over his steepled fingertips. "Please sit down. You too, Sergeant Guest."

I sat down on one of the two seats in front of the desk; Lonnie sat in the other.

Johnston stared across the desk at me. I had a feeling he was waiting for me to speak. I didn't. What could I say?

Finally, he broke the silence.

"How long have you been with the department, Lieutenant?"

That took me by surprise.

"Thirteen years," I said, wondering what the hell he wanted. He knew good and well how long; he knew everything about me, and about everybody else in the department, but there was more to come, a lot more. He began to question me in depth, about both the professional and personal aspects of my life. Questions about my career were okay, and to be expected, but I was decidedly uncomfortable when he asked about my relationships, especially with Henry Finkle sitting there grinning like an idiot. So I did my best to bob and weave. But in the end, when the name Harry Starke came up, I drew the line and informed him that my personal life was my own and that I wouldn't talk about it further.

I expected him to push the issue, but he didn't. Instead, he nodded, then asked, "Do you like your job, Catherine?"

Like my job? Catherine? Nobody calls me that. What the hell?

"Yes, Chief. I do. Why do you ask?"

He tilted his head sideways and looked me in the eyes.

"Why, exactly, do you like your job?"

What the hell kind of question is that? Am I about to get fired?

I thought for a minute, then said, "There's no good answer to that, Ch—"

Finkle sniggered, interrupting me. I cut him a sharp look. He grinned back at me, unperturbed. Johnston acted like he hadn't heard.

"As I was saying," I continued, trying hard not to roll my eyes. "There's no good answer to the question. I'm a cop, a good one, and I enjoy it. It's what I do. Always will."

He nodded. "Good enough... So, I have something special, something new, I'd like to try. It has your name written all over it. Do you want it?"

When the chief asks a question like that, there's really only one way to answer. But what the hell, it was time to buck the system.

I held his gaze and said, "That depends on what it is."

I thought he was going to explode.

Finkle sniggered again.

"That's enough, Henry," Johnston said, almost too quietly for me to hear. Finkle nodded and smiled at me like my demise was imminent.

The chief stared sternly at me for a long moment then, to my surprise, he shook his head and chuckled. I was completely taken aback.

"That's my Kate," he said. "All right, Lieutenant, I'll tell you. I've decided to create a new department, a cold case squad if you will, and you're it—you and your partner."

He glanced at Lonnie, then looked back at me and continued. "And when I say, 'you're it,' I mean exactly that, just the two of you. You will, of course, have access to any of our resources you may need, including forensics. I'll consider requests for extra manpower, of course, but those must go through Assistant Chief Finkle. Now, are you up for it?"

"Well...yes, I suppose, but why me?"

"As you said yourself, Lieutenant: you're a good cop. You're an even better detective, one of my best. Your talents are wasted chasing down drive-bys and domestics. We have a backlog of unsolved homicides that goes back decades. I'd like to see some progress on those, and I'd like for you to begin with these."

He leaned forward and pushed a pile of file folders across the desk toward me.

"There are plenty more where they came from, hundreds more. The one on top, the Sullivan case, I'd like you to make a priority. It's...well, let's put it this way, I knew Rhonda Sullivan. No, she wasn't a friend, just someone I knew. It's a strange case, as you'll see when you get into the file—no, don't look at it now, later.

"You should also know that I've scheduled an official launch for the squad, a party... Well, a reception at the Chattanoogan on Wednesday evening at seven o'clock. The mayor has agreed to attend, so will I, along with several senior officers and, of course, so will the press, and so will you and Sergeant Guest. The reception will also be open to the general public."

Oh hell, that sounds like it will be a blast.

The Chattanoogan is an upscale, downtown resort hotel. I'd been to several functions there, so I was quite familiar with it.

I glanced at Lonnie and inwardly shook my head at the supercilious look on his face. I think he was flattered to be included. *Give him time,* I thought. *Give him time.*

I looked at Finkle. He'd not said a word. His face was now expressionless.

"Yes, sir, but I have a question. I have a full caseload—"

"Yes, of course you do," Johnston interrupted. "Henry and I have already discussed it, and he's agreed to take care of it. Please have everything turned over to him by close of day. Well, that's it, I think. Thank you, Lieutenant. I'll see you at the reception. That will be all."

I looked at my watch. The meeting had gone on a lot longer than I thought it had. *Damn, it's already three o'clock.*

"Yes, sir. Thank you, sir!" I said, rising to my feet.

He nodded, looked up at me and said, "Don't let me down, Kate."

"No, sir. I won't."

I gathered up the files, handed them off to Lonnie, and we left. I could feel Finkle's eyes on my ass as I walked to the door and pulled it open. I turned my head and cut him a look I fervently hoped would shrivel his...

Back in my office, I had Lonnie dump the files on my credenza and then go fetch us some coffee while I cleared the open homicide cases off my desk. He was back in a matter of minutes before I'd even made a start. He shouldered through the door bearing two large mugs of what we laughingly called coffee.

"You need some help?" he asked as he plonked himself down in front of my desk, making it clear that he hoped I didn't.

"No, Lonnie. Just sit there, drink your coffee, and watch while I do all the work." The sarcasm was lost on him.

I took a sip of my coffee and looked at my watch. *Less than two hours.*

End of day for Henry Finkle meant five o'clock, and I knew I could expect him to be right on time. *Damn it all to hell! I wanted to at least be able to glance through the chief's file.*

I got busy. I tidied and closed three of the open files I'd been working on that morning and set them to one side. The reports within were up-to-date so I felt good about handing them off as they were. The rest of my workload, more than a dozen open cases, I organized into some sort of order and then shoved them into two plastic postal-style totes. It was all straightforward enough.

Oh, don't run away with the idea that I was done with any of it. That's not the way things happen. I would have to bring the individual detectives who received them up to speed on each case as they assimilated them into their own caseloads, and I'd be on call to answer questions from said detectives for at least a couple of weeks.

"So, what are you thinking?" Lonnie asked as I dumped the last three files into the tote and closed the lid.

As I looked down at my empty desktop that afternoon, I suddenly realized it was a sight I hadn't seen in the more than five years since I'd been promoted back in 2010. *Wow!*

"About what?" I asked as I retrieved the cold case files from the credenza and dropped them in the middle of the desk.

"Come on, LT. You know what. Cold Case Squad? What kinda bull is that? What's the old man thinkin' of?"

"Well, it's been done before, with some success, I believe, especially now with the advances in forensic science."

"Yeah, but—"

"Lonnie," I said as I slapped my hand down on the top of the pile. "These are all homicides, unsolved. That means there are people—families, mothers, fathers, sons, daughters —out there who want answers, justice, not to mention the killers that are roaming around out there, killers that could do it again. Some of them may already have."

I stared thoughtfully down at the pile of manila folders, then looked up at him and said, quietly, "You want out, Lonnie? I can arrange that." I said it with a smile, but he took it literally and bestowed a hurt look on me.

"No. 'Course not. I was just sayin'."

"Yeah, I know," I said as I sat down behind my desk. "Let's just enjoy the moment, okay. I have a feeling our new department will be like a donkey's gallop: soon over. As I said, it's not the first time, and it probably won't be the last. So, let's make a start."

I picked up the folder at the top of the pile, the Sullivan Case, and then the one beneath it. "Here," I said, handing it to him. "Take a look at this one." It was a slim, faded folder, less than a half-inch thick. The name and date *John Doe 367: January 11, 2001* typed on the label. "See what you can make of it."

He nodded, took it from me, sat down facing me across the desk, opened it, and began flipping through its contents.

Me? I picked up the Sullivan file, of course. The one Johnston had made clear was to be my priority. I flipped through the pages: the autopsy report, the detectives' reports, evidence lists, a DVD, and a stack of photographs. Then I set everything aside except for the DVD.

"Hey," I said. "Stick this in the player, would you please?" I handed him the jewel case.

As he did so, I sorted through the clutter in my desk drawer, found the remote, turned on the player, and settled down to watch. Lonnie turned his chair so that he could watch too.

The video was quite short, a little more than fifteen minutes, and was shot entirely inside the victim's apartment. Other than several minutes of footage of the victim lying face down on her bed, there was little of interest. The videographer had, with the exception of the body and the bedroom, shot only overall views of the two-bedroom apartment. The place was pristine: the bathroom clean, spotless. The personal items on the vanity were tidy and unremarkable. Her clothes were hung neatly in her closet. The interiors of the dresser, nightstand, and bathroom drawers were tidy. Everything was neatly arranged. *Maybe too neat. Was she OCD, I wonder?*

The kitchen was the same. It looked as if it had never been used and likewise the second bedroom. It was also spotless and tidy. The one anomaly was the body in the victim's bedroom.

The victim, as I said, was lying face down, and I do mean *face down,* at an angle across her bed. She was wearing a floral dress that appeared to be undisturbed. *Sexual abuse? Doesn't look like it.* I checked the autopsy report—*Nope.*

Her face was hidden in the bed linen, her arms stretched straight down alongside her. Her hands, palms down, were touching her hips, fingers curled, not quite fists. *Looks staged.*

Her feet were bare and sticking out maybe twelve inches off the bed, toes down, and from those alone it was easy to see that she'd been dead for quite some time: from the mid-soles to the tips of her toes, they were almost black. Lividity was fully set. *So, at least eight hours, then.* Again, I checked the autopsy report. *Twenty to twenty-four hours. Time of death on Sunday, sometime between nine PM and midnight.* That according to Doc Sheddon, who attended the crime scene and did the autopsy.

I ran the video several times, hoping something would catch my eye, but there was nothing, not a damn thing. Even her hair looked tidy. I froze the video at a point where we had a good shot of the body.

I stared at it for a moment, then sighed and looked quizzically at Lonnie.

"What d'you make of it?" I asked.

He cocked his head. "Looks staged to me. Someone laid her out like a board, but why would they do that? It makes no sense. It doesn't look natural."

Yeah, that's it, like a board.

"To hide something, maybe?" I said.

"Like what? A weapon? Hardly."

I pushed the file to one side and spread out the stack of eight-by-ten color photographs.

"Come and look," I said as I gazed at the array of images.

He came around the desk and stood behind me.

Most of the images were wide-angle shots taken inside the apartment; several of them were of the body, taken from various angles. Some were taken during the autopsy. One shot, in particular, caught my eye. It was a close-up of the inner fold of her elbow. Now I knew why the arms had been positioned the way they were. The entire underside of the arm was dark purple: lividity, but right in the center of the elbow crease, it was just possible to see a tiny bruise, which was obviously the subject of the photo. What it was, I had no idea.

All except nine of the photos, including those taken at the autopsy, were signed on the back and dated 10/9/2006; the others were taken a day later on Tuesday, October 10.

One was of a detective, whom I didn't recognize, standing inside a dumpster and holding up what appeared to be a large, white plastic bag with red drawstrings. The second photo was a closeup of the bag itself. It was lying on the floor beside the dumpster and appeared to be about three-fourths full. There was another photo of the same bag—open this time with its contents in a pile on the floor. Visible among those contents was a second, smaller plastic bag: a well-known supermarket grocery bag, the top of which had been twisted and tied in a knot. A fourth photograph was a closeup of the grocery bag and its contents.

I picked it up, handed it to Lonnie, and said, "The murder weapon, I think. Where did they find it, I wonder?"

He took it from me, and as I turned back to my desk, I happened to look at my watch. It was just a few minutes short of five o'clock. *No way. Damn. Tiny will be here in a minute. I should—*

"Here, gimme that," I said, snatching the photograph from his hand. "I have to get the rest of my stuff to Finkle. I'll have to continue this tomorrow," I said as I ejected the disk from the player, scooped up the reports and photos and returned everything to the file. But it was too late, the door burst open and in he sauntered.

"Oh, don't stop what you're doing on my account." He dropped his tight little ass into the seat Lonnie had just vacated, crossed his legs, folded his arms, and...yeah, he grinned the grin. Inwardly, I shuddered, but outwardly I smiled at him and said," We're all done, Chief. Just wrapping it up so that I could turn those over to you." I nodded toward the two totes in the corner.

He looked his watch. "A little early, don't you think? You must have a hot date. Anyone I know?"

I ignored the question and said, "Lonnie, give the assistant chief a hand with those two totes. They're probably more than he can handle by himself."

The grin now had teeth and was fixed.

"Now, gentlemen," I said, lightly. "I have some calls to make, work-related of course." That was only partly true, but what the hell?

Somewhat reluctantly, I thought, Finkle stood and waited for Lonnie, who rounded my desk and grabbed one of the totes.

"Where to, Chief?" he asked.

"My office, of course. I'll talk to you later, Lieutenant."

He waited until Lonnie left my office. "You should know, Lieutenant, that I advised Johnston not to give you this assignment. I don't think you're up to it." He glared at me then stepped over to the corner and lifted the remaining tote, one-handed. *The man has something to prove, methinks.*

"Don't think I won't be watching you," he said. "Screw it up and..." He didn't finish his thought. Instead he walked out the door, the tote swinging from his right hand almost dragging on the floor.

I WAITED UNTIL HE CLOSED THE DOOR BEHIND HIM, then called Harry Starke.

Back then, Harry and I had what one might call a semi-serious relationship ever since he'd left the police department more than three years earlier, even longer than that if the truth be told. Serious? Hah, for me more than him, I think. He'd finally crossed the line a few months earlier, during the Harper investigation. He had one little fling too many, so we split up, sort of. I tried to distance myself from him, but he was a tough habit to break.

We were supposed to have a date that evening; I wanted to confirm.

Harry was an ex-cop turned private detective, and he was a good one. He ran a private investigation agency in Chattanooga. He was also something of an anomaly: he was extremely wealthy although, by looking at him then, you'd never have known it. Most of the time he was dressed down: jeans, tee, leather jacket, that sort of thing. When he did bother to dress up, it was rarely anything more than dress pants and a golf shirt. He was extremely tough, and back in the day, my day, he had his weaknesses, especially where women were concerned. Oh, he didn't chase after them, well, rarely, but he had a tough time saying no when they chased after him. He was, after all, single, and he'd made no promises to me, though I'd assumed... Okay, I'm rambling again, so that's enough of that. Let's just say that when all this happened, we were still something of an item.

"Hey, Harry," I said when he answered my call.

"Hey, Kate. What's up?"

"We still on for this evening?"

"Of course. Why d'you ask? I made a reservation at the club. Is that okay? I can cancel it if it's not."

"No reason. I was confirming. The club's fine. Meet you at your place about seven?"

"I can pick you up if you like."

"No, I can't stay over. I need an early night. So, seven?"

"Why's that?"

"Umm...well, I have a new job. Look, I can't talk about it now. I'll tell you about it tonight, okay? So, seven?"

"Seven it is." And he hung up before I could say more.

A couple of times Harry had helped out as a sort of unpaid consultant, to good effect—the Harper case had made him famous. But I caught all sorts of crap for it, both from the chief and Finkle, especially from Finkle. Then the chief's daughter went missing and he, the chief, for reasons he never explained, would let nobody near it but Harry. Harry, however, insisted that the chief turn me loose to work with him which, under protest, he did. Funny how things work out.

So, that night, I wanted to run the Sullivan thing by Harry, to see if he'd heard anything.

I looked thoughtfully at the now black screen of my iPhone, and then placed it face down on my desk, reached for the office phone, called Doc Sheddon, and made an appointment to see him the following afternoon at two o'clock.

Chapter Three

Thursday, May 7, 7 PM – Harry's Condo

Harry's condo was situated on the north side of the river, on Lakeshore Lane. It must have cost him a small fortune, and another one to decorate and furnish it. His place was comfortable, elegant, with a stunning view of the Tennessee River and, in the distance, the Thrasher Bridge. At night, the panoramic view from the huge picture window in his living room was stunning... I loved that condo almost as much as I did Harry.

Knowing where I was going that evening, and with whom, and even though it was only Thursday, I'd dressed with some care. I have a thing for black. I think it complements my hair, but that's just me. I'm not into fashion... Well, not so much. Anyway, I decided to wear a version of the quintessential "little black dress," crimson pumps with four-inch heels, and to carry an envelope clutch that matched the shoes. For jewelry, I wore a slim gold chain with a tiny cross around my neck and my grandmother's antique gold wristwatch. Makeup? I never wear much, usually just some lipstick, mascara, and a little blush.

Advantage to me, Harry, I remember thinking as I did a final check in front of the mirror. *The heels make me six-three, an inch taller than you.* Yeah, I felt good. The more so when I saw his face as I walked into his living room that evening. Yes, I still had a key to his condo.

He was standing in front of the great window with a drink in his hand, looking out over the river. And he looked good: black golf slacks and shirt and black loafers.

He turned and watched as I walked toward him; he was smiling.

"Wow," was all he said. He would probably have said more, but I stopped him with a kiss, just a peck on the lips.

He set the glass down on the coffee table and kissed me properly. I closed my eyes and let my emotions take over, but not for long. Such things had a habit of getting out of hand, and I'm not just talking about Harry. Let's just say I enjoyed the long moment and then pushed him away.

He didn't resist. Above all things, Harry Starke was a gentleman. He did, however, unconsciously lick his lips. I couldn't help but smile.

"Drink?" he asked.

"Of course, but just one. I have to drive home."

"No, you don't," he said. "You can stay here. You always do...did."

"Yes, well not tonight. I have a big day tomorrow." I took the half-glass of red from him and sipped appreciatively. Harry loves fine wine, old scotch whiskey, and strong coffee: the red was glorious, and I suddenly had the feeling that I might be staying over after all.

He looked at his watch.

"It's time we left," he said. "Unless..."

"Uh, *no!*" I said. "I'm hungry. I intend to murder a ten-ounce filet, so?"

He nodded, set his glass down and put his hands on my shoulders.

"Wait," I said, and put my glass down beside his. Then I wrapped my arms around his neck, pulled him to me, and once again let my emotions take over: the filet had to wait.

It was almost nine o'clock when we finally sat down at Harry's favorite table at the club, in the bay window overlooking the ninth green.

The steak was amazing, the wine superb, and I was totally at ease, my hunger—not only for food—satisfied completely.

While we ate, I filled Harry in on the events of the day: I told him about my new assignment. He didn't seem particularly impressed. I asked him why.

"Kate, it's been done so many times before. Rarely does it ever end well for the officer in charge. Most cold cases are cold for a reason—lack of evidence. Most of them are unsolvable, and that makes for soul-destroying work. I don't envy you. I hope it goes well."

He gave me a sly smile before continuing. "By the way. When are you going to take me up on my offer and come work for me?"

"Not going to happen, Harry. Being friends is one thing, coworkers would be quite another."

It wasn't the first time he'd asked the question; he always asked. The answer I gave him was always the same.

"Friends?" he asked. "Is that all we are?"

"You know it is," I said, cutting him a look and quickly changing the subject.

"Harry, do you remember the Sullivan case?"

He sighed, shook his head, sorrowfully, thought for a minute, then said, "Yes...vaguely? In oh-six, I think. As I recall there wasn't much to it. I believe there was a suspect, though, a nurse? They were never able to tag him with it though. Wells, I think was the lead investigator; Steve Wells. He retired years ago. So, you caught that one, huh? Again, I don't envy you."

I often wonder how he does it. I think he must have an eidetic memory. He says he doesn't, but he never forgets even the smallest thing.

"There was a suspect?" I asked. I hadn't gotten that far into the reports, but I had noticed the three headshots among the photos, besides that of the victim.

"Yes, a male nurse. That's about all I remember. I had nothing to do with it. You'll need to talk to Wells if he's still alive. Last I heard, he was pretty sick."

"So, you can't help me, then?"

"Nope, and I'm betting no one else can. Wells was a good detective, one of the best. If he couldn't close it, I very much doubt anyone can. You'll find it's a dead end."

"Gee, Harry. Thanks for the vote of confidence."

He shook his head. "It is what it is. Go see Wells."

And, try as I might, I could drag nothing further out of him, at least about the Sullivan case.

All in all though, it was a lovely evening; evenings with Harry always were. I had no hesitation when he suggested we go back to his place: I agreed.

Chapter Four

Friday, May 8, Morning – Office

Needless to say, I was late into work the following morning and who should be waiting for me in my office? Assistant Chief Henry Finkle of course. *Damn*, I thought. *Any other day...*

"It's almost nine o'clock, Lieutenant," he said, sneering at me without getting up, looking me up and down. "Anything I should know about?" The question was filled with innuendo.

"No, I don't think so," I said as I sat down behind my desk. "Should there be?"

"Why are you late? Another wild night with Starke?"

"That, Chief, is none of your damn business. I'm late because there's a wreck on Amnicola, as Sergeant Mayfield in Traffic will confirm." It wasn't the whole truth, but true enough. "Now, is there anything else I can help you with? If not, I have a busy day."

"What are you going to do about the Sullivan case? Chief Johnston asked me to keep an eye on it—"

"Oh, he did?" I interrupted him. "I wonder why. Let's see, shall we?" I reached for my phone.

"There's no need for that," he said, quickly, rising from his seat. "Just make sure you keep me informed. Understood?"

I nodded, smirking at him, and he left my office, slamming the door behind him.

I buzzed Lonnie.

"Hey, come on back. Let's talk," I said when he picked up. "Oh, and bring the Doe file with you."

I wanted to get on with the Sullivan case, but I needed to clear the decks first. To do that, I needed to sort through the rest of the cold files, and to do that I needed help.

Detective Sergeant Lonnie Guest is an enigma. Back then, in the early days of our partnership, I had it in my head that he was something of an idiot; he could act really stupid. Later, much later, I realized that he wasn't stupid at all. It was a persona he actively cultivated. He was the latest in a growing list of partners I'd had foisted on me, mostly because no one else could work with them. Lonnie was dumped on me right out of uniform while I was working the Congressman Gordon Harper case.

Anyway, as I said, Lonnie's not quite as stupid as he would have you believe. In fact, at times, he can be positively brilliant. Physically, he's a big man... No, damn it—at the risk of being non-PC—back then he was fat. He needed to lose sixty or seventy pounds.

You know, on thinking about it, though, I guess the extra weight was a big part of his problem. For sure, he could be a real ass: obnoxious, arrogant. But underneath it all there was a softer side to Lonnie Guest, and you know what? Even then, I kinda liked him, felt comfortable with him.

So, we spent the next hour that morning sorting through the files. There were nine of them; all more than five years cold. The Sullivan case, even after what I'd learned from Harry the night before, I had no option but to deal with right away. The other eight—well, okay, I'm one of those orderly people that like to deal with my projects one at a time, though that's rarely ever possible in a busy department such as ours... Look, if I'm rambling, you'll have to forgive me, but I have to set the stage.

Anyway, that's what I intended to do with the Sullivan case as soon as I cleared my desk. I set it aside, along with the John Doe file—Lonnie had already made a start on that— and together we skimmed through the other seven files.

We discussed each in turn, briefly, making notes along the way and, finally, prioritizing them as best we could. That done, I turned the whole lot of them over to Lonnie with instructions to go through them all again, in detail, and report back to me with his thoughts.

With Lonnie out of the way, it was my intention to devote the next couple of hours to Sullivan, and I was itching to get at it. I checked the time; it was almost eleven-thirty. I went to get more coffee and, on the way back, put out the word that, unless someone died, I wasn't to be disturbed.

Back in my office, I set my coffee on my desk and picked up the somewhat dog-eared manila file folder labeled, *Rhonda Sullivan, October 9, 2006* which was the date the file was opened and the day after Rhonda died. The back of the folder had been signed by the detectives that had followed up on the case over the years: five of them. I added mine to the bottom of the list and dated it, and then opened the file.

First, I extracted the stack of photos and the DVD and set them aside. Then I made a copy of the autopsy report and set it aside also, returning the original to the folder. That done, I stood and taped the photos to my dry-erase board, the photo of Rhonda Sullivan at the top center. The three headshots—two male and one female—I added side-by-side just below Rhonda's. The names meant nothing to me, not then, but I added them to the board under their respective picture with a marker. *At least I know who's who.*

Finally, I taped the rest of the images to the board and stood back, staring at the three unsmiling faces.

I went back to my chair, leaned back, and stared intently at each of the twenty-six images in turn.

Not a damn thing! I thought. *Nothing... No trace, no prints, no blood, nothing but the grocery bag... It wasn't recovered until the next day. What's that about? I need to read the reports.* And I did, and that pretty much accounted for the next couple of hours, and then some, and I learned almost nothing.

Harry was right; it looked impossible. Rhonda Sullivan's body had been found by her friend, Lisa Marco, lying on her bed at around ten-fifteen on the morning of Monday, October 9, 2006, and she called 911. Detective Steve Wells had been first on the scene. Doc Sheddon, the ME, had arrived at five after eleven. He made a cursory examination of the body, then turned the scene over to Wells who, for some reason not mentioned in the report, didn't like what he saw. He in turn called in Lieutenant Mike Willis, our CSI commander, and his team.

CSI found almost nothing in the victim's apartment. The only physical evidence they recovered was an empty wine bottle and a glass found on the nightstand beside the body. They were dusted for fingerprints and tested for DNA. The only prints they found belonged to the victim; the same with DNA. If it hadn't been for the position of the body, all would have seemed perfectly normal.

It appeared that Sullivan must have been drinking alone when she died; she'd celebrated her twenty-sixth birthday only five days earlier.

It wasn't until the next morning when Wells received a call from Doc Sheddon urging him to go back to the scene that things took a turn for the better. At least that's how it seemed at the time.

Wells, having noted the empty trash can in the apartment kitchen, had decided to check the dumpster that served the small apartment complex. Inside it, he found a "tall" kitchen garbage bag that, from the examination of its contents, had obviously been removed from the trash can in the victim's apartment. The contents of the bag included the usual kitchen garbage, some wet and some—well, you get the idea, and a plastic grocery bag from a nearby supermarket. It also contained several items personal to the victim, mostly bills—utilities and credit cards—along with their envelopes. All had her name and address on them, so it was thereby established beyond a doubt that the kitchen bag had come from the victim's apartment.

It was the contents of the supermarket grocery bag, however, that included the heart stopper, literally: two vials labeled KCL injectable potassium chloride. The grocery bag also contained a—*Oh yeah. Here we go*—hypodermic syringe and cap, and two swabs.

All of the items in the grocery bag were checked for fingerprints. None were found. Everything had been wiped clean; either that, or the killer had worn gloves. DNA recovered from the swabs and syringe was confirmed to be that of Rhonda Sullivan. No other DNA was present.

Okay, I thought. *Why would anyone throw evidence like this away, where it could be found? Why not get rid of it someplace else? On the other hand, who knows why killers do what they do? Arrogance, maybe? Overconfidence? Me? I would have taken the stuff with me and dumped it far, far away. Whoever the killer was didn't think it would be found, I suppose.*

But it was found. According to the autopsy report, Doc Sheddon, Hamilton County's Chief Medical Examiner, had found the injection site—the tiny bruise in the photo—during the post mortem, barely visible amid the lividity. *Surely the killer would have known that it would be found... Then again, it was almost ten years ago. Not so much CSI on TV back then. Still... But that indicates the killer knew all about lividity... Medical background? And why potassium chloride? Maybe the killer had easy access to the drug.* I glanced up at the photographs. *The nurse, Chad Pellman! Had to be.*

And so I continued digging through the case file.

Using the product serial numbers on the vials, Detective Wells had traced the potassium chloride to a local trauma center. Pellman, age twenty-seven, worked there in the emergency room, as did Sullivan's friend, Lisa Marco, who'd found the body; both were ICU nurses.

The two vials had been checked out of an automatic dispenser located inside the ER a week before the murder. And, according to the trauma center's records, it was Pellman who'd checked them out. *Surely, he couldn't have been that stupid.*

Apparently, users of the dispenser had to enter their employee number. The records showed that it was Pellman's employee number that had been used to check out the drug. He, of course, strongly denied it, insisting someone else must have used his number to access the dispenser. And from there the story got even more bizarre. It wasn't the first time that Pellman had been accused of reckless and unauthorized use of the dispenser; he'd done it before, and he'd been disciplined for it. *So why the hell would he do it again? He would have had to have known that the stuff would be traced back to him—if it was found, of course—which, if he did do it, he figured wouldn't happen. Whew.*

Wells narrowed the short list of suspects down to two: Chad Pellman and Sullivan's friend Lisa Marco. The fiancé Yates, the other male headshot, didn't have the medical background that would have been needed to administer the drug, so he was eliminated as a suspect.

Both suspects had alibis. Even so, Wells had managed to build a case, a somewhat weak, circumstantial case, against Pellman. His interview with the male nurse was also weak. Pellman insisted that it wasn't he that had stolen the drug that killed her, but her friend, Lisa Marco. Marco, however, at least as far as Wells could determine, had an alibi for the time of death. She was, however, on duty at the time the drugs were taken from the dispenser, but most important: she had no motive.

Not so Pellman. It was established that he knew the victim and that he had a crush on her, but she managed to keep him at arm's length. So, there you go, you'd think it was cut and dried, right? Detective Wells certainly did. He figured he had a pretty strong case against Pellman, but it was all circumstantial. His—Pellman's—fingerprints had not been found anywhere, not in the apartment, on the tall kitchen bag, the small grocery bag, the vials, syringe, nowhere. So Wells couldn't physically link him to the crime scene, the murder weapon, the potassium chloride—anybody that knew his employee number could have gotten it. And there was even more. Pellman had a rock-solid alibi; he was out of town on October 8 when the murder took place. He was at his mother's home in Winchester, Tennessee.

Wells had asked him to take a polygraph which, on advice from his lawyer, he'd refused.

Eventually, Wells took the case to the District Attorney, but it was a lost cause: no charges were ever filed. What little evidence there was, wasn't strong enough. Pellman was never charged.

I read through the reports until finally I reached Wells' closing report. It was surprising in that it was so short, both on words and information. I got the distinct impression that he, Wells, was somewhat pissed. It was dated November 17, 2007, a little more than a year after the murder. Essentially, he'd given up and shelved the case.

Finally, I leaned back in my chair and stared up at the photographs of Yates, Pellman and Marco.

So, I thought, as I nibbled on a fingernail, *Pellman has an alibi, so does Marco. Yates didn't have the expertise to administer the drug. There's no physical evidence linking either Pellman or Marco to the scene or the weapon. Marco's fingerprints were found only on the doorknob, as you'd expect. No wonder the damn thing went cold... My money's on the male nurse. There are too many coincidences. One is okay, but two? Not likely, and I count at least five: he has a medical background; his code was used to check out the drugs; he knew the victim, had a crush on her, for Pete's sake; he'd been caught using the dispenser without authorization before, and he tried to frame Marco... Oh yeah; it's him, but how the hell am I supposed to prove it nine years after? Damn. I'll have to go back and start at the beginning, I suppose.*

Okay, I'm seeing Doc at two. Who else do I need to see?

I opened Notes on my iPad, and then my mind went blank. I stared at the empty screen, chewed gently on the tip of my thumbnail.

I started a numbered list, typed the word Doc, thought for a bit, looked up at the photos, then typed some more:

1. Doc
2. Chad Pellman – Nurse
3. Lisa Marco – Friend: Accused by Pellman. Alibi for TOD but not Dispenser.
4. Pellman's mother – Alibi?
5. Talk to co-workers
6. Lead detective, Steve Wells

I stared at the short list. *Is that all I've got? This is going to be a bitch... Pellman's co-workers...and what about that alibi? It's either fake, or he's not the killer. No one can be in two places at once. Hmmm... Time of death? No! Doc would not have gotten that wrong. Well maybe, I wouldn't dare ask him about it...but I have to.*

I shook my head, frustrated, then thought for a minute, and decided to move Wells up the list. Then I called him. His voice was breathless. I could barely understand him, but I was able to make an appointment to see him the following morning, Saturday. He seemed excited at the prospect.

And then I wrapped it up for the day, collected Lonnie, and went to keep my appointment with Doc Sheddon. After that...the dreaded reception.

Chapter Five

Friday, May 8, 2 PM – Doc Sheddon

Doc Sheddon was waiting for us in his office.

"Hello Kate, Lonnie," he said, standing up and reached across his desk to shake my hand. "It's nice to see you both. I was surprised to get your call. I'd almost forgotten the Sullivan case; had to read up on my notes."

Doc's a sweet little man, five-eightish, a little overweight, almost totally bald, with a round face and a jolly disposition.

"Take a seat." He waved me toward the single chair set in front of his desk. "Lonnie, drag that one over and sit down."

"So, Kate, I understand you've been assigned the case. That's good, but I hope you do better than those who've gone before you. They didn't do so well."

"Yes, I know, which is why the chief dumped it on me, I suppose."

"You do know we have a good idea who the killer was?" he asked. "We just can't prove it."

"Yes. I read the file and your report. You're talking about Chad Pellman, correct?"

He nodded, squinted at me over the top of his half-glasses, scratched the top of his bald head, and then reached for a slim file that was lying on top of his desk.

"He might have gotten away with it... Yes, yes, I know. He has gotten away with it, so far. But if I hadn't been the ME," he said, not at all modestly, "the potassium chloride might never have been found. The cause of death would probably have been recorded as natural causes due to a heart attack."

He smiled at me, leaned back in his chair, then continued. "There was absolutely nothing untoward about the body: no trauma, no bruises, no wounds, no bleeding. But I could see right away that there was something unusual about the position of the body. It didn't look natural. It looked as if it had been positioned very carefully, the arms in particular." He opened the file, extracted a photo and pushed it across the desk. I'd seen it before; it was on my board, but Lonnie and I looked at it anyway. Doc continued. "Why? I thought. But I already knew: lividity, young lady, lividity."

Young lady? That's funny.

Lividity, or livor mortis, in case you're unfamiliar with it, is the settling of the blood in a body after the heart stops pumping. Blood is a liquid, so it naturally flows to the lowest point; it's all about gravity. It generally becomes noticeable quite quickly and usually becomes fixed some eight to twelve hours after death.

Anyway, I nodded, agreeably. He waited for me to speak. I didn't. He looked at Lonnie; he didn't speak either.

"Lividity? You may ask," he said hopefully.

I didn't. Only smiled. I knew he would get there. He was simply making the most of his moment.

"Lividity," he said, impatiently. "Catherine, people do not lie face down with their arms stretched alongside them in that manner. It was damned unnatural. So that started me thinking that it must have been a homicide, and the killer must have positioned her that way to hide something. What it was I didn't know for sure, not at that moment. But I had a good idea, and I also knew that whoever had killed her knew how lividity works. Yes, I examined the arms while the body was still undisturbed, but I found nothing..."

He paused expectantly, grunted, and then continued. "I found nothing, but I knew damn well it had to be there, had to be, which is why I did the post-mortem examination first thing the next morning. And I found it. A tiny, tiny injection site here." He pointed to the crook of his left arm. "The slight amount of bruising caused by the insertion of the syringe was almost obscured by the *lividity*." He emphasized the word, almost shouted it, then folded his arms, and leaned back in his chair, grinning broadly.

Of course, I knew all that from reading the autopsy report,

but hearing it from the master himself was—well, entertaining, to say the least.

"And?" I asked.

"And?" he asked. "And what? Oh, I see. Well, I sent old Wells right back out to see if he could find anything. I didn't know at the time what the injected substance might be, but I knew it had to be something, and I hoped that some indication of what it was would still be there, somewhere. And, well, well, well." He smiled widely at his terribly unfunny joke. "It was: two empty vials of potassium chloride, along with a hypodermic syringe. Potassium chloride is an extremely strong drug. It's used to treat patients with low levels of potassium in their blood. When injected, it's quickly metabolized into potassium and chloride, both of which are normally present in the body. An overdose, however—even a small one—can cause death very quickly, in a matter of seconds. It causes severe heart arrhythmias, and the heart spasms out of control and finally stops functioning. Essentially, the victim suffers a heart attack or SCD —sudden cardiac death."

"But it didn't show in the tox screen," Lonnie said. "Surely it—"

"No, it didn't, and it wouldn't, because as I mentioned a moment ago, potassium and chloride are normally present in the body. Yes, the levels would be elevated, but even that would normally go unnoticed, because a heart attack in and of itself will also produce elevated levels of potassium and chloride."

"So, for the killer to know all that he must have been a medical professional?" Lonnie asked.

Sheddon nodded. "To administer such a drug? I would say so."

"You were saying, Doc?" I asked.

"During the second search of Sullivan's apartment, Wells noticed that the trash can in the kitchen was empty; no bag, no trash. So he went and checked out the dumpster, and there it was. Boy, did we get lucky? The body was found on a Monday. If it had been found a day later, Tuesday, we would've missed it: the dumpster was scheduled to be emptied first thing Wednesday morning, always on Wednesdays, early, usually around seven. It was obviously a great find, Kate. Not just from an evidentiary point of view, but because I wouldn't normally screen for potassium chloride...but then again who knows?" He tilted his to one side, then said, "I might have."

"Okay," I said. "We have the murder weapon. We know where it came from. And we think we know who the killer is, but we can't prove it. We can't tie Pellman to either the crime scene or the weapon, and he has an alibi." I stared across the desk at Doc Sheddon.

I took a deep breath and took the plunge. "Doctor Sheddon," I said. He straightened in his chair, obviously made wary by the formality of the address. "Is there any chance, any chance at all that you might have gotten the time of death wrong?" Inwardly, I cringed, waiting for the explosion; it never came.

He simply nodded, and said, "I thought you might ask that. The answer, of course, is no. She died between the hours of nine o'clock in the evening and midnight, as it says in my report." He took it from the file and glanced at it. "I arrived at the scene shortly after eleven on the morning of the ninth. Lividity was fully fixed. The application of pressure had no effect; the color remained constant. That alone meant that she'd been dead for more than eight hours."

Again, he glanced at his report, then continued. "The body temperature was eighty-one point two degrees. That indicates a time of death of at least twelve hours. Rigor Mortis? The body was stiff as a damn board... Shall I go on? There's more."

"No," I said. "I'm sorry, Doc, but I had to ask."

"I know. I understand."

I looked at him across the desk.

"You have a question?" he asked.

"Not really... Look, Pellman has a solid alibi. I'm pretty certain that he's our killer, but he couldn't have been in two places at once, so if you're absolutely certain of the time of death—"

He opened his mouth to speak, but I held up my hand and stopped him. "I know," I said. "I know. I'm not questioning you, but how the hell did he do it?"

"That, young lady, is your job. You're the detective."

I sighed, looked at Lonnie, shook my head and said, "Yeah, well. That's a whole lot easier said than done."

I looked up at the clock on the wall behind him. It was just after three o'clock; time for me to call it a day and go get ready for the reception that evening.

"Well," I said. "I guess that's it, then, at least for now. Unless..."

He smiled. "If I think of anything, I'll call you. In the meantime, if there's anything more I can do let me know."

There wasn't, and I never felt more helpless.

I stood. "Thanks, Doc. I'll let you know. Right now, I have a reception to attend."

"Good luck with that," he said as I turned to go.

I nodded, said goodbye, and we left.

Back in the cruiser at the rear of the forensic center, I turned the key, leaned my head back against the headrest and waited for the air to come on. After a couple of minutes of quiet, Lonnie said, "I think we caught us a piece o' crap, LT. That alibi's the kicker. If we can't break it, then he couldn't have done it. Where was he, by the way?"

I looked sideways at him and made a face. "He was with his mother, for Pete's sake."

"You've gotta be kiddin' me. Geez, I don't see it happening. She's not going to give him up, no matter what."

Reluctantly, I had to admit to myself that he was probably right. Pellman's mother wasn't likely to give him up. I could see no way, short of a confession, of solving the case.

"Something will come up," I said, shifting into drive. "In the meantime, we start over. We re-interview everyone, starting with Detective Wells tomorrow morning. We'll get to Pellman soon enough. In the meantime, you need to go home and get ready for the reception tonight. I'll drop you back at the office and then head home myself."

"Oh hell," he said. "I'd forgotten about that. What a great way to spend an evening. Hey, I don't suppose—"

"Don't even think about it. If I have to go, you have to go."

"*Damn!*"

Chapter Six

Friday, May 8 – Cold Case Reception

    I arrived home that afternoon at a little after four-thirty. It had been a long and tiring day and was about to get even longer. I needed to relax, so the first thing I did when I walked into my kitchen was grab a half-bottle of red from the refrigerator and pour myself a glass. Then I sat down in my ratty old recliner—it was comfortable if not stylish—and leaned back, closed my eyes, and sipped slowly and steadily until the glass was empty.

I was still in the chair, half asleep, when my phone buzzed on the coffee table. I picked it up and looked at the lock screen: *Harry*. I accepted the call and leaned back in the chair.

"What?" I said.

"Now is that any way to greet your best buddy, especially after last night?"

I got his drift, but I was in no mood for banter.

"I'm tired, Harry. It's been a very long day, but yes, I had a lovely time. The steak was delicious."

"Only the steak? I thought—"

I interrupted him.

"Harry, I don't have time to chat. I have to be at the reception at seven, and I haven't even begun to get ready. What is it you want?"

"You're still mad at me, aren't you? No, don't answer that; I already know. I was just checking in to see how it went with the Sullivan case today. From your tone, I'm guessing it didn't go well."

I sighed. "You're right. It didn't. You were also right last night when you told me it was a dead end. Unless I can break the nurse's alibi or get him to confess...well... Look, I have to go. Thanks for calling."

"Hey, hang on. When am I going to see you again?"

"We'll see. I'll call you. Bye, Harry."

I disconnected, put the soft rubber case of the iPhone to my lips and nibbled on it gently, thoughtfully. *Damn you, Harry Starke!*

After a few minutes, I finally managed to shake my black mood and headed for the bathroom. I showered, dried myself off, all the while running the details of the Sullivan case around in my mind. Anything was better than agonizing over Harry.

Then I debated long and hard with myself about what I should wear that evening. I decided that to avoid any negative connotations, I would wear my uniform, my dress blues.

I spent the next thirty minutes dressing and styling my hair in a bun. That done, I checked the mirror one last time: *Oh shit! I look like a security guard. I can't go looking like this.*

And so I changed into a pair of skinny jeans, a tan leather jacket over a white blouse, and shoes that made my legs look even longer. I also took my tawny blond hair down and tied it back in a ponytail. I checked the mirror: *Better!*

It was fifteen till seven when I arrived at the reception. The chief was there—he'd also dressed down, thank the Lord— and so was Assistant Chief Henry Finkle, resplendent in his dress blues. *Ha ha, he looks like he's just escaped from Disney World.*

I walked across the huge room to join them.

"Hey, wait for me," came a voice from behind me.

I looked back toward the door, Lonnie was hurrying after me, puffing like an old steam train. I waited until he caught up, and then we made our way through the crowd... Crowd? Not so much: maybe a couple of dozen civilians, many of them relatives of victims hoping for answers; several uniformed cops, including Mike Willis; and representatives from all four TV stations. The event could have been held in the chief's office.

"Good evening, Lieutenant, Sergeant Guest. You had a good day, I hope." Johnston stuck out his hand for me to shake, which I did; Finkle didn't offer his. He didn't speak at all, not then.

"Yes, sir," I replied. "I had a good day. How about you?"

"Good enough, Catherine, good enough. Now, how about we get this show on the road. Join me at the podium, both of you, please. No, Henry. Not you. Just the lieutenant and Sergeant Guest."

Finkle's face was a delight to see: his lips tightened into two white lines; his eyes narrowed to mere slits; the hatred in them was palpable. Me? I managed to keep a straight face; I didn't dare look at Lonnie as we joined the chief on the stage and turned to face the gathering.

The next ten minutes were among the most boring I'd ever endured—and the most embarrassing. The chief explained his plans for the new squad and then proceeded to praise my career and qualifications. Oh yes, it was flattering, but by the time he'd finished I was blushing like a schoolgirl, and then he handed the mike over to me to "say a few words."

I stood for a moment looking out across the room, wondering what the hell to say, and kicking myself, because I should have known I'd be expected to speak.

In the end, I simply thanked the chief for his confidence in me, and for the opportunity, assured the eyes staring up at me that I would do my best to provide the victim's families with some answers, and then I handed the mike back to the chief. It was a disaster, and Finkle lost no time telling me so.

As soon as I stepped down from the stage, he grabbed me by the arm, pulled me out of earshot, and said through clenched teeth, "What the hell was that, Lieutenant? My chihuahua could have done better. You're an embarrassment to the chief and the department."

I snatched my arm away from him and spun on my heel to face him. "Don't you ever lay a finger on me again," I said in a tone that warned him not to mess with me. "If you do, I'll file a sexual harassment complaint against you. Now get the hell away from me."

"One of these days, Gazzara..." He didn't finish. He turned and walked quickly away and out of the room. At that moment, I figured my future looked kind of bleak, and then I brightened up and smiled to myself. *So what's new?* Then I felt something touch my arm, and I flinched.

"Oh dear," the woman said. "I didn't mean to startle you, Lieutenant Gazzara. I was just—well, I was hoping I might have a word with you."

She was about five feet six, nice figure, probably in her mid-forties but somehow looked older. The light gray dress she was wearing looked good on her but had obviously seen better days. Her auburn hair was cropped, pageboy style. Her brown eyes had a hollow look about them.

"You didn't," I said, smiling. "I don't think I know you —do I?"

"No, of course not. My name is Alice Booker. I was hoping I could talk to you about my sister. She disappeared, and nobody seems to care. Nobody's doing anything to find her."

And so it begins!

I looked at her, and then at my watch, considering my options.

"Oh, I'm sorry," she said. "Am I bothering you?" She sounded—not exactly angry—bitter.

"No, no. Of course not. It's just that you're talking about a missing person. I'm a homicide—" I'd seen the expression on her face; she looked pathetic. "I'm sorry," I said. "Would you give me just a minute, please? I'll get my partner."

I looked around the room, searching for Lonnie. He was out of the way in a far corner of the room, talking to Mike Willis. I caught his attention and waved for him to join us.

"Alice Booker, this is my partner, Sergeant Guest. Lonnie Guest, Alice Booker," I said, making the introduction. "She has a...problem she'd like to talk to us about."

They shook hands while I quickly thought about how I was going to handle the situation. Fortunately, I didn't have to. Lonnie took over.

"Mrs. Booker," he said. "I remember you. I was the desk sergeant when you filed a missing person report. It must have been...what, a couple of years ago?"

"Oh my, so you are. You were so nice. Thank you. No, it was three years ago last month. My sister, Jennifer Lewis." The tears welled up in her eyes.

"Yes, I remember," Lonnie said. "So, they didn't find her?"

"No, and they've given up looking. I haven't heard anything from Detective Tracy in more than six months. And he won't return my calls."

Tracy? No way. What the hell?

John Tracy—his nickname was Dick, for obvious reasons—was my ex-partner. He'd been foisted on me back when Harry left the PD in 2008. Apart from being a smartass and a misogynist, he was arrogant and lazy. He was also buddy-buddy with Henry Finkle. *Shit! Why can't I ever catch a break?*

"She's dead, Lieutenant," Mrs. Booker said, breaking into my thoughts. "I've always known it. We talked every day; never missed. If not in person, then on the phone. I haven't heard a word from her in more than three years. She... she's...dead." She looked up at me, tears rolling down her face. *"Can you help me, please?"* she whispered.

I looked at Lonnie. He was standing slightly behind and to her left. He nodded, slightly, though she couldn't see him.

I also nodded. "We can talk about it, but I can't promise anything. If Missing Persons still has it..."

She stared defiantly at me, slowly shaking her head. "They've done nothing in three years. Someone has to do something. Jennifer has two children…" The tears streamed down her cheeks.

"Okay," I said. "I'd like you to come to my office on Monday morning, about ten. Can you do that?"

She nodded. "Yes, I live in Farragut, south of Knoxville, but I'm staying here in town, at the Quality Inn on Shallowford Road. I can be there at ten."

"All right then. For now, I suggest you go back to your hotel and relax and try to have a nice weekend, and we'll talk on Monday.

Again, she nodded, and then, without even saying goodbye, she turned and left.

I looked at Lonnie. "What d'you think?"

"I don't know. I just took the report. I thought no more about it until just a few minutes ago. What are *you* thinking?"

"I'm thinking Tracy is a waste of skin. Other than that, I'm not thinking anything, nor will I until I've heard her story." I glanced around the room, looking for…not a damn thing.

"Geez," I said, finally. "I wish this thing would end and we could get out of here. These people are friggin' depressing."

He grinned at me. "Oh come on, LT. You love it. You know you do."

"The hell I do. And if that creepy little bastard keeps on staring at me…"

Lonnie looked around. As soon as he did, Finkle turned away, smiling. Suddenly, I felt self-conscious, out of place.

"I'm outa here, Lonnie. Go give the chief my apologies. Tell him I suddenly got sick to my stomach, which is not a friggin' lie. I'll see you at the office tomorrow morning."

And I left him standing there, grinning like the idiot he pretended to be.

Chapter Seven

❧

Saturday, May 9 – Sullivan Case

    I was a little early when I arrived at the tiny duplex in the assisted living complex Detective Wells called home, but I thumbed the bell push anyway, and I waited. I was just about to ring the bell again when a disembodied voice emanating from a speaker hidden somewhere above the doorframe asked who the hell I was.

I had to smile. *Typical ex-cop: guns and gadgets, and possibly paranoid.*

"It's Lieutenant Gazzara, sir. We have an appointment."

"You're early, damn it. Eh, come on in."

There was a buzz and then a click. I tried the door knob. It turned, and I pushed the door open and went inside.

Steven Wells had retired from the Chattanooga PD in 2009, which made him seventy-two years old when I met with him for the first time that day. Unfortunately, the years had not treated him well: he looked ninety.

A life-long smoker, he was confined to an electric wheelchair, sucking oxygen from a tank attached to the rear of it. I'd checked his personnel file before I left the office that morning. The man had a distinguished career: he was a closer. *So why did he let this one get away?*

He was single—divorced twice—and entirely dependent upon his caregivers for his daily bread: a small, white-haired old man made even smaller by the chair he rode around in. He wasn't the only retired cop I knew that had seen better days, and I felt for him; I felt for all of them. They devoted their lives to protecting and serving and then... *Oh shit. There but for the grace of God.*

"Don't look at me like that, Lieutenant. I don't want, nor do I need your pity. I enjoyed every cigarette, every drag; no regrets. If I could, I'd still smoke. Now, d'you want to talk about Pellman or not?"

I hadn't been aware that I was staring at him, but I apologized anyway and told him I did.

"Sit yourself down then. I can't sit here lookin' up at you: makes m'neck ache."

I sat down on the sofa under the window. He rolled the chair up so that he was sitting in front of me, and then he stared at me, nodding slowly.

"Good, good," he said. "I've heard a lot about you Lieutenant; you're good, like a dog with a bone. You don't give up. If anyone has a shot at pulling this thing off, it's probably you. Now listen to me: Pellman's your perp. The son of a bitch killed Rhonda Sullivan and tried to tag the friend for it. But there's no doubt about it; it was Pellman. Lot's o' proof, all circumstantial, but he had a rock-solid alibi. All you have to do is break his damned alibi."

"And how would you propose I do that, Detective? You couldn't."

"You're right. I couldn't. And, to be honest, I don't think you will either. He was supposedly with his mother. I met with her a half-dozen times. She's as daffy as that damned cartoon duck, but I couldn't break her. She has a way of looking you straight in the eye and flat out lying to you, and she doesn't seem to care that you know she's lying. I guess she loves that piece o' shit son of hers—"

He sucked air in loudly, gulped, coughed, shook his head. "Freakin' hell," he gasped, then continued. "He even had a backup for his alibi, only I couldn't confirm that either. He also said he went to Walmart in Winchester early that same evening and, sure enough, his mother had a receipt, time-stamped at seven-fifty-four. It's all in my report."

I nodded. "I read that, but as you noted, it's also circumstantial. She's not handicapped so she could have gone there herself."

"Yeah, well. That's true, and I checked it out. Spoke to everyone who'd been working there that Sunday. No one remembered him or her; why would they? It's a Walmart for God's sake."

I thought for a minute, then said, "The time of death was established as being sometime between nine and midnight. It's what, seventy-five miles, give or take, from Winchester to Sullivan's apartment so it's, say; an hour and a half, in traffic or bad weather. He had time to take the groceries home to his mother and drive back to Chattanooga with at least a two-hour window."

He shook his head, slowly. "True, but two things: one, you're forgetting the time change. It was eight-fifty-four here, so by the time he dropped off the groceries... Eh, it still wouldn't have been impossible, I suppose. But there was still the mother. She's adamant that he spent the night up there, and there's no proof that he didn't." He sucked in a deep breath. "Eeeech," he wheezed, then gasped, coughed, and wiped his eyes on a tissue.

"I'm sorry, Lieutenant," he said, with some difficulty. "I wish I could give you something you don't already know, but I can't. The Sullivan case is my nemesis. I'm just hoping you can do what I couldn't, then maybe I can die in peace."

I didn't know what to say to him. I was as stumped as he was.

"Maybe I could get him to confess," I mused, out loud.

"Not a chance, short of waterboarding or puttin' a plastic bag over his head, or hers for that matter. I take it you haven't met him yet."

"No."

"He's one cold son of a bitch. You'll see."

He closed his eyes, breathed raggedly, the air rattling the back of his throat.

I stood, held out my hand. He looked up at me, his eyes watering, and he took it in both hands and squeezed. His grip was strong, the last, lingering clue to what once had been the man.

He turned me loose, but continued to look up at me, expecting...what? I had no idea.

I placed my hand on his shoulder. "Can I come and see you again, Steve?"

"Why the hell would you?"

I smiled down at him. "Because I want to."

He nodded, surprised. "Sure. Anytime. You're a sweetheart. If I was—"

I laughed. "You might not be much, Steve, but you're still a man. Tell you what: why don't I come by one evening and cook dinner for you?"

His eyes opened wide. "You'd do that?"

"I would. I'll give you a call, okay?"

He nodded. "Yeah, okay. I'll look forward to it, and good luck."

"Okay then. I'll see you soon. Take it easy, Steve." I squeezed his shoulder and then left him sitting there, staring at the sofa.

Chapter Eight

Monday, May 11 – Lewis Case

I spent the rest of the weekend taking it easy. Harry called a couple of times, but I let the calls go to voicemail. I still had a lot of thinking to do... I never did really explain that situation, between Harry and me, did I?

Back in January that year, 2015, Harry and I worked a case together, unofficially, which in itself was okay. It was the first case we'd been on together since he left the police department back in 2008. Anyway, Harry and I had been involved in a steady relationship almost since I was a rookie cop. I'd been his partner when he was with the department, and the relationship continued afterward until...

Look, I never had any illusions about Harry. I always knew he had a wandering eye, and I was willing to put up with it. At least I thought I was, until the Harper case, a particularly nasty affair that covered three murders. The case also involved a lady United States senator and a local congressman, Gordon Harper. Damn, he was one corrupt SOB. During the course of the investigation, Harry "interviewed" one of the murder victims—before she was a victim—Olivia Hansen, a rich bitch with a weird sex life. It turned out that Harry went a little beyond interviewing her. His DNA was recovered... Oh hell, you get the idea. He had the gall to claim it was "research," for Pete's sake. Anyway, since then, our relationship has never quite been the same. *Damn, the more I think about it, the more I want to strangle him.*

So, as I said. I ignored his calls that weekend and, instead, I spent some quiet time with the Sullivan file, a good book, and several bottles of a rather nice red wine.

The first thing I did when I got to work that following Monday morning was go find Detective Tracy.

"Well, well," he greeted me from the cubicle he called home on the first floor. He swiveled his chair around to face me. "If it ain't my old partner Lieutenant Tight-Ass Gazzara. What can I do for you, Kate?"

Old partner? Yep, that's yet another story, one I don't even want to think about.

I ignored the taunt. "What are you doing about the Lewis case?"

"The what case?" He looked puzzled.

"Don't act like an idiot, John. The Lewis case; Jennifer Lewis. She was reported missing three years ago by her sister, Alice Booker. It's your case. What's the status?"

"May I ask what business it is of yours?"

"Booker came to me at the reception on Friday and asked me to look into it...so?"

"Ah yes, the reception." He said it like he had a nasty taste in his mouth. "I heard about that. I also heard you pissed off the assistant chief. That right?"

"John, you're so far up Henry Finkle's ass it's pathetic. So, tell me, the Lewis case."

He shrugged. "There's not much to tell. According to her husband, she ran off with another guy; happens all the time."

I waited, but he simply sat there, staring up at me.

"That's it?" I asked, finally. "That's all you've got: she ran off with another guy? You didn't investigate?"

Again, he shrugged. "The husband seems like a nice guy. He said she walked out on him about a month earlier. She had an apartment off Bonny Oaks, in one of those extended stay hotels. I checked. She didn't leave a forwarding address. She worked at the Country Skillet on Shallowford. I talked to some of her co-workers. Sure enough, she'd been having an affair. So yeah, she ran off with another guy."

I stared down at him, breathed deeply. It was all I could do to be civil.

"I'd like to take a look at the file, please?"

He sucked in through his teeth. "Oooh, I dunno about that. I'm still working it."

"Bullshit! You haven't returned Booker's calls in more than a year. I want to see it, *now!*"

"I don't have it. It's down in Records, filed away under 'I don't give a shit.' You want it, you go get it. Oh, and be sure to sign for it."

He swiveled back around to face his computer screen, and I lost it. I grabbed the back of his chair, spun him around, grabbed him by the balls and squeezed. He grabbed the arms of the chair and squeaked like a mouse in a trap; eyes almost popping out of his head.

"This is how we first met, John. Remember?"

His face was a mask of pain, but he managed to nod.

"That's good, John," I said, twisting them a little. His backside rose six inches off the seat. "Now, here's how it's going to be. As soon as I turn you loose, you're going to get up and go fetch the file. Then you're going to deliver it to me in my office, understand?"

He nodded, and I let him down again, but I didn't let go of his package.

Instead, I leaned in close and whispered in his ear, "Don't screw with me, Detective. If you do, you'll regret it. Ten minutes. No more. You hear?"

He nodded, his eyes shut tight. I turned him loose, spun on my heel, and walked quickly away without a backward glance, back to my office.

Less than ten minutes later, the door burst open and Tracy stormed in and flung the file down on my desk in front of me.

"Thank you, John," I called after him as he stormed out again. "If I have any questions—" but the door slammed shut and he was gone. *Son of a bitch!*

Two minutes later, there was a knock on my door, and it opened.

"You okay?" Lonnie asked as he poked his head inside. "What was that all about?"

"Oh yeah. I'm fine. Come on in and take a seat. Dick's pissed at me. I had to put the screws to him, literally. He didn't seem to want me to have this." I picked the thin file up and then dropped it again. "I wonder why?" I said, more to myself than to Lonnie.

"Can I see?" He held out his hand.

"Sure." I handed it to him.

He flipped through it quickly. "Geez, I know why. Here, you take a look."

I barely had time to glance through the file before I received a call informing me that Alice Booker was at the front desk, but I knew what he meant. I shook my head and closed the file.

"She's here. Stay here while I go get her."

He nodded, crossed his legs and pushed back in his chair.

Alice Booker looked a little better than she had on Friday evening, but not much. I showed her into my office and asked her to sit.

Lonnie stood, said hello, and pulled up a chair for her, and she sat down beside him.

"So," I said, as I opened my iPad, "did you have a good weekend, Alice? Is it okay for me to call you Alice?"

"Oh yes, of course. No, Lieutenant, I didn't have a good weekend. I can't remember the last time I did. It's..." She lapsed into silence.

I nodded. "I understand. So, let's get on with it. I have the missing person file." I lifted the top cover and let it drop again. "But I haven't yet had time to look at it in detail. Why don't you tell me your story? Begin at the beginning. Umm. Alice, I'm going to record what you say," I said, as I set my digital recorder on the desk in front of her and turned it on.

"Yes. That's fine."

She lowered her head, looked down at her hands clasped together in her lap, thought for a minute, then looked up at me.

"Well, as I told you on Friday, Jennifer and I talked almost every day, sometimes more than once, especially toward the end... She was having problems."

I tapped notes into my iPad as she talked.

"Problems?" I asked. "What problems?

"She'd left her husband, John, about a month earlier. She was going to divorce him."

"Okay. Go on."

"So, the last time I talked to her was on Saturday, April 14, 2012. The first time quite early, around eight in the morning, and then again around five that same afternoon. She seemed fine. She said she was going out to eat and would be back home by nine, and she'd call me to let me know that she'd gotten home okay. She did, and that's the last I heard from her."

Alice adjusted her position in the chair and pulled a tissue from her purse.

"She didn't call me on Sunday, but I didn't think too much of it until I called her that evening. That was around eight. She didn't answer, so I left her a voicemail. I called her again at nine-thirty, and at ten, and again at eleven. I still wasn't too worried. I thought she might have been on a date. She was seeing someone, not seriously, of course—"

"Do you know who that was?" I asked, interrupting her.

"Yes, his name was Jeff Tobin but, as I said, it was just a casual thing. Anyway, I called her husband, John. I didn't really think she'd be there, but I knew he talked to her all the time. He told me he hadn't seen her or heard from her and didn't know where she was. So, I called Jeff. He said he hadn't seen her either and hadn't talked to her for several days. I also called her best friend, Amber—that's Amber Watts. She told me they'd had dinner together at Provino's on Saturday evening and that Jennifer had driven home just after eight-thirty. She'd heard nothing from her since...and neither had I."

I could see she wasn't really talking to me, or Lonnie. She was staring down at her hands, thinking out loud. I let her get on with it and continued making my own notes.

"I didn't know what to do," she continued. Finally, at around eleven that Monday morning. I drove to her apartment. She wasn't there, but all her belongings were: her clothes, shoes, everything. I spoke to her neighbors. No one had seen Jennifer for at least a couple of days. I knew she hadn't gone off somewhere. She would have told me; she told me everything. So, I came here and reported her missing, at around two o'clock, I think it was."

She glanced sideways at Lonnie; he nodded confirmation.

"And you've heard nothing from her since?" I asked.

She looked at me like I was an idiot, and no wonder. *What the hell am I thinking? Of course, she hasn't.*

She shook her head. I'm not sure if it was in frustration because of the stupid question or simply her way of saying no. Whatever, I didn't follow up on it. Instead, I asked about Jennifer's breakup with her husband, and then I picked up the file and flipped through it while she talked.

"She left him on Friday," she continued, "March twenty-third, after a terrible argument. She said she'd told him she wanted a divorce, and he went absolutely crazy. He hit her; gave her a black eye. They'd been arguing ever since... I never liked him. He's a mean man, drinks, and he went with other women." She looked up at me.

I didn't have to ask. I knew what she was thinking. *Maybe she's right. More often than not, it's the husband, or wife, whichever...*

That male chauvinist Tracy, I thought, as I contemplated the file and its sparse contents: the original missing person report, a single photograph of Jennifer Lewis, several single sheets of paper, each with hand-written notes. One was a report dated April 20, detailing the results of his search of Jennifer's apartment. In it, Detective Tracy stated that he'd found nothing out of the ordinary. On one of the sheets, he'd made notes of an interview he'd conducted with the husband, John Lewis; it was dated April 21. *He didn't record it?*

Another sheet also had notes he'd made while interviewing Jennifer's best friend Amber Watts; it too was dated April 21. And on another sheet also dated the 21st, he'd written a couple of sentences about an interview with Jeff Tobin. On the final sheet of paper, dated April 23, he'd outlined his own conclusions, namely that Jennifer had gone away with an unnamed man with whom she'd been having an affair for several months, that according to his interview with the husband. That was it. There was nothing more in the file.

Just the missing person report, one photo, and five sheets of hand-written notes.

What the hell kind of investigation was this? He didn't record any of the interviews. He didn't go to the apartment until the 20th? That's three full days after the report was filed, and he didn't talk to anyone until the day after that. I leaned back in my seat, holding the file in front of me, staring at it. *And that's all there is? He didn't talk to anyone else? If he did, there's nothing here. What the hell was he doing... More to the point, what the hell was he thinking? I don't know, but I'm going to find out.*

I shuddered to think of the amount of work that now needed to be done because of his, Tracy's, lack of effort over the past three years. As far as I was concerned, the poor woman might as well have been reported missing only yesterday. If I were to agree to take it on... No, if I were to be allowed to take it on, I'd have to start from scratch.

I leaned forward, closed the file and handed it to Lonnie. I looked sharply at him, a warning not to say anything. He got the hint and nodded, discreetly.

"Alice," I said. "Detective Tracy," the words tasted nasty in my mouth, "is of the opinion that Jennifer simply ran off with another man. Who that man was, he doesn't say."

"She didn't!" Alice snapped. "She wouldn't, and even if she did, she would've stayed in touch with me. You're not going to help me, are you?"

"I didn't say that. Alice, I'm going to do what I can, but it's not going to be easy... Look, I happen to know a private investigator." I glanced at Lonnie. He had that idiotic smile on his face. I ignored him and continued. "I can have a word with him."

She started to shake her head. "I can't afford that kind of money."

"Don't worry about the money," I said, crossing my fingers. "We'll figure something out. For now, I want you to go home and leave it to me. Would you do that for me?"

For a long moment, she looked into my eyes—hers were watering—then, slowly, she nodded, rose to her feet, and said, "I'll stay in town for a few more days. You might need to talk to me."

Lonnie and I both stood. I smiled at her, and said, "If you're sure. I think that sounds like a plan."

"I am. I'll be at the hotel if you need me. Goodbye, and thank you for listening, Lieutenant, and you too, Sergeant. I'll look forward to hearing from you."

I waited until the door closed behind her before I let out a deep breath and sat down.

"Oh boy," Lonnie said, as he resumed his seat. "What the hell are you thinking, LT?"

He dropped the file he'd still been holding back on my desk.

"That's a friggin' joke," he continued, referring to the file. "There's nothin' in it. And what was that about Harry Starke? Are you out of your mind?"

I ignored the question about Harry, and said, "You're right. She's right. Tracy barely went through the motions, but I'll get to him later. Right now, I need to talk to the chief."

I picked up the office phone and punched in the number.

"Cathy," I said when his secretary answered. "I need to see the chief, right now if possible."

"One moment, Lieutenant."

The phone went to some annoying music as she put me on hold, and I waited.

"He'll see you now. Don't keep him waiting."

Chapter Nine

Monday, May 11 – **Chief Johnston's Office**

As usual, Chief Johnston was seated like some medieval king behind his desk. Unfortunately, his chief jester Henry Finkle was in the seat beside the desk, his thin face an expressionless mask.

"Good morning, Chief," I said. "Thank you for seeing me."

"Good morning, Lieutenant. Please sit down. I hope you have good news for me."

"The Sullivan case?" I asked, sitting down in front of his desk. "No, sir. Not yet, I'm afraid."

I swear I heard Finkle snigger.

Johnston narrowed his eyes and leaned forward; the huge white eyebrows met in the middle and became one. *How does he do that?*

"Why not?" he asked. "I don't understand. It's clear that the nurse is the perpetrator. Why have you not arrested him yet?"

"Yes, I agree, but I can't prove that he did it. What evidence there is, is all circumstantial. I'm working on it, sir, but unless something breaks... Well, we'll see, but it's going to take time."

He leaned back in his chair, frowned even deeper, folded his arms across his chest. "That's not good enough, Lieutenant. I assigned the case to you because I thought you'd be able to close it out, and quickly."

"Sir—" Finkle turned in his chair toward the chief.

"Not now, Henry," the chief interrupted him.

Finkle turned back to face me. He looked like a hungry rat.

"So why are you here?" Johnston asked.

"I have something else I'd like to look into, but I thought I'd better run it by you first, sir."

He glared at me across the desk. Finkle's face lit up with a huge a grin.

"I told you, Lieutenant," Johnston said with a fist slamming on the desk for emphasis. "I want the Sullivan case closed. I want that son of a bitch Pellman arrested."

"Chief," Finkle said. "If I might suggest. I'm not sure the lieutenant is capable—"

"Damn it, Henry," Johnston interrupted him again. "I said, not now, so shut the hell up."

Finkle's mouth clamped shut, his eyes narrowed and sparkled with anger.

Well, now I know Henry has my back, I thought. Yes, I was being sardonic.

"Tell me," Johnston said, "and it had better be good."

"Before I do, I'd like you to take a look at this, please, sir." I handed him Tracy's file on the Lewis case.

"What is it?" he asked, taking it from me and opening it.

I didn't answer. I let him look through it. It took him less than thirty seconds. He flipped through it again, his lips tightening as he did so. Then, finally, he looked up at me, his face stern, his eyes narrowed.

"What the hell is this, Lieutenant? Is it a joke? I've never seen anything like it."

"It's no joke, sir. It's a missing person file."

"*I can see that, damn it!*" His voice was raised louder than I'd ever heard. "It's more than three years old. There's nothing in it but a couple of reports and a few sheets of paper. It has Detective Tracy's name on it."

Now it was his turn: he twisted in his chair to face Finkle. "Go fetch that son of a bitch in here."

"Err, I'd rather you didn't, sir," I said, as Finkle stood.

"Why the hell not, Lieutenant? This is the worst piece of policing I've seen in all my years on the force."

He threw the file down on his desk.

"How the hell was he allowed to get away with this, Henry? And sit the hell down, will you?"

He didn't wait for Finkle to answer.

He leaned forward in his chair, folded his arms on the top of his desk, and glared at me. "So tell me, Catherine. Why don't you want me to tear Tracy a new one?" His voice was so low and menacing it reminded me of a wolf readying itself for the kill.

"For a couple of reasons that probably make no sense. Yes, I agree with you. It's pretty bad, but I know Tracy, and I think there must be a reason why the investigation is as cursory as it is. Second, I need to talk to him, and that means I also need him to cooperate."

He nodded, leaned back in his chair and looked at me, thoughtfully.

"There's one thing more."

He raised his eyebrows but continued to look me in the eye. "Go on."

I hesitated, then said, "I want to run it by Harry Starke."

Finkle snorted, derisively.

"You want to run it by him?" Johnston asked, quietly. "What exactly does that mean, and why would you want to do that?"

"She's screwing him, is why," Finkle snarled.

"Shut up, Henry," Johnston said. "Catherine?"

"I'm not asking permission to get him involved... well, not exactly, but that," I nodded at the file, "it's not just cold, it's dead. The woman is missing. We don't know if she's alive or dead. I'm betting she's dead, but if so, where's the body? And if she did run away, with whom, and why hasn't she contacted her sister? To get any answers at all, we need to find her. You know how Starke's mind works. Nobody I know thinks like he does."

Again, the derisive snort from Finkle. Johnston cut him a warning look.

"But it's not just that. I want access to his team," I said. "In particular Tim Clarke. He's a wizard at finding people. He's the best there is. If he can't find her, nobody can. I want access to him."

Johnston nodded, thoughtfully, then said, "Starke was a good detective, I must admit. All right, Lieutenant, but I'm not giving you carte blanche. He's no longer one of us, so tread very carefully." He thought for a moment, then continued. "I'll have the case reassigned to you. Keep me in the loop. And *do not* forget the Sullivan case. I want that one closed out soonest. That will be all."

I stood, picked up the file, thanked him, ignored Finkle, and turned to leave.

"You heard what the chief said, Lieutenant?" Finkle said. I turned my head to look at him.

"I heard everything the chief said. What are you talking about?"

"He told you to tread carefully. I reiterate. I'll be watching you."

"You always are, Finkle, especially my tits and ass, so what's new?"

Out of the corner of my eye, I could see that the chief was smiling. I left them to it.

So, IT WAS DONE. THE LEWIS CASE WAS NOW officially mine, and I had permission from the top to ask Harry for help—that is if I could persuade him to agree. He was kinda funny about working for free, especially when his employees were involved; he liked to get paid.

I returned to my office, sat down, and swiped the lock screen on my phone and called his cell. He answered on the third ring.

"Hey, Kate. What's up?"

"I need to talk to you, Harry. I need a favor. Can we meet for lunch, my treat?"

"Uh oh! What d'you want? Is this about the Sullivan case?"

"I can't talk about it now. So, how about it, lunch?"

I heard him sigh, which made me smile. *Gotcha!*

"Okay. Where? When?"

I looked at my watch. "Soon? Say thirty minutes? At the Boathouse?"

"Noon, then. Grab a table, on the terrace if you can. I'll meet you there." And he disconnected.

Okay, then, I thought, smiling to myself. *That's the first step.*

Chapter Ten

Monday, May 11, Lunch – Lewis Case

It was already after eleven-thirty when I left for lunch with Harry that morning. I left Lonnie with instructions to track down Lisa Marco and, if he could, talk to her that afternoon about Rhonda Sullivan. I'd liked to have talked to her myself, but, in deference to the chief's wishes, I didn't want to put it off. Besides, no matter what other people might think of him, I knew I could trust my partner to do a thorough job and get the information we needed. So, I grabbed the Lewis file and headed out the door.

Harry still hadn't arrived when I walked into the Boathouse and, yes, I did manage to grab a table out on the terrace overlooking the river. It was a beautiful, warm day: fluffy white clouds drifted slowly on a startlingly blue sky with just the hint of a breeze blowing in off the water. It had all the makings of a romantic moment, only that wasn't why I was there, nor did I even feel like such a moment. *My, how times do change.*

I ordered a glass of iced tea, placed the file on the table in front of me, and waited for him to arrive. My head a jumble of disconnected thoughts and questions, to which I was almost certain there were no answers.

I was sitting, drink in hand, staring out across the river when Harry pulled out the chair opposite me across the table and sat down.

"Oh, hi," I said. "You look nice." Yeah, I said it without thinking, but he did. He looked gorgeous: deeply tanned, three days of stubble on his chin, white polo shirt that contrasted nicely with the tan, and dark blue, lightweight pants. Yes, gorgeous, and I didn't like the feelings beginning to stir inside of me. Somehow, though, I managed to push them aside, at least for the moment.

"Thanks, so d'you. Have you ordered yet?"

"No. I was waiting for you."

"Why? You know what I like to eat here." He looked around and attracted the waiter's attention.

"You'll take the Veggie Panini?" he asked me, and he was right, that's exactly what I'd have ordered if he hadn't suggested it.

He's still taking me for granted.

"No," I said. "Can I see the menu, please?"

He smiled, shrugged, then ordered his usual, a Smoked Pork Sandwich with a Blue Moon beer, draft in a glass, no orange slice.

Me? I ordered a Grilled Chicken Salad and a refill for my glass of tea.

"So, what's this all about, Kate? And what's that?" he asked, pointing at the file on the table as the waiter walked away with our order.

"Can we eat first and talk later?"

"Sure, but you've piqued my curiosity. I hear nothing from you for days, then here we are. I hope this relationship is not going to turn into something... Well, if you're just using me..."

Damn, does he ever have a way of figuring things out?

"Oh, come on, Harry. Okay, yes. I need your help, but I'm not using you. Okay, yes I am, but it's not what you think."

"Oh, and what do I think?"

"I don't know, Harry. Who the hell ever knows what you're thinking? I just thought—" And it was at that moment that rescue arrived in the form of our lunch. I looked gratefully up at the waiter and Harry smiled: enigmatic as always.

We ate for the most-part in silence until finally Harry pushed away his plate, signaled the waiter, ordered another beer, and waited until I too laid down my fork.

"So," he said, as the waiter left us, "how exactly d'you intend to use me?"

Oh hell! Here we go.

I picked up the Lewis file and, without saying a word, handed it to him. He opened it, glanced through it, looked at me over the top of it, then closed it and laid it down. After cocking his head to one side he said, "Okay. What is it you want?"

He smiled at me; mocking me.

He's making it tough.

"Harry, I need your help," I said, quietly, sincerely, I hoped. *"Please?"*

He picked the file up again, opened it, shook his head, then said, "Not one of Dick's best efforts, is it?"

"No, it's not!"

He sighed, set the file down again, and said, "You know I'll help if I can. There's nothing here. I—"

I interrupted him, saying, "Which is exactly why I need you. If it was simple, I wouldn't. I thought maybe Tim..." I let it tail off and waited, and waited, while he stared off into space until finally:

"Kate, I don't have time to get involved... Wait, now. Hear me out. I don't have time to get involved personally, but," he picked up the file again, "I can run it by Tim. I'll help if I can, when I can, but I don't intend to get sucked into another long, drawn-out investigation for which I'll never get paid. Understood?"

It wasn't exactly what I was hoping for, but I nodded anyway and told him thank you.

"Let me have the file," I said, reaching across the table. "I'll have copies made and send it over."

"Don't send it," he said. "Bring it over yourself. Look, Kate, I know I screwed up, and I'm so sorry."

"Don't sweat it," I said. "I'm over it, as well, you know."

He nodded. He leaned forward, folded his arms on the table and said, "You know how I feel about you. Can we...can we start over?"

Oh how I wanted to say yes, but the right words wouldn't come. Instead, I looked down at the table, shook my head, and said, "I'm sorry, Harry. I'm just not ready, not yet." I looked up, looked him right in the eye, and said, "What you did was—well, let's just wait and see."

He pursed his lips, gave me a wry smile, nodded, then said, "What was the other night, then? I thought..."

So did I, but the following morning...

"It was nice. It's always nice, but there's more to a relationship than just that, a lot more. Harry, I need to be able to trust you, and I don't. So let's just give it some time, please?"

He stood up, grabbed the check from the table, looked down at me smiling and said, "I understand, and it's better than I deserve but, please, bring the file over yourself. I'll take you to dinner; no strings, okay?"

Well, what the hell would you have said? I said okay, and he left, taking with him the check I'd promised to pay. I stayed for a moment, enjoying the moment, the quiet beauty of the great river, and an unexpected feeling of calm. *I think I love the river almost as much as Harry does. What am I going to do about him?*

Finally, after receiving a call from Lonnie wanting to know where the hell I was, I went back to the office; it was almost two o'clock.

"Yeah," I said, as I walked past his desk. "Give me a few minutes to get this copied." I waved the file at him. "Then come to my office. I need to know what you've been doing while I've been out."

Chapter Eleven

❦

Monday, May 11, Afternoon – Sullivan Case

What he'd been doing was tracking down and interviewing Lisa Marco.

"Okay," I said. "Talk to me. Where are we?"

"I found her easy enough. She was at work... So, by the way, was Pellman, but I managed to steer clear of him. Anyway, she had little to add that we didn't already know. She did confirm that Pellman knew Sullivan and that they'd been friends, sort of, for quite a while. She also said Pellman had been trying to get her to go out with him, but she'd turned him down, several times. There was one more thing of interest she added that wasn't in the file... At least, I don't think it was. She said that Sullivan suffered from migraines, and that's maybe why she let Pellman shoot her up with the drug."

"You know," I said, "that drug, when injected, has to be administered by a qualified medical practitioner so, Pellman, then."

Lonnie nodded. "Or Marco. She would have been qualified to administer it, and she was on duty when the drugs were stolen, but she has an alibi. She was with her girlfriend all evening... That's all evening. Get my drift? So I don't see it. Then again, there's nothing so strange as people. Pellman said she did it, but he would, right?"

"So maybe we should talk to her again?"

He shrugged, made a face. "Couldn't hurt, I suppose. I'd say we need to interview Pellman and his mother first, though. Yates? I think we can cross him off the list. He works at Volkswagen—has since he graduated—so he couldn't have done it. He wouldn't have the medical know-how."

We both stared up at the board. After a moment of silence, I sighed and shook my head.

"So, Pellman or his mother?" I said. "Which one first? Pellman, I think." I answered my own question.

"When? Where?" Lonnie asked.

"Tomorrow afternoon, at his place of work. Let's put a little pressure on him to see if anything breaks."

"Why not now? He's there."

"I have other things on my mind. By the way, we have the Lewis case, officially. Johnston turned it over to me this morning."

"No shit? How cool is that?"

"I'm not so sure. It's more than three years cold. That reminds me, I need to make a call... No, no. Stay put. I want you in on this."

I picked up the office phone and buzzed Detective Tracy.

"John," I said when he picked up. "We need to talk, so please come to my office, now."

I put the phone down before he could make any excuses. Lonnie looked at me, nodding, a slight smile on his lips.

"Tracy?" he asked, and without waiting for an answer, continued. "Oh yeah," he said. "I wanna be here for this."

Chapter Twelve

Monday, May 11, 3 PM – Lewis Case

Detective Tracy took his time. I waited exactly fifteen minutes before I picked up the phone to call him again; I didn't have to. There was a sharp knock on my door, it opened, and he walked in. I could see right away, from the thunderous look on his face, that the interview wasn't going to go well.

"What's this all about, Lieutenant? I don't work for you, so why'd you drag me up here? I'm busy. So—"

I interrupted him. "Take a seat, John." I pointed to the chair next to Lonnie.

"If this is about the Lewis case," he said as he sat down. "You have the file. There's nothing more I can tell you."

I leaned back in my chair and stared at him.

"You don't change much, do you, Detective?" I asked.

"What the hell's that supposed to mean?"

"Bad attitude," I said. "You have a bad attitude; always have."

He stood, looked down at me, angrily. "I don't have to take this kinda crap from you, Gazzara."

"Sit down," I said, quietly.

Slowly he lowered himself back onto the chair.

I picked up the file—I'd placed it on my desk right after I'd called him—and waved it in front of him. "What the hell is this, John?" I asked, not raising my voice.

"You're a detective, so they tell me," he said, sneering. "What does it look like?"

I dropped the file back on the desk. "It looks like a half-assed excuse for an investigation. It looks like you didn't give a shit, like you said this morning. What the hell were you thinking?"

"I don't know what you're talking about."

"Yes, you do," I said. "Even back when you worked with me, you were better than this. What the hell happened to you?"

"When I worked with you?" he said, his lip curling into a sneer. "That was a real boost to my career. I haven't recovered from it yet. You really screwed me over."

"I didn't screw you, John. You screwed yourself. As I said, you had a bad attitude then, and you do now, especially where women are concerned. And you haven't changed at all. So, I ask you again. What the hell is this?" I tapped on the file with the back of my hand.

"You're right, *Lieutenant*." The word dripped with sarcasm. "I didn't give a shit, not when I found out what she was..." He let the words tail off, then continued. "Okay, that's not true. Of course, I gave a shit. Look, she was having an affair. She ran off with some guy; end of story."

"So, what was she, Detective?" I asked.

He stared at me across the desk, then said, "She was a freakin' hooker, is what she was."

"And you know that because? There's nothing about that in your file."

"Yeah, well, I left that out in deference to her husband."

"You did *what?*" I was dumbfounded.

"He was a nice guy; didn't deserve the slut, or the shit he would get if it came out. I cut him a break; so what?"

Why the hell would you do that?

"You cut him a break?" I asked. "She's been missing for three years. She's not been heard of in all that time, and you cut him a break? Why would you do that? What about her family? Don't they deserve answers?"

"You talking about Alice Booker? I stayed in touch with her."

"The hell you did, not for the last two years anyway."

"Geez," he said, shaking his head. "What's with you, Gazzara? She was just a freakin' hooker. The world's better off without her." He paused, shook his head. "And you, and you—you're no freakin' better. Geez! Freakin' women! I hate 'em!"

"What the f—" Lonnie exploded, almost said it, then continued. "Who the hell d'you think you're talking to? Show a little respect, you worthless piece of shit."

"Oh yeah, and what are you going to do about it, Fat Ass?"

Lonnie moved faster than I ever thought possible. He stood, spun around and, quick as a striking snake, his hand streaked out and grabbed Tracy by the throat and squeezed. Tracy came out of his seat choking.

Lonnie relaxed his grip a little and snarled. "I'll tell you what I'm gonna do about it, you smart-ass little shit. Step outa line again and I'll rip the tongue right outa your foul mouth. Get it?" he asked as he tightened his grip.

Tracy's face had gone red, his mouth was wide open, his eyes popping.

I stood, quickly. "Let him go, Sergeant. *Now!*"

I thought for a minute he was going to ignore me but, slowly, he lowered Tracy back to his seat and turned him loose.

"You—you crazy bastard," he whispered, hoarsely, massaging his neck. "I'm gonna turn you in for that—"

I interrupted him. "Turn him in for what, Detective?"

"For—oh, I get it. Well screw you, Gazzara."

Lonnie took a half-step forward, but this time Tracy leaped up, staggered a half-step backward, knocking over the chair, then turned and ran for the door, slamming it shut behind him; Lonnie sat down, grinning.

"Thanks," I said, "but you shouldn't have laid hands on him. If it gets back to Finkle..."

"It won't. He doesn't have the balls. And he sure as hell wouldn't want it to get out that I was able to..." He didn't finish, the smile was gone, and suddenly he looked very tired, and miserable.

"What's wrong, Lonnie? It's okay. I have your back. Hey, partner, you look like you just lost a hundred-dollar bill."

"I wish to hell that's all it was." He paused, looked at me.

"Come on," I said. "Out with it. What's bothering you?"

He sighed a deep sigh, looked down at his feet, then said, "You heard what that piece o' crap called me: Fat Ass."

"Yes, well..."

"No, not 'yeah, well.' I've had it with all that. I've been called it, and worse, all my life. High school was a nightmare, so was UT, so was the Academy. I've always been overweight... No, not overweight, fat, and I can't deal with it anymore. I gotta lose some weight, a lot o' weight. The trouble is, I've tried every diet there is; they all work for a while. I lose a few pounds, then it goes right back on again, and each time it's a little more. I don't know what to do anymore."

I sat back in my seat. "Do you know *why* you put the weight back on?"

"Oh yeah: lack of willpower, partly, but dieting just doesn't seem to work in the long run. Hell, I even tried one of them TV diets, where they supply the food. That worked better'n most, but in the end..." He trailed off, stared down at the floor. Then he looked up at me. "I've had it, Kate. I'd be better off out of it, doing something else."

"*What?*" I couldn't believe what I was hearing. "You can't be serious?"

"As a friggin' heart attack," he said. "I'm sick of the assholes we have around here, the looks I get, the fat jokes, the derisive remarks, the name calling behind my back, and the lack of respect. I'm a good cop, Kate, at least I try to be; not like that piece o' crap Tracy."

"So you're going to give up, take your toys and go home? I thought you were better than that. Lonnie, the people that matter do treat you with respect; I do, the chief does."

"What about your boyfriend, Starke? He treats me like shit."

"You can hardly blame—no, no, Lonnie. Hear me out. You can hardly blame him for the way he treats you. I've heard the way you go after him, every chance you get. I've lost count of the number of times you've wanted to arrest him—"

"Not without cause," he interrupted me. "He has no respect for the law, Kate. He treats the rules as if they weren't meant for him. You let him get away with more crap than you ever would me. And he hates my guts. Always has, ever since we were at the Academy together. Now you're letting him loose on us again, and I don't like it."

I sighed, made a wry face, and shook my head. I was in no mood for this kind of self-deprecating crap. I had to shut him down.

"Gotcha," I said, quietly. "You're fat, and because you're fat no one likes you, and it's everyone else's fault but yours. Lonnie, I'm going to tell you something, and you're not going to like it. It's not them, it's you; you're the problem. You can be arrogant, intolerant, and a pain the ass. If you want to quit, go ahead. But I suggest you take stock, grow yourself a pair, and do something about it—the fat, I mean."

He looked at me as if I'd slapped his face, then he stood, turned and walked out of my office.

I stared at the closed door, sighed, and checked my watch. It was almost five and I needed to take the file copy to Harry's office, which I did.

DINNER WITH HARRY THAT EVENING WAS NICE, AND probably would have been even nicer, had I allowed it to be, but I didn't. Instead, we arranged that I should meet him and Tim at his offices the following morning at ten, and he dropped me off at my car, which was safely locked away in his office parking lot.

He opened my car door for me, leaned in close and kissed me, and I let him, and then I pushed him away. He smiled at me, nodded, and went to his car and waited until I'd driven out of the lot.

I drove home that night. How I made it from one place to the other, I'll never know. No, I wasn't drunk; in fact, I'd had nothing to drink at all. Maybe it was because I had a lot on my mind, and not all of it about Harry: Lonnie was a big part of it, and so was Dick Tracy.

By the time I arrived home, I'd made a couple of decisions. One: no matter how much I tried, I couldn't figure out Tracy. Two: I was going to have to do something about Lonnie. Fortunately, I didn't have to.

Chapter Thirteen

❦

Tuesday, May 12, 10 AM

Lonnie was waiting for me when I arrived at my office the following morning. He looked different, somehow; more upbeat. *That's m'boy!*

"You're in a good mood," I said. "Come on in. Sit down."

"I want to apologize for yesterday," he said, as he sat down in front of my desk. "You were right. I was being childish."

I nodded. "Yup, you were. No apology needed. I'd already forgotten about it," I lied.

"Yeah, right. Anyway, I've decided to do something about it. I'm going to have a lap band fitted."

I opened my eyes wide. "Wow! No kidding?"

He nodded. "I called the clinic already this morning and... well, I have an appointment at eleven, if that's okay with you."

"Yes, of course it is, but—"

"Don't go there, LT. There's nothing to discuss. I made up my mind."

"Okay. Well, what can I say? I'm proud of you, Lonnie. If there's anything I can do...well, you know."

"Do?" a male voice, not Lonnie's, said.

I looked up, startled. Finkle was standing just outside the open door. How long he'd been listening, I didn't know. *Long enough, I should think.*

"Do about what, Lieutenant? You *were* talking about the Sullivan case, I hope."

"No, Chief," I said, lightly. "I wasn't, but I can if you think it's important."

"Leave us, Sergeant," Finkle said, to Lonnie.

Lonnie started to get to his feet.

"Stay where you are, Sergeant," I said, never taking my eyes off Finkle's.

"*What?*" Finkle was dumbfounded. "You just counter-manded my direct order. Are you mad, Lieutenant?"

"No, sir, far from it. As a female officer, it's my right to have a witness present. Anything you want to say to me, you can say in front of Sergeant Guest."

He stared hard at me, obviously lost for words. Inwardly, I smiled: *Gotcha!*

Finally, he smiled... No, it was more snarl than smile, and he sat down next to Lonnie.

"I've been talking to Detective Tracy," he said, conversationally, "and I didn't like what I heard."

Oh hell, here we go.

"If you think I'm going to let you run with this Lewis thing, you're mistaken. And if you think that I'm going to allow that—that shyster who poses as a private investigator, Harry Starke, back into this building, you're even more stupid than you appear to be. You are to concentrate on the Sullivan case until it's either closed or shelved. Is that understood, Lieutenant?"

I leaned back in my chair, folded my arms across my stomach, looked at Lonnie, who rewarded me with a wink, and I smiled at him, Finkle.

"Well?" he asked. "D'you understand?"

I shrugged. "Yes, I understand, Chief, but tell me, did you go to Tracy..." I paused for a split second, "or did he come to you?"

"That's none of your damn business. What the hell difference does it make?"

"Oh, it makes a difference. You know it does."

He didn't answer. Instead, he stood and went to the door, hesitated, then turned to look at me and said, "Sullivan!" And then he left.

"Geez, LT," Lonnie said. "That was intense. What was that about Tracy? What difference does it make, who went to who?"

"Not much. Mostly, I was rattling his cage, watching his eyes. Tracy went to him, which is not good."

"How d'you know?"

"You ever play poker, Lonnie? It's a rare player that doesn't have a tell. Finkle does. His eyes left mine, just a flicker, when I asked him, 'Did he come to you?' And if Tracy is reporting everything to him, we could have a problem."

"He didn't tell him about me, though," Lonnie said. "I told you he'd keep it to himself. Chicken shit!"

"That you nearly strangled him? We don't know what Tracy told him. Just be careful, okay?"

He nodded. "So, the Lewis case; it's off?"

"Not hardly. I have Chief Johnston's okay to go ahead with it, and to consult with Harry, in a limited way, of course." I winked at him. "Finkle can go play with himself... if he can find it. Look, I have to go in a few minutes. I have an appointment with Harry and Tim Clarke at ten and I don't want to be late. Good luck with your lap band interview. This afternoon, if you're back, we'll go talk to Pellman. Let's meet back here at one-thirty. Now, I'd like a minute, please."

Lonnie left, and I spent the next ten minutes thinking about what had just happened, searching for answers that didn't come. Unless... *Well, it's a possibility. Nah, couldn't be...could it?*

Chapter Fourteen

✦

Tuesday, May 12, 10 AM – Lewis Case

It was already ten o'clock when I arrived at Harry's offices on Georgia Avenue that morning. I parked in the lot and entered through the side door. Jacque rose from her seat and stepped around her desk to greet me: a kiss on the cheek and a quick hug.

"Hi, Kate," she said. "I'll tell him you're here."

"How is he this morning?" I asked.

"Like he always is. Dat man is an enigma, you know; you never can tell what he's t'inkin'."

Jacque is Jamaican, though she rarely drops into character; only when she's joking, or angry. She's been with Harry since he first opened his doors for business more than ten years ago, even before she graduated university. She has a master's in business administration and a bachelor's in criminology. Back then, in 2015, she was his PA. Today, along with Bob Ryan, she's a full partner in the company. I love her dearly.

"Hey you," Harry said. "Come on through. Jacque, have Tim come to my office, please."

I won't bore you by describing Harry's office, his "inner sanctum." Let's just say, turn of the century luxury would be an understatement.

"Take a load off," he said, leading the way to the coffee table flanked by two elegant sofas. We sat facing each other. "Can I get you some coffee."

"No, thank you."

The door opened and Tim Clarke—well, he almost fell into the room. His arms and hands were, as usual, loaded: a laptop, iPad, a cell phone, the copy of my file under his arm, and a brimming cup of coffee in his hand.

"Whoops," he said, grinning self-consciously. "Hiya, Kate. Can I sit here?" he asked as he began to dump his tech on the end of the coffee table. Harry watched him, smiling indulgently.

Tim is one of those rare people that nothing ever fazes. I've never seen him without a smile on his face. He lives, most of the time, in a weird world all his own. An IT expert, computer geek, hacker, he looks after the tech side of Harry's business. He's worked for him since before he dropped out of college when he was seventeen. Harry found him in an Internet café in North Chattanooga, just one small step ahead of the law. He's twenty-seven years old, looks sixteen; he's tall, skinny, wears glasses that he constantly fiddles with, and...he's a genius. Harry pays him an outrageous salary and treats him like a wayward puppy, which seems to suit both just fine.

"So, I read the file. It's a bit slim, right? What can I do for you?" he asked as he sat down beside me on the sofa and reached for his coffee, which he managed to slop all over the table.

"I need to know all there is to know about these four people."

I handed him the list:

1. Jennifer Lewis
2. John Lewis
3. Jeffery Tobin
4. Amber Watts

He looked at it, sipped on the coffee, set it down again, tilted his head to one side, looked sideways at me. "Okay. No problem—"

"Wait," I said, interrupting him. "Let me have that back, please."

He handed it to me. I took a pen from my inside jacket pocket and added two more names, then I handed it back to him.

He looked at it. His eyes opened wide. He looked at Harry, then at me.

"Are you kidding?" he asked as he shoved his glasses up the bridge of his nose with a forefinger.

Slowly, I shook my head.

"Let me see that," Harry said, reaching across the table.

He read; he smiled; he looked at me. "This could get you into a lot of trouble," he said and handed it back to Tim.

"No more than I'm already in," I said.

"Tracy I can understand," Harry said. "But why Finkle?"

"I think there's something going on that they don't want me to know about. Ostensibly, Jennifer Lewis is just another missing person, a runaway wife. It happens all the time. You know that, Harry." He nodded.

"The case is three years cold. Nobody cares about it, except Jennifer's sister. So why then is Tracy so sensitive about it, and why did Finkle warn me off it this morning? And he sure as hell doesn't want you involved."

"I don't know," Harry said. "Let's see what Tim can come up with." He thought for a moment, then said, "Tread carefully around Finkle and Tracy, Tim. We wouldn't want them to know what we're doing."

Tim gave him an, "are you kidding me," look, and said, "Hmm." He nibbled on his thumbnail. "These four...it depends on how deep you want me to dig."

"I want to know all there is to know."

He nodded. "You got it. Finkle and Tracy," he smiled, "shouldn't be any trouble...say, Friday? For the others, though, who knows where they are or how deep I'll have to dig. I may need a little extra time, Kate."

"That's fine," I said. "The gruesome twosome will do for a start."

He grinned as he got up, gathered up his stuff, and left the room muttering to himself. I couldn't help but smile.

"So," Harry said after Tim had closed the door behind him. "What now?"

"As far as the Lewis case is concerned?" I thought for a second, then said, "I have nothing to work with, not yet. Not until I hear from Tim. So I guess I'll concentrate on Sullivan for a few days. I'm planning to interview Pellman this afternoon. I'll see how that goes, then head up to Winchester either tomorrow or Thursday to interview his mother. That should be a boatload of fun."

"Is there anything I can do to help? I can let you have Bob for a couple of days if you like?"

I shook my head. "Thanks, but no thanks; not yet anyway. That would be like taking a sledgehammer to a thumbtack."

He smiled. "Well, you only have to ask... Would you like to get together this weekend?"

I tilted my head, frowned, narrowed my eyes, pursed my lips, then said, "We'll see. Right now, I have to go. Listen,

Harry, you do know how grateful I am for everything you do, don't you?"

Now it was his turn: he smiled and said, "We'll see."

I laughed, stood, leaned over and pecked him on the cheek. He reached for me, but I managed to dodge him.

"Not today, Buster," I said, dodging away toward the door.

"Kate, you want to go get some lunch, then?"

"I said, not today. I'll talk to you later, okay?" He nodded, obviously disappointed. I left him still sitting on the sofa, and I headed back to the PD.

Chapter Fifteen

✦❀✦

Tuesday, May 12, 2 PM – Sullivan Case

"Hey, you made it back." I slapped Lonnie on the shoulder as I walked by his cubicle. "Come on back to my office. You can tell me all about it. Then we'll go mess with Pellman's head."

"So," I said, as I sat down behind my desk. "How did it go?"

He sat down opposite me and said, "I made an appointment for Monday, June first—if that's okay."

"Of course."

"Good. I have to be at the clinic in Dalton at seven in the morning. Surgery is scheduled for nine, so I should be out of there by one or two." He paused. "I'll be off work for a week."

"That's fine, Lonnie. I'll manage. Will you need a ride?"

He shook his head. "No, I have that covered."

"Great! Well, I wish you luck, partner. Now, how about we go talk to Pellman?"

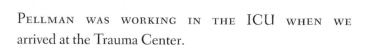

PELLMAN WAS WORKING IN THE ICU WHEN WE arrived at the Trauma Center.

"I'm afraid he might be a while," the nurse acting as the receptionist said.

I flashed her my badge and told her that unless he was assisting with an emergency, I needed to see him right away and that if I had to, I'd go get him.

She made the call, told me he was finishing up and would be no more than ten minutes, then showed me to a waiting room. Twenty minutes later he came bursting into the room, his face bright red with anger.

Great start! I thought. *At least I don't have to wind him up.*

"Who the hell are you?" he began. "And why in God's name have you dragged me out of the ICU?"

I stood. Lonnie stood. We showed him our badges, and as we did so, I said, "We're police officers, Mr. Pellman. My name is Lieutenant Catherine Gazzara, and this is Sergeant Guest. We want to talk to you about the death of Rhonda Sullivan. Now, if there's somewhere quiet—"

He interrupted me. "Damn it all to hell. I thought that was over and done with. I have nothing to say to—"

"Shut the hell up." Lonnie took a step forward. "Either sit down or do as the Lieutenant asked and take us somewhere we can talk without being interrupted."

"Or we can take you to the police department," I said. "Your choice."

He glared at me, then at Lonnie, then seemed to calm down, a little.

He nodded, took a step back, looked at his watch and said, "Okay, there's an office we can use. I can give you five minutes."

Lonnie chuckled. "You'll give us as long as it damn takes," he said. "Let's go."

It was a small, bare office, just a desk, three chairs, and a credenza set against the wall behind the desk. I took the seat behind the desk—no point in giving him any sense of authority. Pellman sat down opposite me, and Lonnie dragged the other chair to one side, set it against the wall slightly in front of and facing our suspect. Then the large cop sat down, folded his arms, shoved his feet out in front of him, crossed his legs at the ankles, lowered his chin, and stared at him. Pellman squirmed uneasily on the seat but said nothing.

He was a nondescript individual, maybe five-ten tall, a hundred and eighty pounds, straight hair parted on the left and swept across his forehead. He was dressed in green scrubs; a surgical mask hung from his neck. He wore glasses and a gold ring with a snake head on his right pinky.

I glanced across the desk at him, opened my iPad and set it on the desk in front of me. Then I made a show of turning on my digital recorder and setting it down on the desktop in front of him.

"So," I said finally, looking him right in the eye. "Tell me about Rhonda Sullivan. How did you pull it off?"

"You've gotta be kiddin' me," he said, shaking his head. "After all this time—"

Lonnie interrupted him. "There's no statute of limitations on murder, asshole."

I shot Lonnie a warning look, then said to Pellman, "He's right. Look, Chad, we know you killed her. Your employee number was used to draw the potassium chloride from the dispenser. You knew her; you were even friendly with her. And we know you had a crush on her—more than a crush, I think. Anyway, she rejected you. So, you had the means, and you had a motive." *I only wish you'd had the opportunity. We'd be done with this!*

"You've gotten it all wrong, Lieutenant," he said, in a calm voice. "As I told Detective Wells, several times: it wasn't me that took the KCL, it was Lisa, Lisa Marco."

"So you did, but she was her friend, her best friend, and she didn't have a motive; you did."

"I was her friend, too. I'm not crazy, Lieutenant. If I was going to kill her, d'you think I'd be stupid enough to check out the drug using my own code? Give me a break, *please*."

"But you'd done it before, hadn't you?"

His eyes narrowed, questioning. "Done what before?" he asked.

"Misappropriated drugs from the dispenser."

"*That?* Are you kidding me? I have a bad back; nerve damage. My prescription for Tramadol had run out, so I took a few pills to tide me over. So what? Everyone does it."

I looked at the notes on my iPad, then up at him and said, "You refused to take a polygraph. Why was that, if you had nothing to hide?"

"I did as I was advised by my attorney. I always do. Why pay for one if you're not going to do as she says." *Damn! Good answer.*

I shrugged. "What d'you think, Sergeant Guest?" I asked, never taking my eyes off Pellman's. "Is he really that stupid, or does he think we are?"

"If he expects us to fall for that old ploy, he is. How many times have we heard that one, Lieutenant? 'D'you think I'd be so stupid' and so on, and so on."

"Yeah, I think he's stupid; stupid, and arrogant, but then, aren't they all? Killers, I mean."

Pellman straightened up in his chair, stared right back at me, and said, "I'm not a killer. I was in North Carolina when Rhonda was murdered, seventy-five miles away in Winchester, with my mother. Detective Wells checked. He interviewed her several times. You can check. Now, I'm not going to say anything more. I want my attorney."

"No, you don't," I said. "You're not under arrest. Is there anyone other than your mother that can corroborate you being in Winchester that evening? Did you go out to eat, to a bar, convenience store, go anywhere at all, Mr. Pellman?"

"Yes, I did. I went to Walmart for Mom. I told Detective Wells. She even kept the receipt."

"She did, and Wells checked. He spoke to every sales clerk and manager that was on duty that evening and, guess what... No one remembered seeing you there. So, let's face it. She could have gone to the store herself."

"She could have, but she didn't. I did, and you can't prove otherwise. I was there all night, at my mother's. I didn't leave until after eight-thirty in the morning, when I went home and got ready for work. My shift started at noon."

"I didn't do it," he said. "Now either arrest me and let me call my attorney, or let me go back to work."

I let him go back to work.

"So much for putting pressure on him," Lonnie said, as he slammed the cruiser door.

"Yup," I said. "And I didn't see any indications that he was lying. Wells said he was tough. I wonder how tough his mother is? I guess we'll find out."

Chapter Sixteen

✦

Thursday, May 14, Morning – Sullivan Case

We traveled to the Pellman residence in Winchester early the following morning, and we timed how long it took: one hour seventeen minutes in very light traffic.

No, we didn't call ahead, which could have been a disastrous mistake if she hadn't been home. But in fact, she was still in bed.

"Come in," she said, resignedly, when she came to the door. "I've been expecting you."

Elizabeth Pellman led the way through to the kitchen.

"Sit," she said, waving a hand at the round, white breakfast table and four chairs.

Hmmm, I thought, *a woman of few words.*

"Coffee?" she asked, opening a cupboard and taking down a jar.

"No, no thank you," I said.

Lonnie looked plaintively at me. I shook my head at him.

"Well, suit yourselves. I've got to have some."

I watched as she set the machine going, trying to size her up. I already knew that she was fifty-two years old. She didn't look it though. I also knew that she'd been divorced from her husband for some eighteen years.

The white, slightly oversized pajamas gaped open at the front, revealing a cleavage that bordered on the spectacular. *Boob job? If it is, it's one of the best I've ever seen.*

Her dark brown hair was close-cropped, almost like a man's. Her eyes were enormous and made even more striking by the eyeliner she'd neglected to remove before going to bed.

She grabbed a large mug and filled it almost to the brim, sat down at the table, cradled it in both hands, placed her elbows on the table, and sipped with her eyes closed.

"Oh wow, that's good," she said and opened her eyes.

"So," she said. "You want to talk to me about Chad?"

She didn't wait for an answer. Instead, she set her mug down on the table and continued. "I don't know why the hell you would. Nothing's changed in the last three years. He was here with me all night. He was here when I went to bed, and he was still here when I got up at six o'clock. Case closed."

She leaned forward slightly, the fingers of both hands lightly stroking the sides of the hot mug; the pajama top gaped even more. I could see her right nipple. I heard Lonnie moving slightly in the chair next to me. *Damn! Those can't be real.*

"Mrs. Pellman," I said, quietly. "Would you please cover yourself up? My partner's about to have a heart attack."

I smiled to myself when I heard Lonnie suck in his breath.

"Oops, sorry," she said, quickly fastening one more button, which still left little to the imagination. "You'll have to forgive me; I'm so used to living alone."

"How did you know we were coming?" I asked.

"Duh! My son called last night. Look, I've been through it all a half-dozen times. My son was here with me from around two on Sunday afternoon, October 8, until eight-thirty the following morning. I know it was nine years ago, but nothing's changed. You're wasting your time."

Okay, so let's give it to her straight.

"Listen to me carefully, Mrs. Pellman."

She smiled indulgently at me.

"I know, and you know, that what you just told me isn't true." I watched her eyes, they narrowed just the tiniest bit; the smile remained but hardened considerably.

"You're calling me a liar," she stated, quietly. "I think you'd better leave, now!"

Lonnie leaned forward, rested his arms on the table, looked her in the eye and said, "No matter what you say, or how often you say it, we know Chad murdered Rhonda Sullivan, in cold blood. He calmly and deliberately injected a lethal dose of potassium chloride into her, enough to kill a *friggin' horse! Your son is an evil piece of garbage, and he'll fry for it!*" he shouted, startling Mrs. Pellman so much she reared back in her chair.

She recovered quickly. "My son didn't kill her. He's not evil. He's a good boy. He'd never hurt anyone, especially Rhonda. He loved her."

"She rejected him," I said, grasping Lonnie's arm and pulling him back. "He made up his mind: If he couldn't have her, no one could. So, he injected her with a lethal drug and watched her die. Doesn't that upset you just a little bit?"

"No, it doesn't because he didn't do it. He was here with me that night, and nothing you can say will change that because it's the truth."

"What time did you go to bed that night, Mrs. Pellman?"

"It was just before eleven." She looked away, then back at me. "I know because I had to take my pills before I went to bed. I checked the time."

She's lying!

"Are you absolutely sure?" I watched her eyes. They narrowed, hardened. There was just the hint of a smile on her lips. She nodded slowly.

"He wasn't here, was he?"

She sighed and stood up. "I've nothing more to say to you. It's time for you to leave."

She walked to the door, opened it, and waited.

I nodded, stood, walked to the door, then paused in front of her, looked her in the eye, and said, "Your son's a sadistic killer, Mrs. Pellman, and I'm going to get him; sooner or later, bet on it."

She didn't answer. I turned and walked out into the morning sunshine. There was a slight breeze blowing across the hillside. *An ill wind, I think.*

"Well, what d'you think?" Lonnie asked when we were back in the car and driving along River Avenue toward Highway 64.

"I think we need to time the ride back to Rhonda Sullivan's old apartment."

"I know that. That's not what I meant. I meant: what d'you think about her?"

I knew that. "I think she was lying."

"Duh, yeah, she was, whenever her freakin' lips were moving. And the titty show; that was a diversion, right?"

I nodded as I swung the big car onto 64. "It was. Did you like that?"

"What's not to like? She's a good-looking woman, a little mature, maybe, but   "

"Yeah, yeah," I said, interrupting his enthusiastic flow.

"Yes," I said, concentrating on the traffic. "She was lying, but most obviously when I asked her what time she went to bed... Hey, I'm hungry. You want to eat?"

"No, I'm trying to watch my intake, especially now that...well, you know."

"Okay, coffee it is then. I think there's a Hardee's down the road a piece." There wasn't. There wasn't one, or anything like it, until we reached Kimball, by which time I thought I was going to die. But I digress.

"Did you notice how she looked away to the left when I asked her?" I said, knowing damn well that he didn't; he had eyes for only one thing...well, two.

"It was a classic tell: when someone looks left like that, they are usually fabricating the answer. If they look to the right, it's likely they are checking their memory. She lied, for sure, but we can't prove it."

I paused, thinking, then said, "I'll tell you this, though: I think she knows he did it... Eleven? That's when she said she went to bed. She knows how long it takes to drive from her house to Chattanooga.

I pulled into the Hardee's at Kimble, checked my watch and said, "Hell, if he was still there when she went to bed, if he was ever there at all, there's no way he could have made this drive back in time. We've been on the road forty-four minutes already and we're still at least another thirty-five minutes from Sullivan's apartment, if we get a clear run through the city. So an hour and a half, or slightly better..."

I pulled up to the drive-through. "Two large coffees, please, black."

"Ninety minutes?" I said as I pulled up to the window. "So, if he left at eleven when she said she went to bed, that would put him at her apartment at around half past midnight, but only if he left right at eleven. That's outside the window for time of death. Which means..." I handed over the cash, grabbed the tray, thanked her, handed the tray to Lonnie, and continued. "Which means—"

"Yeah, I got it," Lonnie interrupted me, impatiently. "We're screwed, and that she was lying, but we already knew that, and we have nothing new. So now what do we do?"

The short answer was that I didn't know. We didn't have a crime scene, not anymore, and I'd already asked Mike Willis to recheck what little physical evidence there was. He'd found nothing new. I was fresh out of ideas; I was stumped.

We were back in the office by two o'clock that afternoon. I left Lonnie at his desk and went to my office. I had a report to write, and I wasn't looking forward to it.

By five o'clock, I'd finished. It wasn't a long report, and I wasn't proud of it, but it would have to do. I'd simply laid out the facts as I saw them.

There was nothing new to report. There had been no progress, and there wasn't likely to be unless a miracle was to happen. I was certain that Pellman had killed her, but I couldn't prove it. We'd re-interviewed Lisa Marco, Pellman, and his mother, to no good result. That there was no point in talking to Sullivan's fiancé, Mark Yates. He had no access to potassium chloride or the medical knowledge to have administered the drug. Lisa Marco had nothing new to add to her previous statements. Pellman insisted he didn't do it —that it was Marco who took the drugs from the dispenser, but there was no way to prove that either. Mrs. Pellman insisted her son was with her when Sullivan died, and neither Sergeant Guest or I could break her. And that was it.

I sighed, shook my head, picked up the office phone and punched in the chief's number.

"Chief Johnston's office. This is Cathy."

"Hey, Cathy. I need to see the chief. It's important."

"Hold for me, Kate."

The line played that annoying music again, but she was back almost immediately. "He wants to know why you want to see him."

"Tell him it's about the Sullivan case."

She was back a few seconds later. "Okay, come on, but I warn you, he's not in a good mood."

Oh crap, that's all I need.

"Okay, thanks, Cathy."

She was right, and she was wrong: he was in a terrible mood.... And who do you think was sitting at his right hand...well to the right of his desk? You got it: Henry Finkle.

"Sit down, Lieutenant," he said. "You're not bearing good news, I assume."

I nodded as I sat down. Finkle was literally beside himself with glee.

"I'm sorry, Chief. The Sullivan case is dead." I placed the file on his desk and handed him my report. He snatched it away from me and proceeded to read it through. His face was like stone, but I could see the anger glittering in his eyes.

"So, you've quit on it," he said, finally, looking up at me.

"No, sir."

"Well, what else would you call it?"

"Sir," Finkle said, "if I may suggest—"

"No, Henry, you may not suggest anything. In fact, you may leave, now."

He looked crushed, stood and glared at me as he walked to the door. I waited for the door to slam. It didn't. He closed it gently behind him.

"So, Kate," Johnston said, his face softening a little. "What's this all about? I figured if anyone could get the son of a bitch, you could."

"That's what I thought too. Without his mother's alibi, I would have. But then, so would Detective Wells have nine years ago, and we wouldn't be here now. She's lying, sir. I know she is. But there's no way to prove that she is. I can't see wasting any more money investigating this thing further. Maybe, sometime in the future we'll catch a break."

I felt horrible letting the chief down. He looked across the desk at me, nodding slowly.

He picked up my report, tore it in half, dropped it in the wastebasket beside him, then pushed the file toward me.

"You're right, Kate. Maybe something will come up. Hang onto it for a while. It's better in your office than it would be in the morgue." He was talking about the basement room where the cold cases were stored.

"Thank you, Chief."

I stood, picked up the file and walked to the door.

"One thing more, Lieutenant."

I turned, my hand on the doorknob.

"Stay out of Henry's way. He means you no good."

"Yes, sir, and thank you." *If you only knew...*

Chapter Seventeen

Friday, May 15, 8:30 AM – Lewis Case

I woke early on Friday morning...real early. I'd had Finkle and Tracy on my mind for most of the night. Finally, around five, I gave up trying to sleep and crawled out of bed, put on some running gear, and drove to the Greenway. By five-thirty, I was running at a good clip along the concrete path. Along the way, I passed several more like-minded fitness freaks—no, I'm not one of those—but I didn't really notice or acknowledge them. I still had Dick and Tiny foremost in my thoughts, and I wasn't sure why; intuition?

Did either of them have personal reasons for not wanting the Lewis investigation to go forward? If so, which one and why? Finkle? Maybe. He didn't seem to tire of trying to get into my pants. He's married but likes to play around. Maybe he knew Jennifer Lewis. If so, he could have told Tracy to go easy. Tracy? He's quirky as hell...

And so it went on, question after question but no answers, other than I was beginning to think Finkle looked good for it... No, no. Ass that he is, I didn't think he had anything to do with Jennifer's disappearance. If he did have anything to hide, it would be something purely selfish. *Maybe Tim will have found something. He said Friday, and I need to talk with Harry, too.*

I completed the five-mile run and was home by six-thirty. By seven, I'd showered, dressed, and was on my second cup of coffee. I scrambled two eggs, burned some toast, and was on my way to the office by eight. There, I made a couple of calls, had a few words with Lonnie, and headed out of the office to Harry Starke's downtown offices; it was eight-thirty.

"Good morning, Jacque," I greeted her as I entered through the side door. "He told you I was coming, right?"

"He did. Tim's with him, but you can go on in. I'll bring you some coffee."

I knocked on his office door and pushed it open. Harry was seated behind his huge desk; Tim was seated opposite him. They looked like high school principal and geeky student. Ah, but looks can deceive. Aside from Jacque and Bob Ryan, Harry thought more of Tim than anyone else on his team. He respected his expertise and never doubted a word he said.

They looked at me when I entered, and they both stood up.

"Hey you," Harry said. "Where've you been? We started without you. Grab a seat; sit down."

"Hello, Kate." Tim smiled self-consciously, looked down at the floor, then up again. "He's pullin' your chain. We haven't started; not yet."

He leaned over the desk, snatched a tissue from a box by the phone, took off his glasses, sat down, and busily went about polishing the lenses.

"So, Kate," Harry said, then paused as the door opened and Jacque handed me a cup of coffee.

"So, Kate," he said again. "Talk to me."

I thought for a moment, sipped my coffee—it was steaming hot—then said, "Tim said he'd have something for me by today. Do you, Tim?"

"He does, but let me go first."

He opened his iPad, flipped through several screens and found the one he wanted. "Henry Finkle was a patrolman back in '97 when I joined the force," Harry said. "So he'd already been on the job for a couple of years. I didn't know him, but I did know of him. He had something of a reputation for crossing the line. Apparently, he'd do just about anything to get ahead.

"Anyway, I contacted some of my old police buddies, and I learned a couple of things: One, he's definitely a lady's man—"

I tried to stifle a laugh, but it snuck out.

He looked up. "What?"

"I could have told you that."

"Yeah, well, I also learned that our boy liked to frequent certain, unsavory bars...and ladies; he'd been known to pay for his delights. He also liked to play rough." He paused, glanced up at me, then continued.

"I, myself, remember hearing a story that an official complaint had been made against him by a lady..." He consulted his iPad. "An escort, one Tina Gonzales. That was, supposedly, sometime in late 2004. Henry was a captain at the time. She claimed—and I got this from two different sources—that he assaulted and injured her; just how or how badly, nobody seems to know." He closed the cover of his iPad, then said, "I asked Tim to check it out. Unfortunately, he was unable to find any reference to that particular incident, so it was either just a rumor or someone went to great lengths to hide it. Which, knowing him as we do, is entirely possible. He's a violent man, is our Henry."

He looked at Tim, and said, "You did find two separate reports accusing him of excessive use of force, though, in 1998 and in 2000, both while he was still a uniformed sergeant. Internal Affairs investigated both, and he was cleared both times. No action was taken in either case."

I looked at Tim; I was in awe. He smiled brightly at me.

"You hacked his personnel file?" I asked.

He nodded, cheerfully, and said, "I did, and Tracy's too."

I shook my head in wonder. I always knew the boy was good, but...

"And?" I asked.

He consulted his laptop, then said, "I'll give you the short version. Detective John Tracy is forty-one years old, joined the force in 1998; he was then twenty-four. He spent his first three years in uniform, and the next seven in Narcotics, undercover." He paused, looked up at me and grinned.

Oh yeah, I knew all about that; that's when Chief Johnston dumped him on me.

"So, in 2008, he was assigned to the then Sergeant Gazzara as her partner." He grinned sideways at me, did the thing with his glasses, and then continued. "That lasted only for a couple of months when for some unknown reason," again, he made with the grin, "he was transferred back to Narcotics." He paused, looked at me, squinted, scratched at the back of his ear, and said, "And this is where it gets interesting. On April 17, 2012, he was transferred to Missing Persons, where he remains to this day."

What the hell?

"April 17, 2012?" I asked, stunned. "Are you sure?"

"Uh, yeah!"

"But...that's the day after Jennifer Lewis was reported missing."

"Again, yeah. And, according to the paperwork in the file, he was assigned the case on...the same day, the 17th."

I looked at Harry, my mouth hanging open.

"That can't be a coincidence," I said. "Who signed off on the transfer?"

"Chief Johnston did," Tim said.

I shook my head, my thoughts whirling. *That can't be right.*

"Okay," I said. "I'm going to need to talk to Johnston. Somebody must have recommended Tracy for that job, and I'm betting it was Finkle. And if it was, he did it for a reason... Who assigned the case to Tracy?"

"There's no signature—"

I interrupted him. "Oh, m'God, you don't suppose..."

"Take it easy, Kate," Harry said. "You're going too fast. You need to slow down, and you sure as hell don't need to poke the bear before you think it through. Johnston will eat your lunch."

I sat back in my chair and stared at the artwork on the wall behind Harry. *Wow! Finkle! And Tracy. What the hell have they done? What, to, do? What, to, do?*

Finally—it could only have been a few seconds—I knew how I was going to handle it. Oh yeah, very carefully.

I looked at Tim.

"Add Tina Gonzales to your list, please."

"Will do." He tapped on his iPad then looked at me and nodded.

"Great! Thank you. What else do you have for me?" I asked.

"That's it, for now. I'm still working on the others. It shouldn't take too long, but I do have other stuff to do."

He cocked his head and pushed the glasses higher on the bridge of his nose. He reminded me of a skinny owl. Somehow, though, I was sure he was a whole lot wiser, well smarter, than any owl.

"Take your time," I said. "The Sullivan case is already nine years cold. A few days is not going to make much difference now."

Tim nodded, closed his laptop, grabbed his phone, stood, and said, "I'll email everything to you. You should have it when you get back to your office. If I find anything I think you should know about, I'll call you. Talk to you later, Kate." And with that, he left us.

"So someone made sure Tracy covered it up," I said, thoughtfully. "But who? I can't believe it's Chief Johnston. The man's a tough SOB, but he's squeaky clean... Had to be Finkle. What d'you think, Harry?"

"I think you're on dangerous ground. I also think Finkle is a nasty piece of work and won't hesitate to discredit—or hurt you—in every way he can. You want me to have him watched?"

I laughed out loud at that. "No, Harry. You keep Ryan away from him. I can handle Finkle, and Tracy, and that's just what I intend to do."

"I believe you," he said with a smile. "Now, what about us? It's Friday. You want to go out tonight?"

I looked him in the eye as he smiled back at me, his eyebrows raised, blue eyes sparkled and...I melted.

"Sure. Why not?"

"Great, I'll cook."

"*Cook?* You said out."

"Out for you; in for me, I hope."

Well...what would you have done?

Chapter Eighteen

Friday, May 15, Late Morning – The Precinct

It was late morning when I arrived back at my office. Lonnie was out somewhere doing something. What, I didn't know, nor did I care. I had some serious thinking to do so I needed to be on my own.

I had my calls forwarded to voicemail, hung my home-made "Do Not Disturb" sign on my office door, which I then closed and locked. Next, I closed the blinds and sat down behind my desk, leaned my chair back against the wall, closed my eyes and began to try to unscramble my aching head. One thing I did know: Harry was right. I needed to think things through before I began to stir the swamp.

I lost all track of time. I might even have dozed, a little— can't remember when that happened before, or since— because it was almost one o'clock when I was startled by a loud and insistent knocking at my office door.

I stood, rubbed my eyes, then walked around my desk and unlocked the door.

"What the hell is this?" Finkle asked, waving the do not disturb sign in my face. "Have you gone mad, Lieutenant? This is a police department, not a freaking hotel. What were you doing?"

"I was working, Chief. What d'you think I was doing? Oh no; don't you dare go there."

He grinned, his teeth bared. He reminded me of an angry wolf.

"What were you working on that required you to lock yourself away with the window shuttered? Not the Sullivan case? I thought you'd closed that out."

"Yes, Chief, the Sullivan case," I lied. "Chief Johnston persuaded me to give it another try, so that's what I'm doing. Now, what can I do for you?"

"It's Friday. I need to know what the hell you're up to."

Damn, I'm glad you don't.

"I'm trying to figure out what my next move is going to be." *That was not a lie. It was exactly what I was doing, but not concerning the Sullivan case.*

"Now, will you leave me alone so that I can get on with it?"

He rewarded me with a snarly smile and backed out of the door. "Keep me informed, Lieutenant. In fact, you can put your intentions on paper and have them on my desk no later than..." he checked his watch, "shall we say, five o'clock today?"

Oh hell. That's screwed it!

I closed the door and went back to my desk, opened my laptop and began to type. Ten minutes later I was done. I hit enter and sent the report to the printer. I grabbed the sheet of paper, read it through, and shook my head. It wasn't going to win me any awards, but it was all I had.

I checked the time—it was almost three—then headed out and down the elevator to the first floor where Finkle's office was located, right next door to Chief Johnston's suite of offices. I knocked, walked in and dropped the single sheet of paper on the desk in front of him.

He didn't ask me to sit, so I crossed my arms and stared down at him.

He picked up the report and read the three short paragraphs, then looked up at me and said, "What the hell is this? There's nothing here, other than you intend to re-interview the suspect and his mother and spend more of the tax payer's money on re-examining the physical evidence."

Yeah, I know. It was all BS I'd made up just to keep him happy. What the hell else was I to do?

"Right, that's the plan," I said, staring him in the eye.

He nodded, his eyes glittering, thought for a moment, then he looked away and said, offhandedly, "And the other thing, the Lewis case?"

"What about it?" I shifted my weight from one foot to the other. "You told me, as did the chief, that Sullivan is the priority and that I was to concentrate on it, and that's exactly what I've done, am doing." It wasn't entirely true, but true enough.

"Hmm. Well then, that will be all, Lieutenant. Keep me informed...about the Sullivan case."

What's he up to?

I left Finkle's office and closed the door behind me. I stood for a moment, looking at Chief Johnston's door, hesitating, then I took a deep breath, knocked once and walked inside. Cathy looked up at me, surprised.

"Lieutenant Gazzara. I didn't know you had an appointment."

"I don't. I was wondering if maybe he could spare me a few minutes, in private."

She tilted her head, stared at me for a moment, then nodded and picked up the phone.

"Chief, Lieutenant Gazzara's here. She'd like a private word." She listened, nodded, and then set the phone back in its cradle.

"He'll see you. Go on in."

"Come on in, Catherine. Sit down. This is...irregular. So, before we begin, I'm going to ask Cathy to join us."

"Of course, sir. If that's what you prefer..."

"It is. I make it a rule never to interview a female officer without a witness present."

That didn't seem to bother you when you kicked Finkle out yesterday.

He picked up the phone. "Cathy, join us, please."

"Don't worry," he said, returning the phone to its cradle. "She's discreet. Whatever you have to say, you can say in front of her."

Cathy entered the room and took the seat usually occupied by Assistant Chief Finkle, which was fine with me, but then she placed a small digital recorder on the desk in front of her, and that *was* a little disconcerting.

"Now, Lieutenant, I know this is not about the Sullivan case, so what is it I can do for you?"

"Sir, I'm not so sure we need to record what I have to say."

He nodded at Cathy. She picked up the recorder and turned it off.

"Be very careful, Lieutenant. Now, talk to me."

I nodded, took a deep breath, and began.

"This is about the Lewis case, Chief."

He leaned back in his chair and folded his arms. "Go on."

"You saw the file, sir. It's...incomplete to say the least." I took another breath. "And there are some troubling anomalies."

I looked at him. He said nothing.

I looked at Cathy. She looked back at me, a slight smile on her lips.

"Sir, you authorized Detective Tracy's transfer to Missing Persons on April 17, 2012. I'd like to know who recommended that transfer."

"And why do you want to know that?"

"Please, sir. Humor me. Who was it?"

"You'd better have one hell of a good reason for this. It was Assistant Chief Finkle," he said.

My heart leaped.

"Did you know, Chief," I said, "that the 17th was the day after Jennifer Lewis was reported missing, and there's no record of who assigned the case to Tracy?"

He stared at me. I felt decidedly uncomfortable. I looked at Cathy; her face was a mask.

"What are you saying, Lieutenant?" he asked, quietly.

Okay, here we go.

"Sir, I'd like to question both Detective Tracy and Chief Finkle—"

"*STOP!* Are you saying that you suspect one or both of those officers had something to do with Lewis' disappearance? If so...by God you'd better be able to back it up."

"Unfortunately, sir, I can't. What I have is circumstantial at best, coincidences, mostly, especially Tracy's transfer and assignment to the case."

He waited. I continued. I laid out everything I had, everything Harry had said, leaving out only Tim's hacking of the PD's computers. How did I manage that? Well, I put it all down to the grapevine and rumors.

"You're right, Lieutenant," he said when I was done. "You have nothing. Nothing concrete. I can, however, confirm the two cases of excessive use of force by the then Sergeant Finkle. The rumors and the allegations about Miss Gonzales well..."

He stared right into my eyes. There was something about that look. *Damn it! He knows. Harry was right.*

He caught my reaction; his lips twitched, slightly. *Was that a smile?*

"I can't confirm any of that, of course," he said. "Nor can I officially sanction what you propose. However, you may talk to the two officers concerned, but," again, he made with the stare, "be very careful, Lieutenant. Henry Finkle is not a man you may wish to cross. I have your back but, for your own protection, keep me informed. You may go now."

"Thank you, sir."

He nodded, and I left the room, my heart beating like I'd just sprinted five miles.

Chapter Nineteen

Friday, May 15, Weekend

To say I was excited when I left the chief's office that Friday afternoon would be an understatement: I was both exhilarated and daunted at the enormity of the task I was about to undertake. Was I on the brink of professional suicide? I was about to take on an extremely savvy senior police officer, and equally devious detective. Compared to Finkle, though, Detective Tracy was inconsequential. Even so, I knew from experience that he was a clever, vengeful individual with the survival instincts of a cornered rat: the man didn't spend seven years undercover among Chattanooga's drug community without learning how to stay alive. Together, the two would pose a formidable threat and, try as I might, I couldn't clear my head of the wandering thoughts and questions that I knew would dog me throughout the weekend.

Harry did indeed cook dinner that Friday evening and, not for the first time in my life was I grateful for the diversion...and the sounding board.

I didn't arrive at his condo on Lakeshore Lane until almost eight o'clock. He was outside, on the patio, with a glass of scotch in his hand.

"I'll have one of those, please," I said, dropping into the seat next to him.

"Whoa, that's not you. Hard day?"

"You have no idea."

He poured a large one for me, dropped a single cube of ice into it, handed it to me, and said, "Well, are you going to tell me about it?"

So I did, and he listened thoughtfully without interrupting me until I was finished. And still he said nothing. He just stared out across the river, seemingly lost in thought.

"*Well*," I said, impatiently. "What d'you think?"

He raised his eyebrows, made a wry face, then said, "I think it's possible you've bitten off more than you can chew, and there's little I can do to help. Johnston might have sanctioned my limited involvement, but he's not going to allow me to interrogate one of his senior officers, or even Tracy for that matter."

"Thanks, buddy," I said, "for the vote of confidence. That's not the kind of help I was looking for. I was looking more for moral support and advice. I can handle the interviews."

"I'm sure you can. I'm sorry, Kate. That's not what I meant."

"Just what did you mean, then?"

"Finkle will block you at every turn. He's an experienced interrogator, vastly outranks you, and he'll do his damnedest to discredit you. He and Tracy will collaborate to bring you down. You think today was tough; you have no idea." He looked at his watch, then stood and said. "It's past time we ate, and I still have to grill the steaks. Let's continue this after dinner, okay?"

"Yes, okay. If you don't mind, though, I'll stay out here and relax, until it's ready." I held out my glass. "Hit me again, please."

Dinner was delicious: some sort of fancy salad, Greek, I think, and a filet mignon the size of a house, cooked to perfection and served with a loaded baked potato. But that's about all I remember of it. I do remember that my head was in a whirl, already living the interviews yet to come, and I was, in Harry's own words, "in dreamland."

Finally, he cleared the table, and we settled down on the sofa in front of the expansive picture window. It was almost dark and beginning to rain. The water was still, motionless except for the needle-like splashes of the raindrops that scattered the reflections of the lights on the Thrasher Bridge. It was, as always, spectacular and, yes, romantic, and any other time... But, as you might guess, I was in no mood for that, at least not then. I needed to talk, and Harry knew that I did.

"So," he said, closing one eye and holding his glass of

Laphroaig up so that one of the lights on the far side of the river shone through it. "I imagine you'll want to get this started first thing on Monday morning?"

He stated it in the form of a question, and it was so simple I hadn't even thought about it.

"Well, yes," I said, hesitantly, "of course."

He nodded. "And how, exactly, will you approach it? More to the point: who will you approach first?"

I hadn't thought about that either. Up until then, all I'd thought about was how I was going to handle Finkle, and I was still trying to figure that out.

"I think...Finkle."

"Why?"

"Because I think he's the reason Tracy did such a lousy job of the investigation. I think Tracy's covering up for him, and that could only be because Finkle was involved with Lewis. What else could it be?"

"You're thinking that because of Finkle's history with women?"

"That, and the way he treats me."

He slowly shook his head. "You'd better be well prepared, Kate. If you're not, he'll eat your lunch. You need a list of specific questions you want him to answer, and it had better be complete. You may not get a second chance."

Hmmm, I mused, staring, unseeing out across the river. The rain had increased, and the surface of the water was a roiling black mass streaked with orange and white reflections. *Food for thought.*

"Okay," he broke into my thoughts. "You'll start with Finkle. He's going to use his rank to try to intimidate you. You'll need to nullify that right at the beginning. Where d'you plan to interview him? His office, or yours? Before you answer that, I suggest you do neither. Treat him just as you would any other suspect; you pick the battleground. Use an interview room. Have Lonnie there, stick to the rules, and record and take video of everything."

Interview room? I thought, inwardly shaking my head. *I don't think so. He wouldn't go for it.* Harry's "full speed ahead and damn the torpedoes" approach might work for him, but it wouldn't work for me; that I knew for sure. No, mine would have to be a much softer, subtler approach, but I wasn't going to tell Harry that.

I sighed. "Harry, I'm an experienced interrogator. I know all that. I can handle it. Don't worry. He will *not* intimidate me."

"So you say, but this is going to be different from anything you've ever dealt with before."

"I know, and I appreciate your concern."

"Okay, can I make one suggestion before you go half-cocked? Talk to Tim first. See what he's come up with."

I sighed. "I can't put it off, Harry. I don't want Finkle fore-warned. And I'm stressed enough already, and tired, and I can't even think straight anymore." I let out an exasperated sigh. "Oh hell, you're right, as always. Okay, but I need to talk to him soon."

"Let me call him." He stood, stepped up to the window, and hit his speed dial.

I watched and tried to listen as Harry talked to Tim, but I managed to get only one side of the conversation: "Yes. Yes. I know. That's good. Yes. Okay, I'll tell her." He discon-nected and sat down again.

"He says to tell you he has a couple more avenues to explore and then he'll be finished. So, eight o'clock Monday morning in my office, will that work?"

I heaved a sigh of relief, and said, "That will work. Now, can we drop it, at least for tonight?"

He nodded. "Sure we can. Are you planning on going home or..."

"Oh come on, Harry. You know better than that. I've had two glasses of that stuff you love to drink and two glasses of wine. I'm not fit to drive...and hell, I want another drink, please?"

And that, as you might imagine, wasn't all I got that night. In fact, I had an amazing weekend.

Chapter Twenty

Monday, May 18, 8 AM

I left Harry early on Sunday morning, not something I would normally have done, but I was antsy and wanted to prepare for what was to come the following morning.

I spent most of the day and evening with a yellow legal pad and pencil—the salient points I transcribed onto my iPad. Old fashioned? Yes, I know, but so easy, and totally visual. By nine o'clock that evening, I'd done all I could; all that was left was to talk to Tim.

My last act that Sunday night before I went to bed was to call Lonnie and ask him to meet me at Harry's offices no later than eight o'clock the following morning.

Typical Lonnie; when I arrived, he was already there waiting for me, outside in the parking lot. Me? I arrived a little before eight and, wouldn't you know it? I was the last one to get there.

Harry and Tim were already in the conference room, heads together, discussing...me, I supposed.

"Ah, there you are," Harry said, getting to his feet. "Hey, Lonnie. Good to see you. Why don't you two grab some coffee and let's get started? I have a nine-thirty appointment."

Good to see you? Wow, that's a first. I thought they hated each other's guts?

Lonnie grudgingly acknowledged Harry's greeting and went to the breakroom to get the coffees.

I dumped my stuff on the table and sat down opposite Tim. Jacque joined us a minute or two later, and Lonnie returned with the coffee a couple of minutes after her.

"Okay, we all ready?" Harry asked when everyone was settled a few minutes later. "Good. Tim, you have the floor. Go!"

"Oh... Er, yeah, yes, okay." He clicked his mouse, stared at his laptop, then cleared his throat and said, "I'll begin with Tina Gonzalez." He looked around the table, quizzically.

I smiled at him, nodded, opened my yellow pad, flipped through it to a blank page, and picked up my pen. They all stared at me. I smiled, tilted my head a little, and raised my eyebrows.

"Wow," Tim said, staring at the pad and shaking his head. "I didn't know they still made those. Okay! Tina Gonzalez; originally from Conyers, Georgia. You had her on the list because of her association with Henry Finkle. She's thirty-nine. She works as a stripper at the Starburst on East Sycamore and has done so since she arrived in Chattanooga at the age of eighteen in 1998. She's been arrested two times for prostitution, and once for public drunkenness. All three arrests resulted in fines; no jail time. I found an ad for her services on the Dark Web as, and I quote, 'a beautiful, sophisticated companion,' and then the ad goes on to list her services. Apparently, she's available for dates, travel, conventions, and so on. Sex is not mentioned. Her last arrest was in 2006, for prostitution, which means she's managed to stay out of trouble for the last nine years, which also indicates that she's either very savvy or someone is looking after her. She has good credit; not great, but okay. She has two bank accounts, checking and savings. There's nothing unusual about the size of the checking account; the savings account, however, is questionable. It seems she's managed to put aside a nice little nest-egg, slightly more than $81,000. Again, that indicates she's savvy and maybe, she's...selling her wares?"

He waited for a reaction, but got none, so he continued, a slightly wounded look on his face. "I could find no references in 2003, 2004 or 2005, to the alleged assault by the then Captain Finkle. If it happened, the records have been thoroughly cleaned." He looked up, and said, "And that's about it... Oh, here's a photo of her."

He handed each of us a glossy eight-by-ten print.

She was indeed lovely, though I wondered how much of it was due to Photoshop. I was the last to lay my copy down.

"You want me to continue?" Tim asked.

"Keep going, Tim," Harry said.

"Jennifer Lewis," Tim said, "missing since April 16, 2012, was born in Dalton, Georgia, in 1974 where she grew up with her older sister Alice. She graduated high school in 1992 and, etcetera, etcetera. I won't go any deeper into her life story other than that she worked for a while in the carpet industry and moved to Chattanooga in 2000; she was then twenty-six. She had several jobs, including a thirteen-month stint at Dillard's as a sales clerk, and two years at J.C. Penney, also as a sales clerk. From October 2003 until she was reported missing, she worked at the Country Skillet on Shallowford Road. Now, this is where it gets interesting. She also worked part-time at the Starburst, for a period of five weeks, from March 12, 2012, until she vanished...as what, I can't say. Maybe as a waitress; maybe as a stripper. Either way, she'd be required to take her clothes off. Well, not all of them if she was a waitress. Only if she was—"

"Yes, yes," Harry interrupted him. "We get the idea. Get *on* with it, Tim."

"Yes...yes, I will. Okay, there's no evidence that she was...a prostitute, but... Okay, she worked at the Country Skillet on April 14 and was supposed to work that evening at the Starburst, but she never arrived. That means," he said, triumphantly, "that we can almost pinpoint the moment

when she was abducted, if she was abducted, or maybe she
did run away..."

He caught Harry's warning look and hurriedly continued.
"Anyway, I couldn't find out when or where she met John
Lewis, but the two were married in 2008; she was then
thirty-four and he forty-six. They had no children and, from
reading the reports," he looked at me, "it seems she left him
on March 2, 2012, and went to work at the Starburst ten
days later. What happened to her from then until she was
reported missing...I don't know. Her cell phone stopped
working at two-thirty-seven in the afternoon of April 15,
and it hasn't worked since. None of her credit cards have
been used since April 13 when she went through the drive-
thru at Taco Bell on Shallowford Road at three-seventeen
that afternoon. I ran her social security number. She's
received no benefits, no unemployment, and she hasn't ever
filed taxes on her own; the last time was in March 2012
when she filed jointly with her husband, John Lewis. She
seems to have vanished from the face of the earth. Questions?" He looked at each of us in turn; we shook our heads.

"All righty then," he said, taking off his glasses and holding
them up to the light. He shook his head, muttered something unintelligible, and grabbed a tissue from the box on
the table. He huffed on and polished each lens in turn, then
jammed them back onto his nose, shoved them higher with a
forefinger, and then turned his attention back to his laptop.

"John Lewis is an interesting character," he said. "He's fifty-
three and comes from Highton, a small town in Walker
County, West Virginia, to the south of Wheeling. He has a

younger brother, Michael. Their parents died when John was three. The two children were brought up by their grandparents on the mother's side, Peter and Martha Howlette. Both brothers attended high school in Highton; both graduated, neither of them went to college. John's been married two times—"

"Whoa, whoa," I interrupted him. "Wait a minute. That's not right. Jennifer Lewis' sister said that Jennifer was his first wife."

Tim's face betrayed a moment of hurt that I was questioning his intel. "Be that as it may, John Lewis married Sapphire Williams on June 6, 1981. He was nineteen; she was eighteen."

Wow, I thought. *That's weird, puts a whole new perspective on things.*

"That marriage didn't last very long. Sapphire left him in August 1982 and divorced him three months later, in November the same year." He paused, clicked his mouse a couple of times, then continued. "So anyway." He paused again, sniffed, tugged at his earlobe, then said, "After the divorce, it seems John moved back in with his grandparents and younger brother, and lived with them until he left Highton sometime in early 1983 when he moved to Louisville, Kentucky and went to work at one of the small whiskey distilleries. He stayed there until early October 1987 when he moved again; this time to Denver... Okay, look: he moved again, several more times in fact, before he finally arrived in Chattanooga in 2007. He's now in real estate. It's all in my report. I can print it or email it to you; whichever you prefer."

"Why don't you do both, please, Tim?" I asked. "But you have more, right?"

He nodded. "I do. John Lewis married Jennifer Tullett on June 14, 2008. He was forty-six, she was thirty-four. He's now a realtor. Does quite well, according to his tax returns—"

"Oh my God, Tim. You hacked the IRS? You can't tell me stuff like that. I'm a cop for Pete's sake."

He grinned at me. "No, Kate. I didn't, but he has his taxes prepared at—oh, well, never mind. You don't need to know. Anyway, his taxable income last year was a little less than $130,000. His credit score is 781, and he hasn't been late on a payment in more than ten years. He keeps his nose pretty clean, I guess."

"Okay, so what about," I checked my notes, "Sapphire Williams Lewis? What about her? And where is she?"

"Uh, I'm still working on that. I'm also still trying to track down John Lewis's brother, Michael. I'm going to need a little more time."

"That's okay, Tim," I said. "You've done great. Thank you. So, maybe tomorrow, d'you think?"

He cocked his head and scrunched his face, causing his glasses to move up his nose. "Maybe. It all depends...well, on a lot of things. I have work to do for Harry, and Bob and Jacque, and—"

"Okay." I held up a hand and stopped him. "I get the idea. Whenever you can. There's no great rush. I have what I need for today, I think. I hope."

"Cool," he said, closing his laptop. "How about I email it to you as I get it? That way you don't have to keep coming back here, okay?" He raised his eyebrows.

"That, Tim, sounds like a plan."

He nodded, gathered up his belongings, and left.

"Jacque, thank you for sitting in on this and for taking notes, too. Harry, I really do appreciate all you do, but we need to go. I want to meet with Finkle as soon as possible, but before I do, I need to call Alice Booker. Talk to you later?"

"Oh yeah," he said, rising to his feet. "I'll be waiting to hear from you. I hope all goes well." He checked his watch. "I have to go too. Talk t'you later. Good luck, Kate. You too, Lonnie."

It was almost nine-thirty when we arrived at the PD. We went straight up to my office where I called Alice Booker.

"Mrs. Booker. How are you this morning? Good. Do you have a minute? I have a couple of things I need to clear up.

Good, thank you. Alice, I think you told me that Jennifer was John Lewis' first wife. Is that correct?"

"Yes, that's right. Why do you ask? Oh my God; he's been married before."

"That's what our research has turned up. It looks like he was married back in 1982, to someone named Sapphire Williams. Have you ever heard that name before?"

"No. This is the first time I've heard it. I—I don't know what to say... Lieutenant Gazzara, that was more than thirty years ago. He must have still been a kid."

"Thirty-three years ago, to be precise and, yes, he was nineteen at the time. Apparently, the marriage didn't last long, just a few months—"

"Where is she, this Williams woman? I want to talk to her," she interrupted me.

"We're still working on that. In the meantime, I'll talk to John Lewis myself. Is there anything more you can tell me about him that I should know before I do?"

She thought for a few minutes, then said, "We never liked him much. He was very quiet. Not talkative at all. There was just something odd about him. He told us that he was an only child and that his mother and father had been killed in an accident—never would talk about that—and that he'd been raised by his grandparents. But they had both passed several years ago, and he had no other family. And he also told us he'd never been married before. That's all I know, I'm afraid. Oh my God, that sounds so ridiculous. He was married to my sister for four years, but I know nothing about him." I heard her sob.

"Well, if that's what he told you, he was certainly lying. He *was* raised by his grandparents, but he was married before, at least once, that we know of, and he also has a brother, Michael. We're still trying to track him down too... No, Alice, it's still early days yet... No, I don't know any more than I've told you... Thank you... Okay, that's good... So, look, if you don't have anything else, I need to let you go... Yes... Yes, of course. As soon as I know something, I'll be in touch. In the meantime, if I have questions, I'll call you. Thank you, Alice."

I stared at the screen of my iPhone for several seconds after she'd disconnected. John Lewis, I now knew, was indeed a liar, but was he also something else? Was he a killer?

I shook my head, looked at Lonnie, and said, "It's time we talked to Finkle."

He smiled, nodded, and slowly got to his feet. "You sure you're ready for that?"

"Oh yes, as ready as I'll ever be." And I was; I was also looking forward to the impending confrontation with some trepidation and a whole lot of excitement, which I hoped didn't show.

Chapter Twenty-One

Monday, May 18, AM – The Precinct

Finkle's movements were always erratic on Monday mornings, but I hoped he was in his office. Yes, I know, I could have called him, but I didn't want to forewarn him. My plan was to beard the lion in his den, so to speak. I smiled at the thought. *He might be able to have me thrown out, but he sure as hell won't be able to walk out on me.*

Instead, I called Chief Johnston's secretary, Cathy, and asked her if Finkle was in his office: he wasn't, so I asked her to give me a buzz when he arrived. Then Lonnie and I settled down to wait, during which time I filled him in on what I planned. He heard me out, his smile growing wider by the minute. When I was done, he just shook his head and said, "Good luck with that!"

The call came at five after ten. At fifteen after ten, I knocked on his door and, without waiting for an invitation, walked right on in, with Lonnie close behind.

I stood aside to let Lonnie by, and then I closed the door and turned to face the desk.

Finkle's office was, in deference to his rank, much larger than mine. Its furniture included, not only the usual office accouterments, but also a mid-sized round table with six chairs; a small conference table, if you will.

I noted that Finkle was seated behind his desk, but I didn't acknowledge him. Instead I dumped my stuff—the Lewis file, laptop, phone, and iPad—on the table, then turned and smiled at him.

He was staring, slack-jawed at me.

"Good morning, Chief," I said, brightly.

"What the hell is the meaning of this?" He began to rise from his seat, both hands on the desk.

"Why are you barging into my office...and why is Sergeant Guest with you?"

"Chief," I said, taking a seat at the table and arranging my stuff in front of me. "We need to talk."

"So, make an appointment, damn it."

"I thought about doing just that, but I didn't think you'd go for it. We really do need to talk, Chief, and right now. So, would you please join us? The sergeant is here because I'm here; you know the policy about men and women alone together in the same office. Lonnie, sit down."

Lonnie sat down next to me. Finkle remained standing behind his desk.

"Have you gone mad, Lieutenant? This is not happening. Now gather up that crap and get the hell out of my office, or I'll have you removed."

"Well now," I said easily. "I can do that, but we'd still have to talk. We could, of course, if you prefer, go to one of the interview r—"

He interrupted me. "What the hell are you talking about?"

There was no easy way to do it, so I took a deep breath and dove right in.

"As you know, Chief, I'm working on the Lewis case, and I need a little help." *Hah, well, I did say I was going to try the soft approach.* "Your help. So, if you wouldn't mind..." I pointed to the seat across the table from me.

"Lieutenant Gazzara, you can't just barge into my office and—"

"Yes, I know, Henry, and I apologize...but it really is necessary that we get it done now. Can we get on with it, please?"

He came around the desk, slowly. For the first time since I'd known him, he looked unsure of himself and, inwardly, I allowed myself a tiny smile. *So far, so good.*

He sat down opposite me. The scowl was intimidating. He clasped his hands on the table in front of him.

"You have five minutes, Lieutenant. Now, what's this about?"

I nodded, made a show of turning on my digital recorder and placing it in the center of the table.

"Please turn that off, Lieutenant."

"No, sir. I can't do that. I need to record this meeting for the record." And then I continued to state for the record the date, time, and those present. That done, I opened my laptop and then my iPad and flipped through the screens until I found my notes.

"Chief Finkle," I began, "as you know, I've taken over the investigation into the disappearance of Jennifer Lewis who was reported missing on Monday, April 16, 2012. You're familiar with the case, correct?"

He nodded.

"Please answer for the record, Chief."

"Yes," he growled. "I'm familiar with it."

For the next several minutes, I led him through the essential details of the case culminating with it being assigned to Detective Tracy. He listened quietly, answering my questions, for the most part, in monosyllables.

Finally, I sat back in my seat, folded my arms, and looked him in the eye. "Assistant Chief Finkle, within hours of Lewis being reported missing, instead of following protocol and allowing the case to be handled in the normal way by the commander of the Missing Persons unit, you took matters into your own hands and *personally* transferred Detective Tracy to the MPU and then assigned the case to him. That's an extraordinary breach of protocol, wouldn't you agree? And I was wondering, why did you do that?"

"How...did, you know that?"

"That's irrelevant, Chief. I ask again: Why did you breach standard procedure and transfer Detective Tracy to the Missing Persons unit and then personally assign the Lewis case to him?"

"I—I." He grabbed the recorder and turned it off.

"What the hell are you doing?" he hissed.

"I'm just trying to find out what your reasoning was. Now, please turn the recorder back on and answer the question. If not, then we'll have to adjourn to an interview room and videotape the interview, that will place it into the official records. Is that what you want, Chief? I think not."

"I don't answer to you, Gazzara. I suggest you think very carefully about what you're doing." He paused, then said, "Does the chief know you're about this?"

I nodded. "He does, and he's sanctioned the interview. Now, will you please turn on the recorder and answer the question?"

He looked down at the recorder still in his hands, contemplated it for a moment, then turned it on and slowly set it down.

He hesitated, then cleared his throat and said, "He was the best man for..." He paused for a second or two and then continued. "He's a good man. He deserved a break. He never recovered from the way you screwed him over when he was your partner. I gave him a helping hand, that's all."

I ignored the comment.

"Do you know Jennifer Lewis, Chief?" I asked.

"I do not."

I nodded. "You're sure?"

"I just said, I don't know her...but it's possible, I suppose, that I might have met her at some time."

Good play, Chief.

Again, I nodded. "Chief Finkle, when I interviewed Detective Tracy on Monday last, I asked him why he didn't properly investigate Jennifer Lewis' disappearance. The reason he gave was, in part, and I quote, "she's a freakin' hooker.' I looked him in the eye and asked, "What do you make of that, sir?"

He hesitated for a moment, then said, "I'm not sure what Detective Tracy was thinking when—if, he said that, but of course I do not condone it. I will question him myself and, if what you say is true, I'll see that he's disciplined and reassigned."

Yes, I'm sure you will.

"Chief Finkle. Are you familiar with a—I'm going to call it a nightclub, but that might be a little too kind. Are you familiar with an establishment," I made a show of consulting my notes, "called The Sorbonne?"

"You well know," he replied, "that, as a police officer, I'm very familiar with that establishment. Where are you going with this, Lieutenant?"

I ignored the question and said, "Have you ever visited The Sorbonne, Chief?"

"In the line of duty, yes. You know I have."

"You've been a police officer for more than twenty years, since 1995 in fact. Chief Finkle, have you ever, during your twenty years as a police officer, visited the Sorbonne socially, outside of the line of duty?"

His face was white. "I—I. Yes, I have."

"Is The Sorbonne, would you say, an appropriate establishment for a senior police officer to visit...socially?"

"This is ridiculous. I enjoy a drink now and then, as do we all. I go to lots of places. I like to keep an eye on the city's underworld, as I know do you, Lieutenant."

"How many times have you visited the Sorbonne socially, would you say?"

"I have no idea."

I thought for a moment, *Okay, now's the time to give it to him. Be careful how you word it, Kate.*

I breathed deeply, then said, "Would it surprise you, Chief, if I were to tell you that the owners of The Sorbonne have identified you as a frequent visitor there?"

"Frequent visitor? Yes, it would. I haven't been inside the place in months." There was an edge to his voice.

Ooh dear, Benny. I fear I may have dealt you a bad hand. Benny Hinkle is the owner of the Sorbonne, and a good friend of mine, and Harry's.

"But in the past...well, never mind. Chief, would it also surprise you if I were to tell you that several witnesses would also confirm that you *are* a regular visitor to The Sorbonne and that you actively solicit prostitutes there?"

I watched his eyes, looking for...well, I didn't see it. What I did see were his eyes bulging with indignation. It did indeed, surprise him. *It would surprise me too.*

"It would indeed." He ground his teeth in anger. "*Because it would be a damned lie.*" He almost shouted it. He was so angry I was glad there was a table between us.

"This is outrageous!" The veins in his neck stood out like purple cords. "I am deeply offended by this line of questioning, so I ask you again, Lieutenant: where the hell are you going with this?"

For a moment, I didn't answer. Instead, I looked down at my iPad, pretending to consult my notes, then asked, quietly, "Chief Finkle, do you know a...Tina Gonzalez?"

Slowly and deliberately, he stood, reached out, grabbed the recorder, and turned it off.

"That's enough," he growled. "I know what you're doing, Gazzara. This is all about..." He hesitated, then said, "Well, you can forget it. If you want to continue this bizarre interrogation; this, this blatant attempt to tarnish my character and good name, I demand to have my attorney present."

I looked up at him and smiled.

"Okay, Henry," I said. "No, it's not what you think. I'm just trying to do my job. There's something hinky about this whole Lewis case, and I need to find out what it is. Now please sit down. It's best for both of us that I get truthful answers to my questions, now rather than later. You'd agree with that, right?" I didn't expect an answer, nor did I get one, so I continued. "Tell you what," I said, trying to calm him down. "We can continue this here, off the record, informally if you like, but I should warn you: I will be taking notes."

Reluctantly he sat down again and nodded his consent. He did, however, keep possession of the recorder.

I leaned back in my chair and glanced at Lonnie. He winked at me.

"Chief," I said. "I know all about the Tina Gonzalez incident. I also know that you were cleared of any wrongdoing. My problem is this: Gonzales is a known prostitute. She works at a strip club, the Starburst which, in and of itself, is not a surprise. What is a surprise, is that the Starburst is the same strip club where Lewis worked. They must have known each other. How well, I don't yet know, but I'll find out. Detective Tracy has stated that Lewis is—was—a prostitute. I, that is we, don't know that. She's never been arrested, for anything.

"I'm sorry, Chief, but all that makes me wonder if Tracy's sudden transfer to the MPU, his assignment to the case assigned him, *and* his lack of investigative effort thereof, are not an attempt to cover up your...possible association with Ms. Gonzalez and Ms. Lewis. Well, you've got to admit, it all looks a bit...coincidental?" I held my breath and waited for the explosion. It didn't come.

He stared at me, seething, then seemed to calm down a little. "Before I address all that, Lieutenant, would you mind answering a question for me?"

"Of course, if I can."

"How did you find out about Ms. Gonzales' accusations? Did Harry Starke's geek hack the police department's records?"

My heart leaped as he looked me in the eye, but I kept it together, held his gaze and didn't hesitate. "I'm sorry, Chief. I can't reveal my confidential source. You know that's not what we do. But you also know, I'm sure, that there is no official record of the Gonzalez incident, at least none that I'm aware of. Is that not so?"

He didn't answer the question. Instead, he said, "I did *not* know Jennifer Lewis. There was no association between Jennifer Lewis and myself. I do *not* consort with prostitutes. The facts you have laid out are nothing more than unfortunate coincidences." He paused, then continued, "They say no good deed goes unpunished, Lieutenant. My providing Detective Tracy with an opportunity to better himself—to leave undercover work—is such a deed." He stood and laid the recorder on the table. "This interview is over. In the interests of professional courtesy and harmony within the department, I'll not hold this interview against you. I would, however, say this: be very careful how you proceed with this investigation. If any of what's been said here today is leaked, either within the department or to the press, I will see to it that—well, I'm sure you understand. Now, I have nothing more to say. Please leave my office."

I nodded. "Very well, Chief. I appreciate your candor. I do, however, reserve the right to question you again, should the need arise."

"I don't think so. Get out, Lieutenant."

LONNIE AND I DIDN'T SPEAK TO EACH OTHER UNTIL WE were back in my office and behind closed doors.

I flung the file down on my desk and set the rest of my stuff down beside it.

I flopped into my desk chair, swiveled around, and stared out through the open blinds into the incident room.

"That was intense," Lonnie said, breaking into my thoughts. "You gonna talk to me, or what?"

I swiveled back around, looked at him and said, "I noticed

you kept your mouth shut in there. You're smarter than you look. You heard what he had to say. What did you think?"

He grinned at me. "Yeah, I did, didn't I? What did I think? I think he's a lying sack o' shit, is what I think. He knew Lewis, I'm certain of it. And what the hell was all that stuff you brought up about the Sorbonne? That was the first I'd heard of any of it."

I smirked, leaning back and clasping my hands behind my head as I recalled the conversation. "I was just jerking his chain. I wanted to get his reactions. I did. He seemed sincere... Look, if Tracy had done his job three years ago, he would have followed up on his premise that Lewis was a hooker. He didn't. We will, though where that will lead us, God only knows. In the meantime, I'm prepared to give Tiny the benefit of the doubt. Maybe that's all there was to it, that he gave Tracy a break... But was there a little quid pro quo involved? I don't know." I thought for a moment, then continued. "I'm not sure we did the right thing: interviewing Finkle first. If he gets to Tracy before we do, well..." I brought my hands down and shrugged.

"I don't think it would have made much difference, either way," Lonnie said. "Tracy would have run straight to Finkle and warned him. No, you did right, LT."

"I sure as hell hope so."

"You haven't yet told me what you think," he said.

"Something's not right. Did you see his reaction when I brought up Gonzalez?"

He nodded.

"I think he knows her. Whether or not he's had relations with her is another matter. Well, she's going to say it happened, but unless she has witnesses, it's all he said, she said. I don't know... What I do know is, I don't believe in multiple coincidences. It just doesn't happen. Was there an ulterior motive behind Tracy's transfer? I think so. I think Finkle knew Jennifer Lewis. How well he knew her, we'll probably never know."

"So where do we go next?"

"Tracy, of course, and we need to talk to John Lewis, but first I need to know what Tim was able to find out about Sapphire Lewis and John's brother, Michael. We also need to talk to the so-called boyfriend, Jeff Tobin, and Amber Watts, but not before I have all the information."

I checked the time. It was almost noon.

I stood. "Let's go get some lunch. I need coffee, in the worst way. We'll do Tracy this afternoon, then I'll give Tim a call."

"Do?" he asked, with a grin.

"Get your mind up out of the gutter, Sergeant. Where d'you want to eat?"

"Arby's would be good. I can get a salad."

"Arby's it is then."

Chapter Twenty-Two

Monday, May 18, Afternoon – The Precinct

I've mentioned before that John Tracy was, some ten years ago, my partner. It lasted only for a few weeks. I couldn't stand the man. He was a nasty little shit: arrogant, lazy, sloppy, and a smartass. He'd been a cop for more than twenty years, yet he'd never climbed higher in the ranks than detective.

His unimposing build was only a little over five-eight—yes, they made a good pair, him and Henry Finkle—and thin, skinny even, with brown hair that he wore almost to his shoulders.

Having told you all that, you'll understand why the interview with Detective Tracy that afternoon did not begin well.

"Well, if it ain't Boris and Natasha," he said, with a sneer, when we arrived at his cubicle on the first floor. "I've been expecting you. Chief Finkle mentioned that you might drop by and that I should cooperate. You want to do this here, or shall we go somewhere more comfortable?"

"That's up to you, shithead," Lonnie snarled. "You want the rest of the squad to hear how you screwed up an inv—"

I placed a hand on Lonnie's arm, interrupting him.

"I think it would be best if we didn't do this here, Detective. My office or an interview room. Either way, I'm going to record you, so it's your choice. What's it to be?"

"Your place, I think."

There was no mistaking the innuendo, or the salacious grin. I still had my hand on Lonnie's arm; I felt him tense up. I squeezed, to let him know it was okay.

"My place it is, then. Let's go."

THE LEWIS FILE WAS STILL ON MY DESK. LONNIE TOOK a seat slightly behind and to Tracy's left.

"Before you begin... Is that thing on? If it is—" he asked, looking at the recorder in front of him.

"It is," I said, interrupting him, and then, for the record, I stated the time, place, and so on. Then I asked him, "You were saying, Detective?"

He flipped the lock screen on his iPad, then said, "I was about to say that I have nothing to add to what I told you last Monday. Jennifer Lewis was having an affair with some guy, name unknown, and she ran off with him. End of story. I interviewed her co-workers and found nothing to indicate otherwise. She had been seeing a Jeff Tobin, and I did interview him, but he said he'd met someone else and had stopped seeing her a couple of weeks earlier. He said he didn't know if she was seeing someone else or not. John Lewis was a nice guy, at least I thought he was. I believed him. That's it."

I'd let him ramble on without interruption because I was looking for anomalies, but he'd stuck strictly to the script. He seemed to know it by heart, which I found incredible for someone who hadn't even looked at the file in more than two years.

"Can I see that, please?" I asked, holding out my hand.

"Why? Wha' for?"

"Just hand it over, John."

He did, reluctantly, and I read through his notes. He'd recited them almost word for word. *He friggin' rehearsed it.*

That troubled me, but I let it go and handed the iPad back to him.

"Why did Chief Finkle transfer you to the MPU?" I asked.

He cocked his head, made a face, looked puzzled at me. "Because I asked him to?"

"I don't know, John. Did you?"

"Yes, I freakin' did. I'd had a gutful of Narcotics." He sighed. "And my freakin' cover was blown."

"How well do you know the assistant chief?" I asked.

Again, he made with the puzzled face. "About as well as anybody, I suppose. He's not so bad. He always treated me well enough, like when he transferred me to Missing Persons."

"What did he tell you when he handed you the Lewis file? Did he give you any special instructions?"

He shrugged. "No, nothing. He told me it had just come in and to get on with it."

"Did he ask you to...how shall I put it?"

"To cover it up?" He finished it for me. "Hell, no he didn't, and I wouldn't have if he had. Are you out of your freakin' mind, Lieutenant?"

"Hey," Lonnie said. "Tone it down."

"Screw you, Guest," he snarled.

"What the hell's going on here, Lieutenant?" Tracy asked. "Am I a suspect, or something? Is the chief?"

Lonnie looked like he was about to say something, probably something he shouldn't, so I raised a hand and shook my head at him. He relaxed a little.

"Do you know Tina Gonzalez?" I asked.

"No," he answered, quickly.

Too quickly I thought. I also didn't believe him.

"Oh come on, John. You spent God only knows how many years in Narcotics, and you never met a known prostitute?"

His face reddened. "Well, I might have, but if I did, I don't remember it. I certainly don't *know* her."

"How about Jennifer Lewis?" I asked. "Did you know her?"

"No, I freakin' did not," he yelled, indignantly. "And I know damned well I never met her."

That one, I believed.

"To your knowledge, Detective, did Assistant Chief Finkle know Jennifer Lewis?"

"Oh, my, God." He was incredulous. "You think it was him she was having an affair with?" He burst out laughing.

No, I didn't think that, but now that you mention it.

"As far as I know," he said, "he never even met her. How the hell would he—"

"You said she was a hooker," I interrupted him.

He just sat there, staring at me, slowly shaking his head. "That's what her husband said. You can't be serious, Lieutenant. You're suggesting that Henry Finkle... Nah, I don't believe it."

"It's been said, John. You've heard the rumors."

"Yes, but that's all malicious bull. You're— You're freakin' crazy."

"Okay, let's talk about something else. You waited four days before you checked her apartment. Why?"

He frowned, looked away to the left, then back again, and said, "As I recall, I was busy, very busy. I'd just been transferred out of Narcotics. I still had a lot of loose ends to deal with there."

You're lying, John.

I nodded. "And when you did finally check it out, you found she'd left all her belongings behind. The only things missing were her cell phone and pocketbook." I looked up at him and frowned. "That didn't seem unusual to you?"

"No. It didn't. Those are the things she *would* have taken with her, so I figured she'd just decided to start over, make a clean break."

I shook my head in disbelief. "I don't believe you, John. I think you were doing just enough to be able to write a report and then shelve the case. How well d'you know John Lewis?"

"I don't know him, well, other than to interview him. As I said, he seemed okay. I had no reason not to believe him. You're not saying he had anything to do with—"

"I'm not saying anything. I'm looking for answers, and you don't seem to have any."

He shrugged. "Whatever!"

"John," I said, looking him right in the eye, "I hope you're clean, because if you're not..." I didn't bother to finish the comment.

"I'd look to your own self, if I were you," he said, his narrow slits glinted with anger. "You're making some powerful enemies, and I'm not just talking about the assistant chief."

"What the hell's that supposed to mean?" Lonnie, said, leaning forward and grasping the back of Tracy's chair.

Tracy jumped up and spun around to face him. "What d'you think it means, Fat Boy? Stay the hell away from me."

He turned his head toward me, still keeping an eye on Lonnie. "You done with me, Lieutenant?"

I nodded, slowly, staring up at him. "Yes, you can go, for now."

He circled around Lonnie, gifted me with a sneer, then closed the door behind him.

"He's right, you know," Lonnie said, sitting down. "Finkle's a nasty little bastard, but he has connections, and not just in the department. So does Tracy. Better be real careful from now on, LT."

"You may be right," I said. "I think we hit a raw nerve; two raw nerves, in fact. Did you believe him?"

"Not for a second."

I nodded. "Me neither. His answers were just a little too pat. He as good as told us that Finkle had warned him, which is exactly what I was afraid of. He's covering something up; they both are. I'm sure of it. We need to interview Gonzales, and quickly. Let's hope they haven't gotten to her."

I leaned forward, my elbows on the desk and chin in my hands as I thought.

"Lonnie, you do realize what this could mean, right?"

"Oh yeah: a cover-up, corruption, and who the hell knows what else. As I said, watch your back."

I leaned back in my chair and stared up at the ceiling. *What the hell's happening to me?*

Three days later, I found out. Lonnie was right: I should have been watching my back.

Chapter Twenty-Three

M**onday, May 18, Evening – Lewis Case**

I was late getting home that evening. I did my usual thing: showered, a little yoga to calm my jangling nerves, got into my pajamas, and then I made myself a sandwich—cheese, lettuce and tomato. That done, I poured myself a large glass of a cheap red wine I'd gotten from the supermarket. Then I settled down with the recorder and pad to listen to the recordings I'd made that day, make notes, and plan my strategy.

It was close to eight o'clock when my cell phone buzzed. I looked at the screen and smiled.

"Hey, Tim. I bet you have some news for me?"

"I do. I'll give you a quick rundown of the main points, then email the report, okay?"

"Good plan. Let's hear it."

"Okay! Sapphire Williams Lewis. As I told you before, she married John Lewis in 1981 and left him fourteen months later in August of 1982. Now get this: she then went to work at a strip club in Wheeling. Crazy stuff, huh?"

Wow, more coincidences? "Okay, so where is she now?"

"I don't know, she turned up for work on the evening of Friday, December 10, 1982, worked a full shift, and left the club at one o'clock on Saturday morning. She didn't turn up for work on Saturday evening. From what little I could find out, she's not been seen since."

"How d'you know all this?" I asked.

"I had to do a lot of digging. The Kitty Kitty Club went out of business in February 1985. It was closed down by the sheriff's office, so that was a dead end. However, Sapphire has a brother, Ryan, eight years older. They grew up in Highton and went to high school there. Ryan lives in Boston now, has since he got out of the army in 1980. I called him. He told me he used to talk to Sapphire at least once a week, usually on Fridays. He talked to her that morning, the tenth. He said she was in an unusually good mood but didn't tell him why. He called her as usual on the seventeenth, but she didn't answer the phone. He said he wasn't worried, not then, not until he called her on Friday, December 24, Christmas Eve and she didn't answer. He called her again on Christmas Day, three times, and then again on the 26th; still no answer. Finally, he called her ex-husband, John Lewis. Lewis told Ryan he didn't know where she was, but that she'd probably gone off with one of her boyfriends. That's all I have."

What the hell! That's the same line Lewis is using about Jennifer's disappearance.

"Why wasn't she reported missing?"

"She was, by her brother, on January 4, 1983, in Wheeling, but nothing came of it."

"Who handled the missing person case, d'you know?"

"It was a detective... Wait, I have it here somewhere... Ah, okay, it was Detective Ellis Benton. Unfortunately, he died in 2016; he was seventy-seven. Old age, I guess. That's all I have on Sapphire, Kate."

"How about Ryan Williams, d'you have his number?"

"Of course."

I wrote the number on my yellow pad intending to call Ryan the following morning.

"Okay, Tim." I heaved a sigh. I was tired, and just about done in. "What else d'you have for me?"

"I also did a little more digging into John Lewis' past, but I didn't find much. I did get hold of some names of high school friends, but I didn't call any of them. I didn't have time. You'll find the list—there are six names—in the email I'm going to send you. As to John's younger brother, Michael, he's a mail carrier. He still lives in Highton with his wife in the old Lewis family home. He has two children, both grown up and moved away. I didn't talk to him either, because I didn't want to step on your toes, say the wrong thing. I do have his number, though. You want it?"

I wrote that down too.

"It appears John Lewis left Highton sometime early in January 1983. I couldn't pin it down exactly, but he started work at the distillery in Louisville on Monday, January 24. As far as I could tell, he's not been seen in Highton since then."

I heard some clicking, and I swear I heard Tim push the glasses up higher on the bridge of his nose. Then he continued.

"Okay, that's all I have for you right now. I'm still trying to track down Tobin and Watts, but I'm really busy with other stuff for Harry and Bob. Don't worry, though. I'll stay with it and get back to you as soon as I have something."

"Thanks, Tim. You're the best. I gotta go. I need to get some sleep. Bye."

And I hung up before he had a chance to digress into one of his long and boring diatribes.

But I wasn't lying. I was exhausted. I turned off my phone, set the alarm for six o'clock, and went to bed. I don't even remember my head hitting the pillow. What I do remember are the dreams. One of them featured me looking up into a bright light with Doc Sheddon looking down at me through a transparent face shield. That one, I'll never forget.

Chapter Twenty-Four

Tuesday, May 19, AM – Lewis Case

I was more than glad to wake up that Tuesday morning, the day after my interviews of Finkle and Tracy. The nightmares were like none I'd ever experienced before. And the final one? Was I really on Doc's autopsy table? I shuddered at the thought and hoped to hell it wasn't a portent of things to come.

Anyway, I arrived at the office in a mood to brook no crap from anyone, but who d'you think was waiting for me by the elevator when I arrived? You got it, Henry Finkle.

"Good morning, Chief," I greeted him brightly, though inwardly I was seething. I didn't need a confrontation with him, not then. "What can I do for you?"

"I was wondering if there had been any progress on the Sullivan case? We're not going to let it go; you do know that?"

Hah, he's fishing.

"I do, but that's not why you're here, is it? You've been talking to Tracy."

I could tell by the look on his face I was right.

He nodded. "Yes, he told me what you're thinking." He hesitated for a moment, and I kept my mouth shut and waited.

Finally, he said, "You're way off the mark, Lieutenant, and you're going to get yourself into a great deal of trouble if you continue with this line of inquiry."

He waited for me to answer; I didn't.

"Very well, then. Carry on. But remember: I'll be watching you."

He turned on his heel and walked back to his office.

I punched the elevator button and rode up to the second floor, shouldered through the door into the situation room, and tapped Lonnie on the shoulder as I walked past his desk. He rose to his feet and followed me to my office.

"Close the door and sit down," I said. "I was just confronted by Finkle. The little creep is on me like a duck on a June bug. He's been talking to Tracy, and he was fishing. I didn't bite, and then he as good as warned me off again."

"That's not good, LT. What're you going to do about it? Maybe you should talk to Chief Johnston?"

"Oh yes," I said. "That would look really good. No, I can't do that. I can't go crying to him every time I hit a bump. I have to handle it myself. Right now, though, I want to talk to Tina Gonzalez. You ready to go?"

He nodded. "Yeah, but can I finish off what I was doing? It will only take a minute."

"Yes, and if I see that game on your screen again... Just get rid of it, all right?"

I didn't tell him about my dreams. I figured I was being paranoid, so I shrugged off my feelings of impending doom, gathered up my gear. Ten minutes later, we were out of the building and heading east on Amnicola in an unmarked cruiser; Lonnie was at the wheel.

As he drove, I filled him in on the intel Tim had shared last night.

Tina Gonzalez lived in one of those apartments off Shallowford Road, just a few blocks from Highway 153.

As per my usual modus, I didn't call ahead. I didn't want to warn her and, knowing that she was a working girl, I was pretty sure she would be home when we arrived at a few minutes to nine that morning, and I was right. She was, in fact, still in bed.

"Oh shit!" she said when she came to the door. "Cops, right?"

"Tina Gonzalez?"

"Yeah. What do ya want?"

"I'm Lieutenant Catherine Ga—"

She shook her head and sighed in exaggerated frustration.

"I know who you are, Detective," she interrupted me, "and I have nothing to say to you. Now piss off and let me go back to bed."

She started to close the door. I took a step forward. She glared at me. "You're not going to leave, are you?"

"Not until you answer my questions."

"Well, I guess you'd better come in, then."

She opened the door wide, stood back, wrapped her robe more tightly around her, and then turned and walked off into the apartment. We followed her into her kitchen.

Even though she was pushing forty, she really was a striking woman: tall, almost as tall as me, nice figure, bright red hair and lips that must need a lot of maintenance.

She hit the button on the coffee maker and said, "You want coffee? No? Well, I do. Sit down, will you?"

She grabbed the mug of coffee and sat down at the kitchen table opposite us.

"So talk to me," she said after taking a careful sip.

"You said you know who we are. How?" I asked.

"That's an easy one. You have 'cop' stamped all over you. And," she grinned at me over the rim of her mug, "you have a badge on your belt."

I knew that wasn't it. She'd been warned we were coming, and she knew that I knew it, but she didn't seem bothered.

"Nobody warned you that we were coming?"

She shook her head, staring at me defiantly.

She put the mug down on the table and said, "Lieutenant—what did you say your name was?"

"I didn't. You didn't give me a chance. It's Gazzara."

"Lieutenant Gazzara. If this is about my work, I'm not going to talk to you."

"It's not about you being an escort, well, not specifically, but I do have some questions. So, if you don't mind…"

She picked up her mug, frowned, but nodded.

"Do you, or have you ever, worked at the Starburst—"

"*Damn,*" she interrupted me. "What did I just tell you?"

"Calm down, Tina. I'm just establishing the parameters."

She pursed her lips, then nodded.

"So, the Starburst?"

"You know damn well that I do."

"How long have you worked there, Tina?"

She shrugged. "I dunno…sixteen, seventeen years, I suppose. I've never worked anywhere else."

"What do you do there?"

"I strip, for God's sake. You know that."

"Are you a prostitute? Do you work as an escort, Tina?"

"Go screw yourself, Lieutenant."

"I'll take that as a yes."

"Take it how the hell you want. I told you I wouldn't talk about my work."

"So you did... Okay, let's move on. Do you know a Jennifer Sullivan?"

She frowned, looked perplexed, then brightened a little and said, "Yeah, I knew her, but I haven't seen her in years. What's she done?"

Boy, is she good, or what?

"She's missing, that's what," Lonnie said, impatiently.

"Wow. I wondered what'd happened to her."

"When was the last time you saw her?" I asked.

"How the hell should I know? I told you, it was years ago."

I nodded, then looked at her and said, "Do you know Assistant Police Chief Henry Finkle?"

She was ready for it. She slammed the mug down on the table and said, "I'm not going to answer that."

"You don't have to, Tina. I already know that you do, and I know your history with the assistant chief."

She glared at me but kept her mouth shut tight.

"You claimed he assaulted you."

Her mouth tightened even further.

"Did you have an affair with him?"

Still no response; her face could have been made of stone.

"Okay, let me ask you this: do you know Detective John Tracy?"

"I'm not going to answer that either."

"I'll take that as a yes, too."

"And you can take that however the hell you want, too. I'm still not answering."

I looked her right in the eye and said, "Fine. I get it. So I'll ask you just one more question, and then you can go back to bed. Think very carefully before you answer." I paused, waited a second, then said, "To your knowledge, did Assistant Chief Finkle know Jennifer Lewis?"

And there it was, barely a blink, but it was enough. She knew.

"I have no idea, Lieutenant. As I recall, she only worked at the Starburst for a few weeks. I didn't know her, not well anyway. Just to say 'Hi' in passing, that's all. Now," she said as she stood up. "I'll show you out."

"There's no need," I said. "We can find our way to the front door. Thank you, Tina. You've been most helpful. I'll be sure to let Chief Finkle know just how helpful."

Her eyes narrowed, and the frown lines deepened. "Get the hell out."

"THAT WAS SHORT AND SWEET," LONNIE SAID AS HE slammed the car door. "I hope you got more out of it than I did."

"I got enough. In fact, I got more than enough." I started counting on my fingers. "One, she knew we were coming. Two, she'd been coached. Three, she as good as confirmed that Finkle knew Jennifer, and that's what I really wanted to know. Four, she sure as hell knows Tracy, too. Five, she also knew Jennifer, though how well, we'll probably never know."

"Geez. How do you do that?" He nodded, thoughtfully, then said, "So, where do we go from here?"

"Right now? Back to the office. I have some thinking to do... By the way, when did you say you're scheduled for the surgery?"

"Monday, June first, why?"

"Well, it's just that I was thinking that maybe I might travel to Wheeling...or Boston."

"That's not happenin', Kate." He turned his head and grinned at me. "Johnston's not going to turn that kind of money loose, not with what little we've got."

I sighed. He was right, of course.

Chapter Twenty-Five

❦

Tuesday/Wednesday, May 19 & 20 – On Call

Unfortunately, I didn't get to work much more on the Lewis case that day or, indeed, the next several days. Cold Case Squad not notwithstanding, I was still attached to the Major Crimes Unit and as such, still a member of the Homicide Division. As a result, I was expected to take my turn "on call." Lonnie too.

Oh, don't get the wrong idea, I didn't have an assigned caseload per se, but I *was* obliged to work the first forty-eight hours of any cases I caught while on call before I could hand them off. If you watch any TV at all, you'll know that after that, the case becomes more and more difficult. If you can't find a lead within the first forty-eight hours, the chances of solving the case decrease dramatically. The first forty-eight are when witnesses' memories are still fresh; when you have the opportunity to find clues and follow them from one to the next, and then the next. As time goes by, evidence gets contaminated, witnesses disappear, and surveillance video gets copied over.

Well, wouldn't you know it? We caught two homicides that day, one after the other: a gas station robbery gone bad, and a drug deal, also gone bad. Both were simple enough, but time-consuming all the same.

The first was a "shots fired" call that came in over the radio as we were driving back to the office. We were the closest unit, so we had to respond and were directed to a small white house in Highland Park. Thus, I became the first detective at the scene. That's a sure-fire way to end up with the investigation.

When we arrived, there were two blue and white cruisers already on site, and a dead, black male aged about nineteen lying on the kitchen floor in a pool of blood. He'd been shot several times. There were dollar bills—mostly small denominations—scattered all over the kitchen table and floor. Two large caliber handguns lay on the floor, and there was an open brick of marijuana on the table.

I recognized the boy as one I'd dealt with several times in the past. He was...well, he was a product of the environment, and seeing him lying there, I couldn't help but feel sorry for him. I already had a couple of ideas as to who might have shot him, and I was right. I arrested the young man early that same evening; he hadn't even bothered to change his pants, upon which the blood spatter was easy to see. When I pointed it out to him, he simply shrugged and held out his hands to receive the cuffs. I wish they were all that easy.

And later that same evening—well, it was actually early the following morning: one-twenty-three, to be precise—we were called out to a convenience store in the East Lake area. The owner decided he wasn't going to hand over the contents of his cash register and had died for it. Fortunately, he had good security cameras. Unfortunately, the robber knew about them and managed to keep his head down.

But most gas station robbers are usually pretty dumb, and this one was no exception: he made his getaway on a Suzuki motorcycle. He parked it behind the convenience store on a side road, where it was dark, but didn't notice the camera on the back of the building. No, he didn't turn his lights on, but he did hit the brakes and that lit up the license plate, providing the camera with a good image of the number.

No, it wasn't quite that easy. We tracked down the owner of the bike, who claimed it had been stolen, and that he had an alibi. It turned out that it was, stolen, and that his alibi was good. It took some time, but we questioned his friends and, eventually, we found one who fit the description: an eighteen-year-old with an attitude. He was, well, antsy during questioning, but he did give us his permission to search the house where he lived. I guess he didn't think we'd find the bike hidden in a ditch *behind* his house. He looked quite outraged when we charged him. They always do.

All of that took us through Wednesday. By the time we got through, it was almost seven o'clock, and I was exhausted. John Lewis would have to wait until morning.

Chapter Twenty-Six

✥✥✥

Thursday, May 21, Morning – Lewis Case

I wasn't surprised to get a call from Chief Johnston when I arrived at the office that Thursday morning. In fact, I'd been expecting it.

"Sit down, Lieutenant," he said as Cathy ushered me into his office. "You too," he said to her.

He assumed his usual position—leaned back in his chair, folded his arms, and stared at me across the desk.

"Just what do you think you're doing?" he asked me. "I haven't talked to Tracy yet, but I have spoken to Chief Finkle. He is..." He shook his head, seemingly lost for words. "He's furious. It was all I could do to dissuade him from filing a formal complaint against you. Kate, your interview with the assistant chief crossed the line. I warned you—"

"Yes, sir, you did," I interrupted him. "And I was mindful of that, but I had to push him. I had to know if either one of them, or both, was involved in some sort of cover-up."

He rocked his chair slowly back and forth, his chin down, looking at me through hooded eyes.

"And?" he asked, so quietly I could barely hear him.

I closed my eyes and shook my head. "I'm not sure."

For a long moment, he stared at me across the desk, then said, "I hate to hear that, Catherine. It presents me with something of a problem, as I'm sure you must realize. Assistant Chief Finkle is insisting that I put a stop to what- ever it is you're doing and, unless you can provide me with a good reason why I shouldn't, I'm inclined to acquiesce."

"Chief, you really need to let me run with this."

He leaned forward, placed his folded arms on the desktop, and waited.

"I talked to both of them," I said, "and I do think they're trying to cover something up, but what it is—I don't know, not for sure. Chief, I'm almost certain that Chief Finkle knew Jennifer Lewis, but how well, I don't know that either. I really don't think he had anything to do with her disap- pearance. I think it's something else. I think that he may have—that maybe he... Look, sir, Tracy told me that Lewis was a hooker. I don't know if she was or not. If she was, and if the assistant chief... Oh shit, sir. You know what I'm getting at. It wouldn't look good if, it, got out." I shut up and waited.

Johnston leaned back, steepled his fingers, and stared at me over them. I glanced at Cathy; she was looking down at her hands.

Finally, he nodded, and said, "Very well, you may continue, but finish it, quickly, Lieutenant. That will be all, for now."

"Er...sir?"

"What?"

"I may need to go to Boston...and Wheeling."

"Don't push it, Catherine. Cathy will see you out."

"Wow, you've got nerve, I'll give you that," Cathy said after she'd closed the door behind us.

I grinned at her. "You noticed he didn't say no, right?"

She rolled her eyes. "Good luck with that!"

JOHN LEWIS HAD A SMALL REAL ESTATE BUSINESS located in a strip mall on Bonny Oaks Drive. It was just after ten o'clock that morning when Lonnie and I arrived there. A pretty young woman seated behind a desk in the front office greeted us with a smile.

"Good morning. Welcome to Lewis Realty. What can I do for you?"

I made the introductions and told her I would like a word with her boss. She frowned, hesitated for a moment, stood, asked us to please wait, and then she disappeared.

"Let me do the talking, okay?" I whispered to Lonnie.

He nodded.

She was gone only for a moment.

"He said he'll see you. I'll show you the way."

She led us through a door and along a long, narrow corridor with doors equally spaced on either side: small offices, I assumed.

She knocked once on the closed door at the end of the corridor and pushed it open. Lewis was seated behind a desk at the far side of a fairly spacious office; not huge, but bigger than mine.

"Please, come in," he said as he stood up behind the desk. "Lucy said you're with the police. Please sit down. What can I do for you?"

"I'm Lieutenant Gazzara," I said as we sat down. "This is Sergeant Guest. We'd like to talk to you about your wife."

"Jennifer? Have—have you found her?" He sounded concerned, even hopeful, but he also looked agitated.

That doesn't sound natural. Damned if he isn't faking it. I made a show of opening my iPad as I watched him in my peripheral vision.

"I was handed the case only a couple of days ago, Mr. Lewis," I said. "I'm just getting started, so no, not yet. I do have some questions, though, if you wouldn't mind."

"Of course. Anything."

I reached into my jacket pocket and took out my digital recorder.

"I'm going to record our conversation," I said, as I turned it on and set it down on the desk between us. "It's routine; just for the record. Do you have any objections?"

He looked at the little machine, frowned, but shook his head.

"Out loud, if you don't mind, Mr. Lewis."

"No, I have no objections, but what's this all about? I haven't—"

"One moment please, sir," I said, interrupting him. Then I spoke into the machine adding the date, time, and pertinent details. That done, I settled against the backrest.

"I'm sorry this is taking so long," I said as I picked up my iPad. "Just one more minute, and I'll be ready."

He didn't answer.

I swiped the iPad screen and brought up an old, faded photograph of him—and Sapphire? I studied him over the top of the device. The years had been kind to him. In the photo he was slim, thin-featured with what they used to call a "bowl" haircut. Still do, I suppose. Anyway, he looked like a geek, but thirty-odd years later, though he was now fifty-three—he still retained something of his youth. His hair had thinned a little and was receding. His face had filled out; he must have been at least thirty pounds heavier, but he looked fit and healthy. But there was something about his eyes. They were light gray; most unusual.

He moved slightly in his seat as if he was uncomfortable under my scrutiny, but he smiled at me, a set smile that had no humor in it, or his eyes.

"Yes," I said, lowering the iPad a little and repeating what I'd said so the recorder could pick it up. "It's about Jennifer and, no, we haven't found her, not yet."

"You think she's dead, don't you?"

"I don't know," I said. "Do you?"

He shook his head. "No...but it's possible, I suppose. I haven't heard from her in more than two years."

"*Two years?*" I said. "She was reported missing in May 2012. That's three years."

"Yes. I know. She called me. She wanted money."

"*What?*"

He shrugged, then said, "She called me," he tapped the keyboard of his computer "in February 2013. She was in some kind of trouble. I asked her what. She wouldn't tell me." He shrugged.

"You didn't send the money?"

"Hell no. She left me in a mess. I was glad to see her gone. If I'd have sent her money, she'd have asked for more. I wasn't gonna start that mess."

"Where was she?" Lonnie asked.

"I don't know."

"You didn't ask her?" Lonnie asked, skeptically.

"No."

"No? Weren't you at least a little bit curious?" I asked.

"No! I didn't give a damn."

"Your wife had been gone for more than a year—and you didn't give a damn?" Lonnie asked. "I don't believe you."

"Believe what the hell you like. I didn't care then, and I don't care now. Are we done, here? I have work to do."

I ignored the question and said, "When exactly did she call you?"

He glanced at the computer screen. "February 19, in the evening sometime."

"What time?"

"I didn't make a note of it."

"How about the number?"

"I didn't make a note of that either."

"No problem, I'll check your phone records. I'll need the phone number please."

He grabbed a pad of sticky notes, scribbled down the number and handed it to me. "Go ahead," he said smirking. "Knock yourselves out."

The son of a bitch. He planned it. He set it up. "And you never tried to call her back?"

"No."

"Why didn't you report that call to Missing Persons? They would have followed up on it."

He shrugged, looked away and said, "I don't know. It didn't seem important, at the time. I told you, she went away with some guy. I simply assumed..." He didn't finish his thought.

"What did you assume?"

"To be honest, I was worried that she might have left him and wanted to come home. *That,* I didn't want."

I nodded, thought for a minute, then said, "Was Jennifer your first wife, Mr. Lewis?"

He looked startled, hesitated, just for a split second, then said, "No. I was married before, briefly, in 1981. I was nineteen. Why d'you ask?"

"Mr. Lewis, you told Jennifer and her family that you were a bachelor, that you'd never been married before. Why did you do that?"

"That's not true. I told Jennifer I'd been married when I was a kid. I didn't tell anyone else. It was none of their business."

"So, you're telling me that Jennifer knew about your first wife and that she didn't tell anyone else?"

"If she did, she didn't tell me."

"You also told Alice Booker you came from Indiana, but that's not true. You're from Highton, in West Virginia. Why did you lie to her?"

"I didn't tell her that."

"You also told her you were from a dysfunctional family."

"So?"

"Well, are you?" I asked.

"Depends what you call dysfunctional."

"What do *you* call dysfunctional?"

"My parents died when I was three years old. I was brought up by my grandparents. I'd call that dysfunctional. Wouldn't you?"

"No. That's not at all unusual."

Again, he shrugged.

"Did they provide you and your brother with a good home?"

"My brother? I don't—" He paused, narrowed his eyes, hesitated, then said, "How d'you know about him?"

I dodged the question. "You told Alice Booker that you were an only child."

He shook his head. "That's not true either. Look, me and Alice Booker didn't get along, okay? She's an interfering bitch. She doesn't like me, and I don't like her. When Jennifer ran off, she accused me of every kind of abuse, mental and physical, you can think of. None of it was true."

"During your interview with Detective Tracy, you stated that Jennifer was having an affair, and that she had," I looked down at my iPad, "run away with the guy. What was his name?"

"I don't know."

"You were pretty angry when Jennifer told you that she was going to divorce you," Lonnie said. "Isn't that right, Mr. Lewis?"

"Yeah, I was *freakin'* angry. Wouldn't you be?"

He closed his eyes, shook his head, and muttered something I couldn't understand.

"What was that, Mr. Lewis?"

"Nothing. Look, this shit has got to stop. I've told you every-thing I know—"

I interrupted him, and said, "Did you know that Jennifer worked as a stripper, and possibly as a prostitute as well?"

He laughed. "You've got to be kidding me. That's crap. You're talking about those few weeks she spent working part-time at that club, the Starlight, or some such. She worked there as a waitress, that's all. Look, she met this guy there a couple of weeks before she ran away with him.

That's the end of it. Now, if we're done..." He was becoming annoyed.

"No, we're not done, Mr. Lewis. Did you ever visit the Starburst? That's the name of the club by the way."

"Occasionally."

"How often is occasionally?"

He adjusted in his seat. "I don't know—three, maybe four times?"

"Why?"

"Why what?"

"Don't be stupid, Mr. Lewis," I said. "It's a simple question. Why did you visit the Starburst?"

Oh, that pissed him off, as I intended.

"I'm *not* freaking stupid, Lieutenant. Yes, I have. I like to go out occasionally. Who doesn't? I visit several clubs, *occasionally*. I like a drink; I like women, and I'm single for God's sake."

"No, you're not. You're still married to Jennifer, at least you were last time I checked."

"Yeah, right!" He made a wry expression, rolled his eyes, and shook his head.

"Were you there because you knew Jennifer would be there?" I asked.

"No."

"But she was there, correct?"

His eyelids flickered. "Yes."

I nodded and changed the subject. "Do you associate with prostitutes, Mr. Lewis?" I asked.

"*What?* Hell no. What the hell has all this got to do with anything?" His face was flush with color, his voice rising.

Lonnie leaned forward, placed his elbows on his knees, clasped his hands together, and glared at him. Lewis got the point and seemed to calm down, some.

I flipped through several screens, found what I was looking for, then showed it to him.

"Do you know this man?" I asked.

He took the device from me and looked closely at the photograph of Henry Finkle.

"Yes, well, maybe. I think I've seen him around."

"At the Starburst?"

"Yes. Maybe. I don't know."

"More than once?"

"*I, don't, know!* Eh, a couple of times, I suppose."

"Who was he with?" Lonnie asked.

Again, his eyelids flickered as he glanced away to the left.

"Some girl. I didn't take any notice."

"Was it Jennifer?" Lonnie asked.

The eyelids flickered again. He shook his head, then said, "No."

"Were you stalking Jennifer, Mr. Lewis?" I asked.

"No! *Hell no!*"

"Then why were you at the Starburst, watching her?"

"I wasn't, damn it, watching her. I was—I wasn't watching her... Okay, I was. She was my wife, for God's sake. I saw her with a guy; yeah, I watched her. That's all. Wouldn't you?" That last question he directed at Lonnie.

Lonnie simply smiled at him.

I nodded, took the iPad back, flipped screens, and said, "How about him? Did you ever see him in the Starburst?"

He took a quick look at the photo of Detective Tracy, looked at me stupefied, then said, "Are you out of your freaking mind? That's Detective Tracy. He interviewed me three years ago. No, I've not seen him anywhere since. He's not even contacted me."

Oh hell, don't remind me.

"Your first wife's name was Sapphire, I believe."

He nodded but said nothing.

I looked him in the eye. "You know what bothers me, Mr. Lewis?"

Again, he didn't answer.

"Coincidence. That's what bothers me."

Again, I waited for him to answer, but he didn't. He simply stared at me, almost unblinking, so I continued.

"We know that Sapphire also worked at a strip club, in Wheeling. So, that means you have two wives both of whom worked in strip clubs. That's a bit of a coincidence, don't you think?"

No answer; no reaction.

"Sapphire has a brother, Ryan, but you knew that."

I watched his eyes: no reaction.

"Several days ago, one of my associates interviewed Ryan. Did you know he hasn't seen his sister since 1982?"

He sat rigid in his chair, hands clasped together on the desk in front of him.

"Would you like to know what else Ryan told my associate?"

"Quite frankly, my dear," he ground the famous quote out through his clenched teeth.

"No? Well, I'll tell you anyway. Ryan told my associate that he called you the day after Christmas 1982, two weeks after he last talked to Sapphire. He asked you if you knew where she was. Do you remember what you told him, Mr. Lewis?"

He didn't answer. He just sat with his hands clasped together on the desk in front of him and stared at me.

"You don't?" I asked. "Well, I'll remind you." I looked at my iPad—the image of John Tracy stared right back at me. I looked up at Lewis, and continued, "You said, and I quote, 'I don't know where she is. She's probably gone off with one of her boyfriends,' end quote."

I watched his eyes; I've seen warmer eyes on a dead fish.

"Sound familiar, Mr. Lewis? You see what I mean about coincidence?"

His lips were two thin white lines. The muscles in his jaw were tight, bulging.

"Where the hell are they, John? Where are Jennifer and Sapphire?"

His lips twitched slightly and then, suddenly, his mood changed, and the gray eyes seemed to be laughing at me.

"Well," he said, brightly, as he stood up and offered me his hand across the desk. "If that's all, Lieutenant. I really do have work to do. So, if you'll excuse me, I'll get on with it."

"Sit the hell down—"

I put a hand on Lonnie's arm, interrupting him.

"It's all right, Sergeant," I said, also rising to my feet.

I ignored Lewis' hand, picked up my recorder, turned it off, looked him in the eye, and said, "You're one cool, sick son of a bitch, Mr. Lewis. I know you killed them, and what's worse, you know I know. Don't you?"

He cocked his head to one side, smiled, then said, "I have no idea what you're talking about, Lieutenant. You really should be very, *very* careful though," he paused. The menace in his voice was palpable, chilling, and then, with an obvious lack of concern in his voice, he continued. "You should be very careful what you accuse people of, especially when you have no proof. It could...well, get you into serious trouble. Now, are we done?"

"Is that a threat, Mr. Lewis?" I asked.

He didn't answer, but the evil smile he gifted me with told me all I needed to know.

"Get us out of here, now," I snarled at Lonnie as I slammed the car door. Oh, I was pissed, and I wanted to get as far away from Lewis as I could get.

He reversed out onto Bonny Oaks, put the big car in drive and, with a whole lot more restraint than I would have been capable of, drove west toward Highway 153.

"That, LT," he said, as he exited the on-ramp and eased into the traffic, "was intense. Did you lose it in there, or did you really mean to accuse him?"

"No, I didn't lose it, but I wouldn't have done it... I wouldn't have done it but for the patronizing look he gave me. That smart-ass piece of shit was laughing at us, well me."

"You really think he done it?"

"You heard what I said about coincidences. This case—and the Sullivan case—is one great basketful of coincidences. Yes, I think he killed both of them. Maybe others too. He's one cold bastard. Did you notice he was about to deny that he had a brother, then thought better of it? Oh yes, he's smart—and careful. I already know there's not one damn incriminating syllable on the tape. John Lewis just became my prime suspect. We need to get back to the office. I want to run his phone records."

And we did, and sure enough, Lewis had received a call on February 19 at seven-nineteen PM that lasted for almost nine minutes. *Son of a bitch. How the hell did he pull that off?*

There was only one way I knew of to find out: I called Tim Clarke and asked him to run the number for me. Guess what? He couldn't.

"The call originated from a fake phone number," he said when he called me back. "I'm fairly certain it was obtained from an app, such as NoTrace."

"What are you talking about, Tim? You're telling me that the call was made from a burner phone?"

"No. I mean yes, but not really; better than that. Whoever made the call downloaded the number from an app. It's done all the time in dating circles. The app provides the user with a temporary phone number that essentially turns the phone—any phone—into a burner. Except that you don't have to burn it, throw it away, the phone I mean, when you're done. Instead, you simply delete the number from your phone, and it can't be traced back to you. It does, however, leave the number in the recipients call log and, of course, the phone company's records. Neat, huh?"

"Oh my God. Are you kidding me? Burners are out, apps are in?"

"Essentially, yes. You got it. Burner apps have been around for a couple of years, since early 2014."

"So where did the call come from?" I asked.

"We'll never know. It could have originated in Alaska or right here in Chattanooga."

"You're saying he could have placed that call himself?"

"Yup. All he needed was a second phone and the app. They could have been right next to each other... Okay, let me give you an example. Did you ever get a call from a local cell phone number, a number you didn't recognize, but you answered it anyway because you saw it was a local number, only to find it was a computerized sales call? That's how they did it. They used an app like the one I just described."

"Oh wow, what will they think of next. No, no, no; don't tell me. I don't have time to listen. I have to go. Thanks, Tim. I'll talk to you later. Tell Harry hello for me."

Damn, damn, damn, I thought, after I'd hung up. *Lewis is one sneaky son of a bitch. I need to talk to the brother, Michael Lewis, and not on the phone. I need to check flights to Wheeling. The big guy isn't going to like it, but what the hell?*

I was right, Johnston didn't like the idea of my flying to West Virginia, not one bit. But after he heard my pitch and listened to some of my interview with Lewis, and knowing the drive would take a couple of days and cost almost as much as the airfare, he grudgingly okayed it.

I didn't want Michael Lewis to know that I was coming because I didn't want him to call his brother. But I needed to be sure he would be home. I figured that the weekend would give me my best shot, so I decided to go the following Saturday morning. Even so, I still couldn't be absolutely sure. So what to do? I couldn't call him. Hell, I couldn't even hang-up call him—caller ID is a bitch, sometimes.

In the end, I decided I needed some local help, so I called the local sheriff, Ben Jacobson. It was a call I had to make anyway: I was going to be in his patch, so protocol dictated that I let him know. I did that, and then I asked the favor, which caused him to laugh. At first I was taken aback, a little, but it turned out that he wasn't laughing at me.

Highton is a small country town, one of those sleepy little places—much like Mayberry—where everybody knows everybody; the sheriff knew Michael Lewis. Now that was one coincidence I was happy about.

Anyway, it turned out that Lewis and a bunch of his friends ate breakfast every morning at the local diner; so did Sheriff Jacobson. He claimed that Lewis hadn't missed a Saturday morning in more than ten years. *Hah, with my luck, this one will be the first.*

Chapter Twenty-Seven

Friday, May 22, Morning – Lewis Case

I spent most of Friday morning going over my interview with John Lewis. The more I listened to it, the more convinced I became that he had done away with both of his wives. He'd been careful in what he said, but in my mind's eye, I remembered each one of the little giveaways that told me when he was lying: the facial tics, the flickering eyelids, slight dilation of his pupils, the sideways glances, the hesitations. He was good, though. I never would have seen them had I not been looking for them.

And then there were the coincidences. There were way too many of them, but the one that stood out above all the others, at least to me, was his story—stories—that both women had run off with lovers unknown never to be heard from again.

The frustrating thing about the case, though, was that I knew that somewhere out there were two bodies, and unless we could find either one of them, he was in the clear: no body, no murder, no evidence of foul play. They were just missing persons.

And the morning dragged on, interminably until I was jerked out of my reverie by the buzzing of my iPhone.

I looked at the screen, swiped it and said, "Hey, Tim. How are you?"

"I'm good, Kate, very good. So, I have a little more information for you, but you're not going to like it."

I sighed. That was all I needed, more bad news.

"Go ahead, Tim. Make my day."

"You asked me to find Amber Watts and Jeffery Tobin and run backgrounds on them."

"Yes, for the Lewis case. Watts is the friend and Tobin a supposed boyfriend."

"I did... Well, sort of... Tobin, yes, but—"

Oh, come on, Tim. I don't have the patience for this today.

"Yes, Tim," I said, hoping my frustration wasn't too obvious. If it was, he didn't seem to notice.

"Kate, I couldn't find any reference to Amber Watts after Saturday, May 5, 2012. That was the last time she used her debit card. And believe me, I looked. That's not all, though. The last call she made on her cell phone was also on May 5. Her bank account is still open and shows a balance of nineteen thousand, three hundred and fifty-one dollars and seventeen cents, but there's been no activity on the account since Friday, May 4, 2012, when she deposited seven hundred dollars, in cash. I found out where she lived. She doesn't live there...not now... Anyway, so I called her former landlord. It seems someone cleaned out her apartment and paid the remaining balance on the lease, also in cash, on Monday, May 7. The landlord can't remember if it was a woman or a man."

"Are you serious?" I asked, dumbfounded. Amber Watts had disappeared only a couple weeks after Jennifer Lewis.

"Oh yeah, very serious, and—"

"Hold on, Tim. I need to make a quick call."

I grabbed the desk phone and buzzed through to Missing Persons.

"Hey, Laura," I said. "I need a favor, a quickie, please. Okay, great. I need you to look up a missing person report on an Amber Watts. It would have been sometime in 2012, after May first. I gotta go. I have someone waiting on another line. You'll call me, right?"

She said she would, and I dropped the handset back in its cradle.

"Okay, Tim. I'm back. I was just checking with Missing Persons. Laura's going to call me back."

"There's no need for that. I already checked. She won't find anything."

"Oh shit, Tim. You hacked the computers again? Please stop doing that. If you get caught—"

"Oh yeah, as if—"

"Okay, okay," I interrupted him. "Amber Watts; there's more, right?"

"There is. She has no relatives, at least none that I could find, not without going very deep. She's a product of the foster care system. She aged out of the system sixteen years ago. I also called her last foster parent, a Mrs. Judy Brownlee. She hasn't heard from Amber since she moved out... Kate, you're gonna love this: Amber Watts worked at the Starburst."

"No frickin' way!" I swear I heard him laugh.

"I assure you she did, but she hasn't been seen there either. Her last day was Thursday, May 3. She was supposed to work Friday, but she never showed. That's it, Kate. That's all I have, on her anyway."

The desk phone buzzed.

"Hold on, Tim."

I picked up the handset. "Gazzara. Hey, Laura... There isn't? Well, okay. Thanks for looking... No, not right now. I'll talk to you later. Thanks again."

"That, Tim," I said, "was Missing Persons. You're right. She has not been reported missing, ever."

"That's what I told you. Now, Jeffery Tobin. Nothing bad; nothing good. He's a sales manager at one of the nicer used car dealers. He's thirty-six, has fair credit—his score is 710—divorced twice, no outstanding warrants. Lives in Hixson with his girlfriend, Tonya Wix. He's clean. Do you want his number?"

I made a note of the number, told him thank you and goodbye, and then I hung up.

I spent the next half-hour lost in thought. The Amber Watts thing had thrown me. I now had three missing women. And I was certain all three were tied together and that John Lewis was the one who'd tied the knot, maybe literally.

I badly wanted to talk to him again, but the more I thought about it, the more convinced I became that I needed to wait. The extra knowledge gave me a certain advantage, and the Lord knew I needed all of that I could get.

Finally, I buzzed Lonnie and had him join me, and then spent another half-hour filling him in on what I'd learned and discussing the ramifications of the new information.

I say half an hour, but the arrival of Assistant Chief Henry Finkle cut it short.

As usual, he burst into my office without knocking, but then why would he? To my certain knowledge, the only door on which he ever did bother to knock was the chief's.

"Good Morning, Chief," I said, as he parked his butt in the chair next to Lonnie. "Is there something I can do for you?"

"It's Friday, Lieutenant. I haven't heard a word from you since our little talk on Monday. I was hoping you'd keep me updated. What's the status of the Sullivan case?"

Hah! That's not what you're after, and playing Mr. Nice doesn't impress me...at all.

"Chief," I said, weariness in my voice. "If I'd had any news you would have been the first to know. I turned Sullivan back in, you know that, but the chief asked me to keep at it for a while. D'you want to look at it?"

"That won't be necessary... What about the other thing, the Lewis case?"

Ah ha! Here we go.

"Lonnie," I said. "I need a private minute with the chief, please."

He grinned at me, caught the look on Finkle's face, wiped off the smile, and stood up.

"Look, Chief," I said after Lonnie had closed the door behind him. It was time to ingratiate myself a little. "I'm sorry about Monday, but it had to be done; you know that, right?"

He looked warily at me but made no response.

I sighed and shook my head. "Okay, this is what I have so far..." And there went another fifteen minutes as I brought him up to date on the case, leaving out only the parts that affected him and ending with what I just learned about Amber Watts.

"Now," I said, finally, "you know as much as I do. I'm going to try to talk to Tobin this afternoon and Michael Lewis tomorrow."

"So you think John Lewis is a serial killer, then?"

"I don't know, Chief, and if that gets leaked to the press, I never will know. So please, keep everything I've told you to yourself." I had no doubt that he would. It wouldn't have been in his best interests to do otherwise.

He stared thoughtfully at me. Strangely, there was no animosity in the look and, for a moment, I was tempted to think I was maybe dealing with a softer, kinder Henry Finkle. It was but a fleeting moment. I knew the man too well.

Finally, he nodded and said, "I understand."

You do? Wow!

"Good work, Lieutenant. Keep it up. Come see me on Monday and let me know how it goes in Wheeling."

Then he stood, smiled benignly, and left me sitting there with my mouth wide open.

I buzzed Lonnie.

"What was that about?" he asked.

"You really don't want to know. Let's go find Jeff Tobin."

We found him in his office at Skyler's Auto Brokers; brokers being an upscale definition of what was essentially a used car lot.

I was expecting a version of the caricature used car salesman; he wasn't. He was smartly dressed, clean-shaven, trim and obviously fit.

"Hey," he said brightly as he came around his desk. "You looking for a nice clean ride? If so—"

"No, Mr. Tobin," I said, interrupting his flow. "I'm Lieutenant Gazzara, Chattanooga Police, and this is Sergeant Guest. I need a word, please."

"Sure, sit down. What's this all about? I'm not in any trouble, am I?"

"I don't know," I said as we sat. "Are you?" I said it with a smile, but he looked uncomfortable.

"No. *No!* Of course not. How can I help you?"

"I want to talk to you about Jennifer Lewis," I said.

"Whew, you do? Wow. I haven't thought about her in years. Has she turned up, then?"

"You knew her when she worked at the Starburst?" I said.

"That's right. She was a nice kid."

Kid? She's about the same age as you. "You had an affair with her," I said.

"*Affair?* Not hardly. I had a bit of a fling with her. I went out with her a few times, but that's all there was to it. It wasn't an *affair*. Look, the Starburst; it's a strange place, but you know that, right? She was waiting tables there, maybe more. I don't know. She wasn't exactly the sort of—look, I wasn't sure if maybe she was an escort, or not. If she was, I didn't want..." He shook his head, frustrated, then continued. "Maybe she was, maybe she wasn't. She never asked me for money. We just went out a few times. That's all. I told that detective." And somehow, I believed him.

"We've been led to understand that she was having an affair with someone. You say it wasn't you. Do you know who it was?"

He was slowly shaking his head. "No. If she was seeing someone else, she kept it to herself."

"When did you last see her, Mr. Tobin?" I asked.

"Oh Lord, I don't know. I can't even remember what month it was. Just before she left, maybe a week, or so."

I changed the subject, flipped through several screens on my iPad, found the photo I was looking for, and said, "How about this woman? She worked at the Starburst at the same time as Jennifer Lewis." I turned the iPad and showed him the photo of Amber Watts.

He looked at the photo and shook his head. "No, I don't think so. She's lovely. I would have remembered."

I nodded, flipped through several more screens, then turned the device toward him again.

"How about him?" I asked as I showed him a photo of Henry Finkle.

He nodded. "Yes, in the Starburst, among other places. Who is he?"

I ignored the question, and asked, "When Jennifer Lewis worked there?"

He shrugged. "I suppose. He's often in there. Likes the ladies."

"He is? Oh. How often?" No, I didn't really care, but hell, I was curious.

"A couple of times a month, I suppose."

Sheesh, Henry. You need to be more careful. "Did you ever see him with Jennifer Lewis?"

He hesitated. "No, I don't think so, but he does look familiar. Who is he?"

Again, I ignored the question. My problem now was how to get out of there without arousing his curiosity any more than it already was. If he figured out who Finkle was...

"So, when you took Jennifer out, did you ever notice anything unusual? Were you ever followed? Anything at all?"

"You mean that creep of a husband?" he asked, leaning back in his chair and smiling. "Yeah. In fact, he threatened me. I'd just dropped her off at her apartment. I was about to get into my car when he crept up behind me and pushed my car door shut. The son of a bitch grabbed me by the shirt and said if I ever went near her again, he'd break my legs. And, by God, I believed him. That was the last time I saw her."

"Why didn't you mention that before?" I asked.

"I did. I told that other detective. I don't think he believed me."

Oh, John. That's something else you left out of your report.

I stared at Tobin. He held my gaze. I believed the man. I was ready to get out of there, but I asked him several more questions, mainly to make sure he'd forgotten about Finkle. Then I stood, thanked him, gave him my card, and we left.

"HE'S TELLING THE TRUTH," I SAID TO LONNIE AS HE drove out of the car lot. "John Tracy really screwed this one up. I'm not sure what to do about him."

"Yeah, I thought that too, that he was telling the truth. Hey, did you see that Beamer in the lot? I wonder what they're asking for it. I could see me in that sucker."

"That's it?" I asked. "That's all you're good for, a frickin' used BMW? I want to know what you're thinking about the case, damn it."

"Sorry, LT. You gotta admit, though: it's sweet."

"Damn," I whispered, shaking my head. "Lonnie, where the hell is your head? Did you listen to any of the conversation at all?"

"I did, and I agree with you: he's telling the truth. My question is, though: where does Finkle fit into all this? And what the hell were you two talking about this morning, by the way?"

I smiled, and said, "You're right, Lonnie. That Beamer is a sweet-looking ride."

"Right!" he said. "Okay, so don't tell me."

Chapter Twenty-Eight

Saturday, May 23, Morning – Lewis Case

When I landed at Wheeling that following Saturday morning, Ben Jacobson was waiting for me and, even before we'd had time to properly introduce ourselves, I knew he was my kind of sheriff.

He had a caustic sense of humor, an infectious laugh, a never-ending smile, and blue eyes that twinkled whenever he spoke, which was often, and not always appropriately. He was a fun kind of guy; even so, there was a serious side to him too, as I found out when I filled him in.

By the time I'd finished, the smile was gone, and he was shaking his head in disbelief.

"I was at high school with John Lewis," he said. "He's a crazy son of a bitch, and Sapphire was all it took to set him off. I remember her too. We were a year ahead of her. She loved to push his buttons, always flirting and fooling around."

"Fooling around?" I asked.

"Not what you think. She was a happy little thing, a flirt, as I said, liked to joke around a lot. But as far as I know, she never stepped out on John, although he always claimed she did."

He continued to fill me in as we drove to the Lewis family home, obviously enjoying reminiscing about the past. By the time we got there, I knew everything he knew, which was, in fact, not a whole lot.

He parked the cruiser in front of the house, and together we mounted the steps to the porch. I stood back while he thumbed the bell push.

"Hey, Mike," he said when the door opened.

I found myself looking at a mirror image of his brother, only younger, but older...if you get what I mean. He had a hollow look about his eyes, sported a beer belly, and his hair was almost white. *He's what, forty-five? What's that all about, I wonder?*

"Ben?" he said. "What? Who's that with you?"

Jacobson introduced me, and I flashed my badge.

"I need to ask you a few questions, Michael, if you don't mind."

"But, you're from Chattanooga. I've never been there. What d'you want with me?"

"I'd like to talk to you about your brother John."

"Oh. *Oh!* Well, I haven't seen him years... You'd—I guess you'd better come in then."

He stood aside, and we entered and followed him into the kitchen.

"Where's Amy?" Jacobson asked. "She not here?"

"No. She went to Wheeling, shopping. She'll be back this afternoon. Can I get you anything, coffee, water, anything? No? Well...okay. Sit, please."

Wow, the guy's nervous. "I need to tell you that I'm going to record this interview, Mr. Lewis," I said as I turned the tiny machine on.

"Why? What for? I don't know how I can help you. John left here more than thirty years ago. We haven't really stayed in touch." He looked at Jacobson, frowning. "Ben? D'you know what this is all about?"

"It's okay, Mike," Jacobson said. "The tape is mostly for your protection. Just answer the lieutenant's questions truthfully, okay?"

He nodded, and said "okay," but I could tell he wasn't happy about it. His face had lost all color.

We talked for several minutes about things long since passed. The man's memory wasn't too good, but maybe that was just a put-on. I tried to take him back through the months leading up to Sapphire's disappearance, but it was uphill going. I had to drag it out of him syllable by syllable. It wasn't until I asked him what had happened after the divorce that he began to open up, a little.

"I understand that after he divorced Sapphire, he moved back in with you and your grandparents, here, correct?"

He nodded. "Yes, ma'am."

"When would that have been, exactly?"

"Exactly? I don't know. As I told you, it was more than thirty years ago. November '82, maybe?"

"And you two got along okay?"

"Yeah, for the most part, I suppose."

"What does that mean?" I asked.

"Well, he kept to himself. Stayed in his room, mostly. Look, John and me...we never was what you'd call friends. Tell the truth, he was a miserable brother. I was glad when he left."

"When did he leave?"

"We knew he was planning on going, but he went kinda sudden-like, on a Sunday. January 16, I think. He just packed his things, loaded 'em into his truck, and drove. Didn't even tell us goodbye."

Hmm, that was a full week before he started work. Why the hurry? Where did he go, I wonder?

"You knew he was planning to leave? Did he say why?"

"Yeah. He'd gotten himself a good job in Louisville. He told me about it a week or so earlier, then he dropped it on me that Sunday afternoon that he was leaving that day. I was kinda shocked because I knew he wasn't supposed to start his new job for another week. Anyway, I told Grandpa. He was shocked too and said he wanted to talk to him. We found him in the garage packing his stuff. He was stuffing clothes into a big old wood box."

My heart started to race. "What kind of box?"

"A wood box. I helped him make it a few days earlier. He said he was going to use it to store some of Sapphire's clothes, in case she came back for them. He took it away with him when he left. We thought no more about it."

That doesn't make any sense.

"Mike," I said, "you said he made the box to store her clothes in case she came back for them, so why would he take them with him?"

He stuck out his bottom lip and frowned, obviously thinking about it.

"I dunno," he said. "I never thought about it."

"And you didn't see him again for what, four years?"

"Almost five."

"How so?"

"Well, one day, I got a call from Hank Tully—he's the guy who runs the Triple A storage units in town. He told me that John hadn't paid the rent on his unit in a couple of months and he couldn't get hold of him. I didn't even know he had a unit."

He shrugged, and then continued. "Anyway, I figured I better go pay the rent...for John, so I did. It wasn't much back then, just seven dollars a month. I gave Hank twenty-one dollars, that's three months' rent, includin' the past due, and then..." He hesitated, coughed, then said, "Then I called John and asked him to send me the money—"

There's something going on here. He can't look me in the eye.

"Just a minute, Michael," I interrupted him. "Did you enter the unit?"

He hesitated, then looked at me and said, "Yeah, I did. Tully had a spare key."

"And?"

"There was a lot of old stuff in there."

"What old stuff?"

Again, he hesitated, then said, "You know: furniture, an old bike, stuff we played with when we were kids...bags of old clothes. Paint cans. Tools, an old file cabinet. Several wooden boxes—"

"Wooden boxes? Was one of them the box you saw him putting Sapphire's clothes into in your grandparents' garage?"

He nodded.

"Did you open it?"

"I—no. No. I didn't?"

"I don't believe you, Michael. You were curious, right? You *had* to open it. What was in it?"

"I didn't open it, I tell you. That was the first thing John asked when I told him I'd paid the rent on the unit. Look, Lieutenant, you don't screw with John. He's—he's freakin' crazy. He scares the shit outa me. I watched him almost kill a guy one night, just for looking at Sapphire wrong, and they was already divorced then. He beat him half to death with a tire iron. If they hadn't stopped him...well, you don't mess with him, is all. Hell no. I didn't open the box."

"You told him you saw the box? Why would you do that? It was just one of a number of stored items. Why did you mention that particular one to him?"

"I didn't. He asked me. It was the first thing he said after I told him I'd paid the rent: 'Did you open any of the boxes?' I told him no."

"But you did, didn't you?"

"No!" He looked away, wouldn't look at me.

I glanced at Ben Jacobson. He was shaking his head.

"Okay," I said, "then what?"

"He came and got the box."

"*What?* When?"

"That same damned night. He drove straight over from Louisville; three hundred and fifty miles. It must've took him five or six hours. He was here just before ten. I helped him load the box into the back of his pickup. Then he drove away. He wasn't here but a few minutes. He told me to keep m'mouth shut or else."

"Okay, Michael," I said. "I need to know exactly when this happened."

He thought for a minute, shook his head, sucked air in through his teeth, then said, "Geez, it was so long ago. I know it was on a Monday in 1987 that Hank called me, but what month it was...I can't remember... Wait...wait a minute. I do remember. It was Labor Day. I know 'cause it was a holiday and I had the day off."

I looked at Jacobson. He shrugged.

"Labor Day, 1987," I said, more to myself than Lewis and Jacobson. "Okay. So, it would have been around ten o'clock that same night when he arrived here, yes?"

"Yes, the same night. He told me he was leaving right away and that I wasn't to touch anything."

"What about the other boxes? Did he take them too?"

He shook his head. "No. Just the one. We loaded it into the back of his truck, then he slammed down the storage unit door and asked me for the key. I gave it to him and he locked up. Then he left."

"What about the unit? Does he still have it?"

"No. A couple of months or so later, I got another call from Hank Tully. The rent was overdue, again. I told him, 'tough,' and I gave him John's number. He called back an hour later and told me the number was disconnected. He told me if I'd pay the past due rent, I could take the stuff out of the unit. If not, he was going to get rid of it. I told him to do just that, and I never heard from him again."

"When did you hear from John again, after he left that night?"

"I didn't. I called him a couple of days later, to see if he got home okay, but Hank was right. The phone was disconnected. That was it for me. It must have been a couple of years later that I heard from him again. Since then I've talked to him maybe a half-dozen times, basically just to say hello how are ya."

"When did you last hear from him?"

He looked quickly away, then said, quietly, almost in a whisper, "Four days ago."

No shit? Why am I not surprised?

"What did he want?"

"He said—he said I'd be hearing from the police."

"And?"

"And I was to keep my mouth shut about the box. If I didn't... He killed her, didn't he? Sapphire. He said he would, that night when he beat that guy. He called her a slut that didn't deserve to live... Lieutenant, John is family, but I haven't been able to sleep since he carted that damned box away. That's why I told you about it. I have nightmares about the frickin' thing. No, ma'am. I swear to God I didn't open it, but I sure as hell had a good idea what was in it. It was her, wasn't it?"

Now I believe you.

"I don't know, Michael. I surely don't know, but I'm going to find out. If he calls you, be careful what you tell him."

"Are you kiddin' me? He calls, I ain't even gonna talk to 'im."

"So WHAT THE HELL HAPPENED TO THE BOX?" Jacobson asked as he drove me to the airport. "And what was in it?"

"I don't know what happened to it, but I think we can guess what was in it...or should I say who?"

"You think John Lewis killed Sapphire?"

I stared straight ahead through the windshield, nodding. "Yes, and maybe others too. His second wife has been missing since April 2012, which is why I'm here."

"No kidding? You didn't tell me about that. Well, as I said, he was one crazy son of a bitch. Double murder though? Wow! Well, he wouldn't be the first."

We drove the rest of the way to the airport for the most part in silence. I had a lot on my mind and so, it seemed, did he.

"Listen, Kate... It's okay if I call you that, right?"

"Sure. Everyone does."

"Good. So if you ever need anything, anything at all...follow-up interviews, whatever. You only have to give me a call. I'll help if I can."

I thanked him, said goodbye, and passed quickly through security to my gate. I was back in Chattanooga and walking up the steps to my apartment by nine o'clock that evening, tired out and ready for bed, but, as I put the key in the lock, I suddenly had the darnedest feeling I was being watched.

Chapter Twenty-Nine

Sunday, May 24 – Lewis Case

The rest of the weekend passed quietly enough. On Sunday I had lunch with Harry and his father at the Club. That could have turned into an all-day thing, but I had my head full of what I'd learned in West Virginia about Sapphire Williams Lewis. And, of course, I was on call. So I spent Sunday afternoon and evening alone in my apartment with pencil, paper, iPad, and laptop computer.

Where the hell is that box, and what was in it?

I knew that without the answers to those two questions, my investigation of John Lewis was going nowhere. I considered calling Ryan Williams, Sapphire's brother, but then I figured it would be a waste of my time. Tim had already talked to him and he, Tim, was nothing if he wasn't thorough. No, I'd learn nothing Tim hadn't already learned.

I thought about my interview with Michael Lewis. I listened to the recording, two times, and one thing I became certain of; the mysterious wood box contained the remains of Sapphire Williams Lewis. I was also pretty sure that Lewis would have been in one hell of a hurry to dispose of the box. After all, he'd been in one hell of a hurry to retrieve it when he learned that his brother had found it. And, let's face it: if it contained Sapphire's body, he sure as hell wouldn't want to get caught with it. He would have wanted to get it as far away from Highton as possible, but he would also have been desperate to get it out of the truck ASAP. That being so, I figured I knew approximately when—probably after midnight, but while it was still dark, on the Tuesday after Labor Day, 1987.

Probably closer to midnight than dawn, I thought. *Say two to three hours after he left Highton. So that would have been early hours of the morning on September 8... But where? Somewhere say four hours tops... He wouldn't have taken the Interstate—too many cops; couldn't risk getting stopped. And he wouldn't have driven over the speed limit, for the same reason. So somewhere within a two-hundred-mile radius of Highton.*

I pulled up Google Maps on my laptop.

So, he'd be wanting to get back to Louisville as soon as he could, maybe... I would... So, West Virginia? No, I don't think so. He'd want to get it out of the state, but I can't rule it out. Ohio, then, and Kentucky... Maybe even western Pennsylvania. Indiana? Don't think so. Virginia? Nah! Couldn't hurt to include either one, or both... Six states? Wow, that's a lot of territory.

And so it went on. By the time I called it a night, my phone showed nearly eleven o'clock. I was bushed; the traveling and long hours were beginning to catch up with me. But I went to bed happy in the knowledge that I was getting close, and that I had a plan. Not much of a plan, but better than I had forty-eight hours earlier.

Chapter Thirty

Monday, May 25 thru June 1 – Lewis Case

This first thing I did when I arrived at the office the following morning was grab Lonnie and have him come to my office.

I filled him in on the events of the weekend and all that I'd learned from Michael Lewis. Then I had him send an email to every sheriff's office and police department in the six states, the gist of which was this:

I wanted to know if anyone had a record of finding a handmade, wooden box sometime after Labor Day 1987. If so, would they please contact me. Yeah, I know: it was one hell of a long shot, a twenty-five-year-old long shot, but it was all I had. That done, there was nothing left to do but wait. That's the worst part of what we do. It can take months before a multi-state query bears fruit. In the meantime, I had six more files I was working on and plenty more where they came from.

Five of the six were solved quite quickly. We ran DNA harvested from the victims through CODIS—the Combined DNA Index System—and were rewarded with three matches. Of the remaining three cases, we were not so lucky. Then, when we reran the latent fingerprints found at the crime scenes through the constantly updated AFIS—the Automated Fingerprint Identification System—we nailed two more bad guys. So, five down and one to go.

The last case was a bummer. It should have been a simple solve. The naked body of a woman aged about twenty-six had been found in a storm drain. She'd been raped and stabbed eleven times. We had the body, possibly the killer's DNA, and his fingerprints; we even had the murder weapon, a skinning knife. None of it was helpful because we were missing the single most vital clue to solving the case, any case: the identity of the corpse. Without that...well, we were screwed, as were the detectives more than a decade ago. The investigation had stalled then and gone cold and, even with the advances in technology...nothing we did could breathe new life into it.

I had no option but to send the file back where it came from. We called that place the morgue, the storage room in the basement where it would be revisited, officially once a year. Too bad, that because of the shortage of manpower, it might be another decade before it again saw daylight.

I wondered if Amber Watts was in a file down in the morgue. An unidentified body never claimed.

By June first when Lonnie was scheduled for surgery, I'd had no hits on the email search for the wooden box, and I was becoming decidedly discouraged. I was convinced I had a killer, but unlike the case I'd just consigned to the depths, I had no bodies. I needed a body: no body, no murder.

And that wasn't my only concern: I still had the Sullivan folder on my credenza. Like a sore tooth, the daily sight of it niggled away at me, until finally, I grabbed the thing and flung it into my desk drawer: out of sight, out of mind...not!

Chapter Thirty-One

❧❀❧

Monday, June 1, Late Morning – Sullivan Case

It was just after eleven-thirty on the morning of June first when my cell phone rang. I looked at the screen and was surprised when I saw the number. *Lonnie? What the hell? He can't be out of surgery already.*

"Hey Lonnie. I wasn't expecting to hear—"

"Kate, listen to me," he interrupted. "I had to call. Something's happened—" He sounded breathless.

"What do you mean, something happened?" I interrupted *him*. "What's wrong. Are you all right? Did something go wrong with your procedure?"

"No, no, no, nothing like that. It went fine. I'm in recovery. I would have called you earlier, but the nurses wouldn't let me have my phone. Listen, Kate, this is important."

And then he proceeded to tell me.

I listened to him without interrupting for what seemed like a very long time; it wasn't, but what he said stunned me.

"Wow!" I said when he'd finished. "I've got it. Lonnie, that's one hell of a stretch, and something I never would have thought of, but it's sure as hell worth a try. Well done. I'll get right on it... Hey, are you sure you're okay? Would you like for me to come and get you?"

He declined the offer, said he was okay. He was tired and feeling a little woozy, but he had a ride home and would call me later that evening. Then he hung up.

I sat back in my chair, put my hands together behind my neck, stared up at the ceiling, then closed my eyes and whispered a prayer.

I sat like that for several minutes, mulling over the crazy idea Lonnie had just described to me. The weirdest thing about it was that he was able to back it up with experience. My brain was in turmoil. Surely it couldn't be that simple, could it? What Lonnie had described was entirely viable; hell, I'd even seen it myself. I still couldn't believe we could get that lucky, but I hoped. Oh, how I hoped.

Finally, I opened my eyes, picked up the phone and punched Mike Willis' button.

"Hey, Mike. You got a minute?"

"Sure. What d'you need?"

"Mike, it's the Sullivan case. I need a favor."

"Okay, if I can."

"You remember I asked you to recheck the DNA on the two swabs and the syringe?"

"Of course, and I did. I told you, and it's in my report. It was Rhonda Sullivan's. Nothing's changed."

I took a deep breath, then said, "Right! Okay, this is what I want you to do..."

"No freakin' way," he said when I'd finished.

He sounded skeptical, and I wasn't surprised. I didn't believe it myself.

"How long, Mike?"

"Five days...six at the most."

"Great," I said. "Soon as you can."

And there I was again, playing the waiting game.

Chapter Thirty-Two

❦

Monday, June 8, AM – Sullivan Case

When Lonnie called me from the recovery room the morning he had his lap band fitted, he'd had something of an epiphany.

He'd been lying on his bed in pre-op waiting to be taken into surgery when the nurse came in to administer a sedative. As he watched, he noted that she removed the syringe cap with her teeth. Apparently, it didn't register immediately what she'd done. He was already getting the anesthesia and counting down from one hundred when he realized the significance of what he'd seen, but by then it was too late; he was already in la-la land.

It must have had one heck of an impact on him, though, because it was the first thing he remembered when he came to in recovery. He figured that whoever had injected the potassium chloride into Rhonda Sullivan might have done the same. I knew when he told me exactly what he was talking about. I'd seen it done myself, several times when I'd had blood work done. Most nurses will take off the syringe cap and lay it down, but some are in the habit of using one hand to steady the injection site and the other to hold the syringe: in which case, the only way to remove the cap is to use their teeth.

And that meant what? Well, if that's what had happened, there would be DNA on the cap. And in the Sullivan case, the DNA would belong to Pellman.

When Mike Willis called me on Monday morning a week later, I had no real hopes of hearing anything good. As I told Lonnie more than a week earlier, it was one hell of a stretch. Even so, sometimes you catch a break, right?

"Hey Mike," I said. "I need some good news, my friend."

"Well, I'm sorry, Kate," he said, and my heart sank.

"I have bad news and some not so bad news," he said.

"The DNA doesn't match, right?"

"Right. Well—no and yes—"

"What the hell's that supposed to mean?" I asked, interrupting him.

"It's not Pellman's saliva."

Shit, shit, shit!

"That's the bad news," he said. "But here's the thing: while it's not a match for Pellman himself, it does belong to a *close* member of his family. A female."

"You're kidding me?" I was stunned. "You're sure?"

"No doubt about it. It's impossible to pin it down to a single person, but when the DNA test came back negative for Pellman, they ran a mitochondrial test. They kind of reverse engineered it, traced it backward. The saliva belongs to a female member of Pellman's family. A sister, maybe?"

"But he doesn't have any sisters... Oh, my God. Mike. You, you, you frickin' angel. So what are the odds?"

"Better than one-in-thirty...million." I could almost see him smiling.

"Oh, my, God. Thanks, Mike. Thanks. I gotta go."

I hung up and pumped my fist. "*Yes!*"

I picked up the desk phone, punched in the number, and when he picked up, I said, "Lonnie, get your ass in here, *now*."

"No fricking way," he said after I'd given him the news. "You're frickin' kidding me?"

"The hell I am."

"But if the DNA is not Pellman's, it's...?"

"It's his mother's," I finished for him.

"Yeah...yeah...hell *yeah!* But how? Why? *How?*"

"The why is easy. He's an only child; his mother is besotted with him. Sullivan rejected him, and then she humiliated him. Overprotective mommy couldn't allow that to go unpunished. So she killed Sullivan. The how is going to be the problem. She also has an alibi—Pellman. Kind of ironic, isn't it?"

"Ya think?"

"Pellman always maintained that he was out of town during the time-of-death window, at his mother's home in Winchester, Tennessee. That works for her too, unless..." I thought for a minute, shook my head, exasperated.

"I wonder how many female relatives she has?" I said it out loud, but I was really talking to myself. "We need to know."

I grabbed my cell phone and called Tim Clarke.

"Hey, Tim. It's Kate. You got a minute?"

"Sure, Kate. What's up?" Tim asked.

"You ran a full background check on Elizabeth Pellman, right?" I held my breath.

"No. You didn't ask for one."

Shit! "I'm sorry, Tim. I should have. This is time sensitive. How long will it take you to run one?"

"Not long... Well, I say not long, but it depends on how deep you want me to dig. If all you want is—"

"The works, Tim. I need to know all her family secrets, job history, social media—everything. I want to know what makes the woman tick."

"Wow! Okay, I'll get right on it. I'll call you later today."

"Tim, wait—" But I was too late. He was gone. *Damn it, Tim. I don't know how Harry puts up with you. Ugh, maybe I'd better call him too.* My stomach knotted. *Maybe later.*

It was a couple of hours later when Tim called back. Harry should pay him more.

"You ready?" he asked.

I said I was, and he began to reel off Mother Pellman's background information. There wasn't a whole lot that interested me about her childhood, but then it got interesting.

"She spent the early, formative years of her life in the army; well, I guess they were formative. Anyway, she graduated high school in 1982, went to community college for two years, and then enlisted in the army. She was honorably discharged in July 1988 with the rank of E4, or specialist, after serving a term of four years." He paused, took a breath.

"She married Harvey Pellman a month later, and Chad was born seven months after that. The marriage lasted roughly nine years. She divorced Harvey in February 1997, citing abuse and infidelity—"

I interrupted him. "What does her work history after discharge look like?"

"Well, she was already pregnant, so she didn't go to work until January 1990, and then only part-time at Sears in the Hamilton Place Mall. After her divorce, she went full time but injured her back. She's been on disability ever since."

"So she doesn't work, then?"

"No, not according to her tax returns."

"Hmm. Do you know if she has any close female relatives?"

"Only one that I could find, her mother Mrs. Elsie Billing-ham. She's seventy-seven, lives in Florida, at The Villages. Why d'you want to know about her relatives? Is there some-thing I can do?"

"I don't know. Maybe I'd better explain."

I told him about the partial DNA match and its implica-tions. For once, he listened without interruption, almost.

"So," I said, finally, "what I need to know is—"

"It wasn't her mother," he interrupted me. "Couldn't have been. She's in an assisted living facility. I doubt she's able to travel."

Well, that rules that out, I guess. Damn! I still don't have what I need. What I need is a live sample of Elizabeth Pell-man's DNA. Even then... Oh hell, I don't know.

Then I had a thought.

"Tim, what did she do when she was in the army?"

"She was a 68W."

"Oh-kay, and what, exactly, is a 68W?"

"She was a healthcare specialist, a medic. These days she would be called a combat medic."

"Ah-hah!"

And there it was, the medical expertise to administer the drug and know about the technicalities of death: rigor mortis, lividity, and so on. I had another key to the puzzle.

"What?" Lonnie mouthed at me.

I held up a hand. "One minute, Lonnie."

"What?" Tim asked.

"I don't know, Tim. I need to think about what you just told me. Thank you so much for all this. Listen, tell Harry hello for me, and that I'll call him later. Tell him I said I owe him dinner." And I hung up and smiled broadly across the desk at Lonnie.

"She was a freaking army nurse, Lonnie, a medic."

He grinned and said, "No shit? That's fantastic. Now we have means and motive."

"We do, but opportunity is going to be tough. As I said, what worked for Chad also works for her."

"But the DNA? One in thirty million? Surely that's conclusive, right? What is it Harry always says? 'When you've eliminated the impossible, whoever's left is who done it,' right?"

I had to smile at that. "Not quite, Lonnie, but you have the right idea. And it wasn't Harry, it was Sherlock Holmes. The correct quote is 'When you have eliminated the impossible, whatever remains, however improbable, must be the truth.'"

"Whatever! We got her, right?"

I sighed. "That, Lonnie, depends on the DA. Maybe I should give Larry Spruce a call."

Hell, what can it hurt?

I picked up my iPhone, scanned through my contact list, and called him. Lonnie leaned back in his chair, frowning.

It rang once, then, "Mr. Spruce's office."

"This is Lieutenant Gazzara, Chattanooga PD. I'd like to have a quick word with him if I can."

"Hold please."

It wasn't but a minute when I heard a click and then, "Hey Kate. I haven't heard from you in a while. How the hell are you?"

"I'm good, Larry. How about yourself?"

"Me, I just keep on keepin' on, but you didn't call me to make small talk. What can I do for you, Kate?"

"I'd like my partner, Lonnie Guest, to hear this, so if it's okay with you, I'm going to put you on speaker."

"Sure. Go ahead."

I took a deep breath, and then I laid it all out for him finally asking the DNA question.

"So," I said, "is the partial match, on its own, and considering her alibi, enough for you to charge her with murder?"

"Hmm, good question. So, all you really have is some odds and ends of circumstantial evidence and a mitochondrial DNA match to one or more of your prime suspect's relatives—"

"No, not relatives," I interrupted him. "One relative; there *is* only one: his mother."

"Ye-es," he sounded like he was thinking. "Thirty million to one... Those are good odds, and juries are very tech savvy these days, thanks to the TV. I'd need to look at all of the evidence in context but, considering... Hmm. Yes, I think it could work, but I'd feel a whole lot more comfortable if you could get a confession."

"I'm thinking that's probably not going to happen," I said.

"You'll never know, Kate. Not unless you try. Now, I have to go. Let me know. If you decide to charge her, I'll back you, but you'd better get it right." And then he disconnected.

I stared for a moment at the phone, then up at Lonnie.

"You heard all that. What do you think?"

"I think you're right. She ain't gonna confess. D'you think we have enough to charge her, then? And if you do, what about him, the son?"

As it turned out, the answers to those questions didn't matter...not then.

Chapter Thirty-Three

Monday, June 8, Late Morning – Sullivan Case

"So," Lonnie said, "are we just going to question her, or are we going to arrest her?

"Question her, for sure, but I'm thinking we'll do better if we bring her in and interrogate her here. The problem is, Lonnie, we can't just go breezing into Franklin County and arrest her. We have no jurisdiction there."

"So what do we do? Not the TBI, surely?"

"No, not them. Not if I can help it."

I thought about it for a minute, then said, "I think what we'll do is arrest Chad."

He grinned at me and raised his eyebrows. "*Chad? Pellman?* There's nothing that would tickle me more, but what the hell?"

I didn't answer. I tilted my head a little to one side and grinned back at him.

He continued smiling, then said, "What? Let me think. Well, he is in our jurisdiction. Oh, I gotcha." Then he frowned and said, "I think. Ah, maybe not."

"Who loves Chad more than anything else in the world?" I asked. "Who loves him enough to kill for him?"

"Well, his mom." He stopped frowning. "But how does that help us get her?" He squinted at me quizzically.

"Come on, Lonnie, it's simple enough. We arrest Chad Pellman and give him his phone call. Who d'you think he'll call?"

"His attorney?"

I rolled my eyes. "No, he's a momma's boy. He'll call his mother."

"Okay, maybe, maybe not, but even if he does..." And then his eyebrows raised. "She hightails it in here? And we have her; she's in our jurisdiction. Nah, it can't be that easy, can it?"

"Why don't we give it a shot and see? You want to go get him? Take a couple of uniforms with you. Let me know when you get back."

He was right, it wasn't that easy. Lonnie called an hour later and informed me that Pellman wasn't at work—he had the day off—and he wasn't at home either. I told him to come on back.

"So what now?" he asked as he sat down. "Do we call him, find out where he is?"

"Can't. I don't want him to know we're after him. When will he be back at work?"

"Tomorrow."

"Shoot! The minute he walks in the door he'll know; someone will tell him."

"So what, then?"

I shook my head. "There's no telling where he is or when he'll be back. There's only one thing we can do: you'll have to go sit outside his apartment."

"Oh, hell. Are you serious?"

I made a face and nodded. "Yep! Off you go. Stay in touch."

And wouldn't you know it? Pellman didn't arrive home until fifteen after ten that evening.

"You want me to go ahead and haul his ass in, LT?" he asked when he called it in.

I was at home, still dressed, and could have gone back out again. But by the time we would have gotten him comfortably settled in an interrogation room, it would have been after eleven. And by the time Mrs. Pellman arrived, I was thinking well after midnight. So I hesitated.

I was standing by the window, gazing out across the wasteland toward East Brainerd Road about two hundred and fifty yards away to the north, thinking.

"No, I don't think so. It's late. Go home, Lonnie. Get some sleep. You can grab him first thing tomorrow morning."

"You got it. See you tomorrow."

He disconnected. I glanced at the screen, thinking, not really seeing it. Lost in thought, I raised the iPhone to my lips and nibbled the edge of the soft, neoprene case, staring out into the darkness... And then something off in the distance caught my eye. It wasn't much, just a tiny glitter of light that came and went as the seconds passed.

What the hell is that? Looks like... Shit. It's in the parking lot of the gift shop. Someone's freakin' watching someone... Me? And then I realized it wasn't the first time. *Oh my God, that could be a scope—a rifle. Take it easy, Kate. No sudden moves.*

I turned and moved away from the window, out of the line of sight. I thought about turning the light off but decided against it. Instead, I grabbed my Glock, racked one into the chamber, and headed out the door, making sure I couldn't be seen through the window.

I crept out through the front door and ran, keeping as low as I could, the few yards to where my car was parked. I hit the button on my key fob and... *Damn, damn, damn...* The lights flashed, and the interior light came on as the doors unlocked. *Why the hell didn't I think of that?*

And right then I knew it was a lost cause. No matter, I had to check it out. I drove up to the automatic gates and waited for them to open, cursing myself for my stupidity, and then I drove out and onto the access road. A minute later I swung the unmarked cruiser into the gift shop lot and hit the brakes.

There was nothing there. I got out of the car and walked the lot, my Glock in my hand at my side: nothing. I looked out toward East Brainerd Road: all was quiet. Even so, I had that God-awful tickling feeling that I wasn't alone.

Finally, I went back to my car and drove back to my apartment.

I turned off the lights and went to the window: nothing, just the street lights and the occasional headlights on Brainerd. *Maybe I was wrong. Must be getting paranoid.*

I made some hot cider in the coffee machine and went to bed.

Sleep...did not come easy that night.

Chapter Thirty-Four

Tuesday, June 9, Morning – The Precinct

Sleep did come, eventually, but it was a rocky night full of dreams and nightmares. As you might imagine, I rose early that Tuesday morning.

A long, hot shower washed away the night terrors, and when I arrived at the police department, I said nothing of the events of the night before. Lonnie already had Chad Pellman stewing in an interview room.

Lonnie and I stood side by side watching Pellman through the one-way glass. He was seated at the steel table, dressed in green scrubs, staring down at his hands. They were in his lap, and he was twisting the snakehead ring around and around on his finger. He looked nervous. *He's had a haircut since I last saw him.*

"Are we going to talk to him?" Lonnie asked, without taking his eyes off his prey.

"Of course, but we'll let him stew a little longer, say an hour."

Lonnie looked at me, smiling. "You know you can be a wicked bi—"

"Don't say it," I said, interrupting him. "Let's go get some coffee."

As it turned out, we kept him waiting way more than an hour, because while we were in my office going over our notes, I received a phone call.

"Gazzara," I said.

"You have a call from a Sheriff Gene Drake," the receptionist said. "You want me to put him through?"

"Gene Drake?" I asked.

"That's what he said."

I don't know any Gene Drake.

"Okay, put him through."

The phone clicked. "This is Lieutenant Gazzara. How can I help you, Sheriff?"

"Hello, Lieutenant. This is Gene Drake. I'm Sheriff of Bolton County, Ohio. I don't know if you can help me or not, maybe you can, maybe I can help you."

"O-kay."

"I received an email from you a couple of weeks ago... Yeah, I know. Sorry. I didn't recognize the sender, so I didn't open it right away. Lucky I didn't trash it. Anyway—"

By then I knew what he was calling about, and I was tingling with anticipation.

"Sheriff Drake," I said, interrupting him. "Hold on while I put you on speaker. I need for my partner to hear this. Okay, Sergeant Guest, say hello to Sheriff Gene Drake."

They greeted each other, and then Drake told us his story.

He told us that a state trooper had found a weird-looking wooden box on a county road. It contained, among other things, a dismembered, skeletonized body of a young woman. Drake, then a deputy, as one of only two county detectives had caught the case.

"So," he said, "when I opened your email and read that you were hunting a box, I remembered my box. So I checked the dates and all the other details, and I figured, hey, I think that's the one. So here we are."

"Hold on, Gene... It's all right for me to call you Gene? Okay, good. I need to pull up a map. Where exactly is Bolton County?"

I opened Google maps and found the tiny county some one hundred and sixty miles southwest of Highton, West Virginia, via State Route 7—a three-hour drive, maybe a little more. *Oh shit,* I thought, barely able to believe it. *This is it. This is freakin' it. If he left Highton at ten, as his brother said, that would put him at the dumpsite around one in the morning. Yes!*

"Okay, I got it," I said, barely able to contain my excitement. "You found the box. I need the exact date."

"It was Tuesday, September 8, 1987, the day after Labor Day."

"At what time, exactly?"

"Now that, I ain't sure, but in the morning, early-ish, say around ten."

"Were you able to determine exactly when the box was dumped?" I asked, my fingers crossed.

"It hadn't been there long. Old man Cackleton—he was the coroner back then. He's dead now, of course—well, he reckoned from the condition of the grass under the box that it hadn't been there but a few hours. Strange thing is though, the vic' had been dead for years: five, maybe six: strangled."

It's her. It has to be. Everything fits.

"Did you get her DNA?" Lonnie asked.

"In 1987? Are you kidding? Listen, I'd forgotten about her until I received your email. We, that is me, I worked the case for almost eighteen months before I gave up on it. We buried her bones in the churchyard... Well, not all of them. I kept the skull."

"*You what?*" I asked, stunned.

"I kept the skull. She had nice teeth; good dental work, and well, you know... I figured if ever anyone came looking for her, and we needed to do a dental comparison, we wouldn't have to dig her up. Like I said, she's in the churchyard, here in Raglan. The pastor was kind enough to donate the plot."

"O-kay. You kept the skull. What about the box, and the stuff she was wrapped in?"

"Yeah, we kept all that too. Hey, how'd you know about that, the clothes and the blanket?"

"It's a long story, Gene. Can we keep it for another day when I have more time?"

"Sure. Everything is in the basement. So, d'you think she's what you're looking for?"

"Could be. Gene, I need all that stuff, including the skull. Would you, could you..."

"Sure. I'll have it packed up and FedEx it to you. I'm gonna have to bill you the shipping charges, though. So, are you gonna tell me who she is?"

"Gene, I would, but the truth is, I don't know, not for sure, which is why I need it all. As soon as I know, you'll know. Is that okay?"

"Yup, but how about the rest of her. We buried her in a child-sized casket. You want me to dig her up and send that too?"

"No, not right now, but if it's who we think she is, we'll need it for the family."

"Sounds good. Glad I can help. You can expect the package next couple of days. Give me a call and let me know it arrived safely. Bye for now, and good luck, Lieutenant. You too, Sergeant."

He hung up. I tapped the button on the desk unit to end the call.

"So what d'you think of that?" I asked Lonnie.

"Sounds too damn good to be true, if you ask me."

"I agree," I said, "but we deserve a break, for Pete's sake. This could be it. It's gotta be it, Lonnie. Everything fits. It's her. It's Sapphire. I know it is."

He nodded. "Sure does sound like it. So what about Pellman?"

"Oh shit. I'd forgotten about him. Let's go."

Chapter Thirty-Five

Tuesday, June 9, 10 AM – Sullivan Case

"At frickin' last," he said when I walked into the interrogation room. "What the hell am I doing here? Why did you leave me here? It's been more than two frickin' hours."

"Hello, Chad," I said, amiably. Yes, I was feeling pre-tty good. "Can I get you some coffee?"

"Hell no. You can let me outa here, is what you can do. And when you do, I'm calling my frickin' attorney. I'm pissed off with you keeping on harassing me, and I'm not having any more of it."

"Let you go?" I said, smiling at him. "Oh, I don't think so."

I nodded at Lonnie. "Turn on the camera and recorder, please, Sergeant."

"So. Chad," I said, brightly, after I'd stated the time, place and all the usual details for the record. "I know, and you know, that you killed Rhonda Sullivan. So how about you tell me all about it?"

"Screw you," he snarled. "I didn't. I—I loved her I, frickin', didn't, kill, her. You can't prove I did."

"Oh, I don't know."

I smiled a big smile at him. He didn't like that. In fact, he looked decidedly disconcerted.

"Are you going to charge me? Because if you are, I need to call my attorney."

And right then, I knew I'd screwed up. *Damn, damn, damn it!*

My feeling of euphoria generated by the call from Gene Drake had caused me to forget the goal. I wanted him to call his mother, not his attorney. *Now what?*

I stared at him, no longer smiling, and he noticed and smiled right back at me. *He's confident; too damn confident. I need to smack him down.*

"No, Chad, that's not why you're here. I just have a few questions. Do you mind?"

He shrugged and rolled his eyes.

"Is that a yes?" I asked.

He sighed, loudly, then said, "Yes, go ahead. Ask your questions. It won't do you any good."

"You're going to stick with your alibi, that you were in Winchester, with your mother?"

"Of course, because it's true."

I nodded and said, "Okay, so let's say that what you say is true, that you were in Winchester that Sunday. What about your mother? Where was she when Rhonda was murdered?"

His mouth dropped open. His eyes widened in disbelief.

"What? What the fri—"

I interrupted him. "Now you can make your phone call; your *one* phone call." I stood up, picked up the phone from the nook in the wall and slammed it down in front of him.

"Let's give him a little privacy, Sergeant." I walked out of the room, followed by Lonnie.

I looked through the glass, and I had to smile. He was sitting at the table staring at the phone like it was a rattlesnake readying itself to strike. Now all we had to do was watch and wait. If he made the call, we'd know who to: it would be on speaker and recorded. Attorney or mother? I needed him to lure her into town. Either way, I'd have to let him go... *Eventually!* I smiled at the thought.

"What're you smiling about?" Lonnie asked.

"Myself, mostly. Is he going to make a call, or what?"

He must have sat there ten minutes before he made a move. When he did, he reached slowly, picked up the handset, and dialed. It rang three times before it was answered.

"Yes? Who is this?"

I slapped Lonnie on the shoulder and whispered, "*Yes!*"

"It's me, Mom. They arrested me."

"*What?* They arrested you? Who arrested you? Where are you?"

"I'm at the police department in Chattanooga. That bitch lieutenant sent some fat ass sergeant, and he grabbed me as I left for work. You have to come and get me, Mom."

"Did you call our attorney? Did you call Kelly Roberts?"

"No. I only get one call. I wanted to talk to you. I figured you'd call her."

"I will. I'll call her right now. You sit tight. Don't say a word until she gets there. I'm on my way. I'll be there as soon as I can. You say *nothing*. You understand?"

"Yeah, okay. Thanks. Listen, Mom, I think they know you—"

Holy shit. That, I wasn't expecting.

"*Shut up*, you—you stupid..." she spluttered, interrupting him. Then she got hold of herself and said, "Honey, just remember what I said: keep your mouth shut. Don't say another word unless Kelly tells you to. I'll be there soon, sweetie."

Click! She'd hung up the phone.

"Oh, my God," I grabbed Lonnie's arm. "Got her!" I was jubilant.

"Yeah, but I don't think we can use it. Her attorney will get that call thrown out."

"Doesn't matter. Larry Spruce can deal with that. The call's not enough on its own anyway. She'll just make something up to explain it away, but now we know; now we freakin' know. I'll hold him until his mother gets here, then we'll grab her."

Chapter Thirty-Six

Tuesday, June 9, 1 PM – Sullivan Case

Kelly Roberts, the Pellman's attorney, arrived first and insisted that we either charge her client or turn him loose. I told her that I would do neither. I was holding him for questioning and would begin doing so as soon as possible, and she was welcome to wait with him or by herself in a waiting room. She chose neither. Instead she kept on insisting that I had no right to hold him. It was a debatable point, and one I chose to ignore.

To say that she was annoyed would be something of an understatement; she was pissed. I couldn't get the woman to shut up. Eventually, I decided I'd had enough and walked out, leaving her with her client in the interrogation room.

By that time it was twelve-thirty in the afternoon, and I was famished, but I couldn't go to lunch. I had to wait for Elizabeth Pellman to arrive. I settled for a tall mug of paint stripper—PD coffee—and a Snickers bar from the machine.

I was in my office when I was notified that Elizabeth Pellman was in the lobby. I downed what was left of my coffee, grabbed my iPad and briefcase, and headed for the elevator. On my way through the incident room, I circled by Lonnie's cubicle, tapped him on the shoulder, and signaled for him to follow me.

On the ground floor, the elevator is located just beyond the lobby, reception area. As we stepped out into the corridor, I could see her through the glass door; she was pacing back and forth like an angry tiger in its cage at the zoo.

I smiled to myself, nudged Lonnie, then nodded to the receptionist to buzz the door. She did, and I pushed it open.

"Good afternoon, Mrs. Pellman," I said, brightly. "It's so nice to see you. You can come on through."

"Where the hell is he?" she asked as she stormed through the doorway. "Where's my boy? You had no right to arrest him."

"Calm down please, Mrs. Pellman," I said, soothingly. "I haven't arrested him. I just brought him in to answer a few questions. If you'll follow me, please."

She followed me, chattering all the way like an angry gibbon. Lonnie followed behind, grinning like an idiot.

"In here, Mrs. Pellman," I said, standing to one side to allow her to enter the vacant interrogation room.

She walked through the door, stopped, turned around and said, "Where the hell is he?"

"Please sit down, Mrs. Pellman," I said, backing out of the door. "I'll be just a minute." I closed the door behind me, clapped Lonnie on the back, smiled at him and said, "This should be fun. Let's go relocate Chad."

"Cool," he replied, grinning widely.

"Yeah, cool," I said, rolling my eyes. "Here's what I want you to do."

I opened the door to the room where Chad and his attorney were still seated together at the table and strode inside.

"Okay, Chad," I said, smiling brightly. "Let's go. Sergeant Guest will show you the way."

"But my mother should be here soon."

"Really," I said, frowning. "Well, you can't wait here. Please show him where he can wait, Sergeant."

They both stood, then walked out together into the corridor.

"Oh, just a moment, counselor. I'd like a word, if I may."

They both stopped.

"Just you, Ms. Roberts."

I waited until Lonnie and Chad had rounded the corner and were out of sight. Lonnie was taking him to a holding cell.

"Please step this way, Ms. Roberts," I said, opening the door to the room where we were holding Mrs. Pellman.

"Kelly," Mrs. Pellman said, rising to her feet. "What are you —where's Chad?"

"Oh," I said. "He's waiting for you. I need to ask you some questions, then you can see him. Please sit down, both of you."

"What questions?" Mrs. Pellman asked as they sat.

I ignored the question and made a show of opening my iPad and briefcase, and then I signaled through the glass for the camera to be turned on.

"Before we begin," I said. "I must inform you that everything that's said in this room will be recorded, audio and video. Do you understand, Mrs. Pellman?"

They both stared at me, like a couple of owls, across the steel table.

"*What* are you doing, Lieutenant?" Roberts asked. She sounded outraged.

"My job. Oh, there you are," I said as Lonnie entered the room. "Sit down Sergeant. You both know Sergeant Guest, so we'll dispense with introductions."

I stared across the desk at them for a couple of seconds, and then I began.

"Elizabeth Pellman, I'm arresting you for the murder of Rhonda Sullivan—"

"*What?*" she screamed and jumped to her feet. "What the hell are you doing? Kelly, say something."

"Please sit down," I said, quietly.

She did, slowly, and I started over. "Elizabeth Pellman, I'm arresting you for the murder of Rhonda Sullivan. You have the right to remain silent. Anything you say can and will be used against you in a court of law. You have the right to an attorney," I looked at Kelly Roberts. She stared back at me, her eyes narrowed. "If you cannot afford an attorney," I continued, "one will be appointed for you. Do you understand these rights, Mrs. Pellman?"

She slowly shook her head, then said, "You're frickin' crazy. Kelly, for God's sake, say something, do something."

I held up my hand and stopped Roberts before she could speak.

"I'll ask you again: Do you understand your rights as I have read them to you, or would you like me to read them again?"

"Screw you, you crazy bitch."

"I think you'd better answer her," Roberts said, quietly.

"Screw her."

I nodded. "In that case, there's nothing more to be said. Sergeant Guest, please take Mrs. Pellman away and lock her in a cell."

"*What?*" Mrs. Pellman screamed as Lonnie stood and walked around the table. "No. *No! Wait!* Okay, okay, I understand. Now stop."

I nodded to Lonnie. He came back around and sat down again.

"Now," I said. "Is this person sitting next to you—Ms. Kelly Roberts—your attorney, and do you wish for her to be present during this interview?"

She looked wildly around at Roberts, who nodded.

Pellman looked at me and nodded.

"Out loud, please."

"Yes, for God's sake, *yes*. But you can't charge me with murder. I didn't do it. You have no proof."

"Oh, but I do. I have everything I need: motive, opportunity, and means. And I *can* prove it."

"Don't say anything, Beth," Roberts said.

She didn't listen. "You can prove I murdered her? That's crazy. You're crazy. Why would I do that? How would I do that?"

"If you give me a minute, I'll tell you. Oh, and I should also tell you that I'll be charging your son as an accessory."

They both stared at me, seemingly not comprehending what I was saying.

"Mrs. Pellman, is it not correct that you spent four years in the United States Army?"

"Yes—"

"I told you not to answer any questions," Roberts interrupted her.

"Shut up, Kelly."

"And you received an honorable discharge with the rank of E4?"

"Yes."

"What, exactly, were your duties during the time you were in the army?"

"I was a medic."

"Yes, you were," I said, quietly.

I reached into my briefcase and took out a photograph of the contents of the grocery bag Detective Wells had found in the dumpster.

"Do you recognize these items?" I asked, knowing full well that she'd deny it.

"No," she said, staring me right in the eye.

"Do you know what the items are?"

She glanced down at the photo, then said, "Looks like two vials of something, a syringe, and some swabs."

I nodded. "That's right. The vials contain, no, they contained potassium chloride. As a medic, you'd know what that is, correct?"

"Yes. So what?"

"And this—you know what that is?"

"Yes, it's a syringe."

"Not that, Mrs. Pellman. This," I picked up the photo, held it up for both of them to see, and pointed to the syringe cap.

"Yes, it's the syr—" She stopped talking. Her face had drained of its color.

I nodded. "Of course you do. Do you remember how you removed it from the syringe?"

"I—I didn't," she stuttered, looked at Roberts, then said, "I'm not saying anything else."

"That's all right, Mrs. Pellman. I have everything I need, so let me tell you how it went down. Your son was in love with Rhonda Sullivan, and he told her he was. Unfortunately, she didn't love him, and she told him. And that would probably have been the end of it, but she told her friends. She also told them that Chad was a stupid idiot that reminded her of Dopey, the big-eared dwarf in Disney's Snow White. And guess what? One of her friends told Chad what she'd said, and it upset him, badly. It upset him so much that he told you too, which in turn upset you. You love your son very much, Mrs. Pellman. We know that, and we know that you're very protective of him. You hated her for what she'd done, which is why you decided to punish her. How am I doing so far?"

She didn't answer. She just stared at me, wide-eyed and white-faced.

"Not good, right? Because you didn't decide to punish her, did you? You decided to kill her, but how? That was the easy part, wasn't it? Being an ex-nurse—okay, a medic—you figured you'd inject her with potassium chloride. That way her death would look like a heart attack.

"You knew that Chad had access to the drug, so you had him steal some, which means, Mrs. Pellman, that *Chad knew what you did*. And he told you on the phone that we knew. We recorded that call. That makes him an accessory. I can charge you both with first-degree murder."

"You, can't, prove, any, of, that," she said.

I nodded, then said, "As I understand it, Mrs. Pellman, you have no living female relatives other than your mother, is that not correct?"

She nodded. "Ye-es. Why d'you want to know that?"

"Well, you see this?" I tapped the image of the syringe cap in the photo. She stared down at it, mesmerized. "When you removed it from the syringe, you used your teeth, remember?"

She looked up at me, shaking her head, but she didn't answer.

"So, here's the thing," I continued, softly. "We always figured it was Chad that injected the drug into Rhonda. But then we sent that cap away for DNA testing and, well, there was no match, at least not for Chad." I paused and looked her right in the eye.

"Do you know what mitochondrial DNA is, Mrs. Pellman?"

She stared back at me, uncomprehending. And then she got it.

"*You frickin' bitch,*" she said, jumping up and swinging her fist at me across the table.

She took me totally by surprise, Lonnie too. Her fist clipped the side of my jaw and knocked me sideways out of my chair, and then she was over the top of the table grabbing for me. Fortunately for me, Lonnie recovered before I did, and he grabbed her and threw her to the floor.

I struggled to my knees, my jaw hurting like nothing I'd felt before.

Slowly I rose to my feet, shaking my head. I put my hand to my jaw, feeling it already beginning to swell.

I stood upright, took a step back. By then, Lonnie had the cuffs on her and was dragging her toward the door.

"*Wait,*" I gasped. "Sit the hell back down. I'm not finished yet."

Lonnie had her by the arm, he swung her around and marched her back to her seat and sat her down.

"Damn it, Beth," I said, massaging my jaw. "What the hell did you do that for? By the way, glad to see your back is feeling better." My voice was heavy with sarcasm. And I couldn't resist rolling my eyes.

"Screw you, bitch."

"Okay," I said. "I get it. Now, where was I? Oh yes, mito-chondrial DNA. As I said, the DNA results came back no match for Chad, but when the lab got that result, they decided to go a step further: they decided to do an mtDNA scan. That one did deliver a match, not for Chad, but for a close female member of his family. The odds against a mistake are one in thirty million." I watched her; she didn't flinch. *Boy is she a cold one.*

"And that, Beth," I said, "means that either you or your mother removed that cap from the syringe and pumped the drug into Rhonda's arm. And I don't think it was your moth-er," I said, still trying to regain some of my composure.

"How did you do it, Beth?" I asked.

"Do not say a word," Roberts said, putting a hand on her arm.

Pellman calmed down, some, looked at me through slitted eyes, smiled, then said, "What about Chad? He had nothing to do with anything."

I shook my head. "He knew what you did and covered up for you. That makes him an accessory. He'll probably be charged with first-degree murder along with you."

"Screw that, Lieutenant. Chad goes free. That's it. If not, you'll not get another word out of me."

I thought about it for a minute. I doubted Larry Spruce would charge him with anything more than manslaughter, and I could have told her that, but I needed a full confession.

I stood up, and said, "I need to make a phone call. I'll be back in a minute." I left the room.

I returned a couple of minutes later, resumed my seat, and said, "I just talked to the district attorney. He's prepared to offer you a deal—confess, admit to what you did, and he won't bring charges for murder against Chad."

That wasn't exactly what Larry said. He said he'd reduce the charges against Chad to manslaughter, but what the hell. I needed to dig it out of her. But she was smarter than I gave her credit for.

"That's not good enough. He goes free, or you can go to hell."

I smiled, shook my head, then said, "The best the DA's office would go for was involuntary manslaughter: twelve months prison, suspended, and five years of supervised release. Yes, he'll go free, but he'll have to stay out of trouble."

She turned and looked at her attorney. Roberts nodded.

"You can guarantee that?" Roberts asked.

I shrugged. "That's what Assistant District Attorney Spruce said. You can call him."

"It's acceptable," she said. "Beth, be careful what you say. Lieutenant, I will stop her if I need to."

"Go ahead, Beth," I said.

She glared at me for a moment, then shrugged nonchalantly and said, "Frickin' bitch deserved all she got. I hope she went straight to hell."

Suddenly, the pain was gone. Adrenaline? Maybe, I don't know.

"It was so frickin' easy," she continued. "I knew Chad was treating her for potassium deficiency. She had no medical insurance, and couldn't afford to go to a doctor, so he'd been dosing her with a diluted solution of KCL, potassium chloride. She called him that night. 'Oh, Chad, I feel awful. I'm hurting really bad. Can you come over?'" She mimicked a little girl's voice.

"Chad, the stupid fool," she continued, "said he'd be right there. I told him not to go, but he insisted, so I said I'd go with him. He introduced me to her, told her I was a nurse. That impressed her, so I asked if she'd like me to administer the drug. Poor little bitch was in a lot of pain. Her legs were cramping like hell. She told me she would... I injected thirty milligrams of undiluted KCL into her arm." She shrugged, looked down at the photograph still on the table. "It stopped her heart. She was gone in seconds," she said more to herself than to us.

All three of us were stunned, even Kelly Roberts. I stared into Mrs. Pellman's cold, unblinking eyes and, I couldn't help myself; I shuddered. She smiled.

I shook off the feeling of utter repulsion and said, "And then you laid her out, hoping lividity would hide the injection site... You cold, wicked bitch."

"Yeah, I didn't think it would be found; should have known better. Eh, it is what it is. I got my revenge... We done now?"

We were, and I couldn't get out of there fast enough: my jaw was aching, and I was totally disgusted by what I'd heard. I needed coffee and some ibuprofen, fast.

"Have her make a written statement, Sergeant, then make her comfortable and come find me." *Make her comfortable. Sadly, we no longer use the electric chair.*

Chapter Thirty-Seven

Tuesday, June 9, 3 PM

The first thing I did when I got back to my office was call Chief Johnston and tell him the good news, that we had Rhonda Sullivan's killer.

Weirdly, so I thought, he didn't seem overly impressed by it, but then he rarely ever was impressed by much. His attitude being that it was our job to solve cases: it's what we were paid for. What he was interested in, though, was the Lewis case. *What's that about?*

"I'm making progress," I said. "You want me to come by your office, Chief, and bring you up to speed?"

"That won't be necessary, Lieutenant. Please tell me it's not going to take much longer."

"I think not, but you know how these things go. Right now, I'm waiting for FedEx to deliver a package from Bolton County, Ohio."

"A package?"

"Yes, sir. The sheriff has the remains of Lewis' first wife, Sapphire. He's sending...well, he's sending some artifacts—"

"I see," he interrupted me. "Let me know how it goes." And he hung up. *Damn! No, thank you, Kate, you did a great job. Not even a goodbye when he hung up. Maybe I should reconsider Harry's offer... Nah!*

I took my cell phone from my jacket pocket and tapped the speed dial.

"Hello, Kate," Harry said when he picked up. "How the heck are you?"

"I'm good. You?"

"Good. You sound tense. What's up?"

"Well, one, I owe you dinner...and two, I solved the Sullivan case."

"You *did?* Congratulations. Want to tell me about it?"

"Not now. I don't have time. Tomorrow night, though, over dinner?"

"Geez, Kate. You're going to make me wait. That's just plain mean."

I couldn't help but smile at that. He sounded like a spoiled little boy.

∾

I'M GOING TO SKIP OVER THE NEXT PART OF THE STORY. It's kind of personal and well... Oh, just use your imagination. Suffice it to say that the following night, Wednesday, Harry and I had a nice meal at St. John's and then we went to the club for a nightcap. By ten-thirty, I was done, tired and ready for bed; so was Harry, but not to sleep. Any other night—well, you get the idea.

Anyway, I decided not to stay at Harry's that night. He drove me back to his apartment where I'd left my car, and I kissed him goodnight and left; it was just after eleven.

The drive from Harry's apartment on Lakeshore Lane to my own apartment took about fifteen minutes. I remember little of the drive home. I was on automatic, my head full of the events of the past couple of days: one case closed and a second well on the way, I hoped.

I was almost home and about to turn into my apartment complex when I noticed the lights of another vehicle close behind me. Then they followed me down the drive to the gates. I stopped the car, punched in my number while the other vehicle waited behind me. *Must belong to another resident.*

The gates opened and, sure enough, the vehicle followed me through. I pulled into my parking space and turned off the engine, but I didn't get out, not right away.

I watched as the driver of the other car pulled into a space two stalls away and turned off their lights. I thought no more about it. I took a moment to gather my things from the passenger seat. Needless to say, I looked around before I turned my attention to my belongings. With my trusty leather bag in one hand and my keys in the other, I exited the car and walked the few yards to my front door. I was about to put my key into the door lock when something hard slammed into the back of my head. There was a blinding flash of white light, pain searing through my head, and then...nothing.

Chapter Thirty-Eight

Wednesday, June 10, Midnight

When I came to, it was dark, and I was lying spread-eagled on a bed, a bare mattress, my hands and feet fastened to the bedframe and...I was naked, and oh so cold. My mouth was dry. I tried to lick my lips. I couldn't. My mouth was taped shut. My head was aching. I could move it, but I couldn't see much. Just enough light emanated from the small, darkened windows high up in the wall to my right, for me to realize that I was in some sort of small basement room.

I hadn't been awake more than a couple of minutes when the door opened. The overhead light flickered and then came on, momentarily blinding me.

"Ah, you're awake. Good."

John Lewis!

He came to the side of the bed and looked down at me. He was holding what looked like a large fileting knife: the long, thin blade glinted under the fluorescent light.

"Nice tits."

I guess you'll believe me when I say I didn't take it as a compliment.

He leaned over me. *Oh shit, what—*

But all he did was rip the tape from my mouth.

"That better?" he asked.

I licked my lips, swallowed noisily, and nodded, and then screwed my eyes tight shut as the movement caused pain to sear through my brain.

"Thirsty?" he asked as he reached for a bottle of purified water on a small table set against the wall.

He put the bottle to my lips and I drank greedily, my eyes locked on his. They twinkled, full of mirth. *The son of a bitch is laughing at me.*

"What the hell have you done, John?" I asked, my voice cracking. "You won't get away with it. I'm a police officer. They'll know it's you. They'll hunt you down."

"Oh, come on, Kate. It's okay if I call you that, isn't it?"

"You're sick, John. You need help. Just let me go and—"

"Sick? *I'm sick?* Yeah, I'm frickin' sick. Sick of... You have no idea how much I hate women. They lead you on, all sweetness, big eyes and promises. And then they get their claws into you, and they suck, and they suck, and they suck...the frickin' life out of you."

He paused, stared at my breasts, licked his lips... *Oh hell. He's going to kill me.*

"Let me go, John... *Please?*"

"Hah, as if. You were about to spoil everything," he said, never for a moment taking his eyes off my breasts. "Everything I've worked for all these years. I couldn't have that, now could I? I have to stop you."

He pulled up a chair and sat down.

"This is not going to stop it, John," I said, quietly. "They'll have the box with Sapphire's remains tomorrow. When they do, they'll identify her, and they'll come for you."

"It won't matter," he said, gently trailing the tip of the knife down my chest between my breasts. "I'll be gone by then. There's a little place I have picked out...but that's enough of that," he said as he started to get up. *Oh shit. I have to keep him talking.*

"How did you know we were onto you, John?"

He looked down at me, then slowly lowered himself back onto the seat.

"Typical for a woman. You all think you're so damn smart, so clever. I was way ahead of you. You remember your visit to my brother, Mikey? I'm sure you do. Well, he played you like a fish on the hook. Right after you left him, he called me and filled me in on what you two had discussed... Yes, Kate. I know what he told you: that he wouldn't call me, or even talk to me. He always was a frickin' little liar. He tells me *everything*. He hates women almost as much as I do. You do realize he's whacko, right?"

And you're not? Damn!

"Loves to play mind games, he does. I'd told him to expect you. He was supposed to find out what you know, not spill his guts. He called me the minute you left him."

He paused, stood, walked around the bed, staring down at me, whistling almost soundlessly.

"Damn, Kate. You're a good-lookin' woman," he whispered, almost as if he was talking to himself.

"Sapphire," he said, thoughtfully, "was... She was white trailer trash, screwing anybody she could get her hands on. Then the little bitch decided she was going to divorce me. Well, what would you do?"

"What would I do? Are you serious, John?"

"Anyway," he continued, "I knew back in '87 that they'd found that box. It was on the news the next morning. It couldn't be helped, though. My brother, Mikey, found it in the lock-up unit, so I had to get rid of it." He paused, obviously experiencing some sort of flashback.

"See, Mikey knew she was inside it. Yeah, yeah, I know, he told you he didn't look. Hah, and you believed him. The little prick couldn't help himself. Anyway, after he found it, the box, he called me. Told me he'd found it, and that he knew what was in it. I had to go get it." He lapsed into silence once more, then continued.

"Kate, you have no idea what that drive from Highton with that box in the back of my truck was like that night. I was scared shitless I'd be discovered, all the damn way, till I could stand it no longer. I had to get rid of it. So, finally, I pulled over and dumped the thing among the trees at the side of the road. I had no idea where I was. Then I hauled ass outa there. Next day, it was on the news that they'd found it. They never did trace the damn thing back to me though... Not until you turned up."

By now he was standing at the foot of the bed, staring at me, at my crotch. *Oh shit, he's going to rape me before he kills me! I have to keep him talking.*

"What about Jennifer, John? Why did you kill her?"

He smiled. "That bitch..." He paused, stared down at me, his eyes unblinking. Maybe he was remembering.

"She was like all the rest," he said. "Loved only me one minute, putting it around to anyone and everyone the next. Typical woman."

"So you killed her!"

He shrugged but didn't answer.

"What about Amber? Did you kill her too?"

"Freakin' little busybody had her nose stuck in where it didn't belong. Got it chopped off, didn't she?"

"What did you do with the bodies, John?"

His eyes glittered in the low light. He laughed, then he said, "Gone, but not forgotten. Isn't that what they say, Kate?"

I stared up at him and shuddered. I knew what was coming next, but I was only half right.

"See the box over there, Kate?" He pointed with the tip of the knife. It was on a table, on the dark side of the room to my left.

"That will be your final resting place, but not before—"

He was interrupted by a loud crash as the door burst open and someone—I wasn't able to see who—stumbled headlong into the room.

Lewis was taken completely by surprise. He spun around, the knife high in the air, then BAM, BAM, BAM. He shuddered under the impact of the bullets, fell sideways, and landed on top of me, crushing the breath from my lungs.

I couldn't move; I couldn't breathe. Then someone was pulling Lewis off me. I looked up and saw a grinning face, one I knew well. One I never thought I'd be happy to see.

What the hell? Detective Tracy? How?

"Surprise!" my former partner said as he dropped the body. There was a dull thud as it landed on the concrete floor. "Hold on, Kate," he said, flipping open a pocket knife. "Backup's on the way. I'll cut you loose."

I felt first my right hand drop onto the mattress, then my right leg, and I immediately tried to roll onto my left side in a vain attempt to hide my naked body.

"Hey, hey, take it easy. I'm not looking at you. Here," he said as he cut the final cable tie, the one holding my left wrist, and handed me my clothes. "Get dressed, I'll wait." And he turned his back to me while I put them on, which in itself was an ordeal. I was aching all over, and my head... *Shit, I think that son of a bitch Lewis has cracked my skull.*

"What are you doing here?" I asked. "How the hell did you find me?"

"You're welcome, Kate," he said, grinning. "No need to thank me... Truth is, I've been following you for weeks, and him too, but not for as long. I chanced on him watching your apartment a couple of Saturdays ago. First chance I got, I slipped a GPS tracker under his rear fender. I've had one on your car too, since day one. Shit, that boy owns a lot of properties. Anyway, I was sitting in my car on East Brainerd. I already knew where you were, more or less. I'd followed you to Harry Starke's place—"

I interrupted him. "Wait a minute. Day one? You sneaky son of a bitch. You put a tracker on my car?"

"Ain'tcha glad I did? Hehehe, Kate. That piece o'shit might have gotten you preg—"

"Oh, for God's sake, John. Stop trying to screw with my head. Get on with it."

"Okay, so when you left Starke's place, I headed back toward your apartment. I parked on Brainerd and watched your blip, and you came right past me. I knew you were heading home, so I figured I'd go home too. I was heading back toward I-75 when for some reason—curiosity, I suppose—I flipped screens to see what Lewis was doing, and damned if his blip didn't pass right by me going the other way. It took me by surprise, and it didn't really register for a couple of minutes. Then I figured he was following you, so I turned around. But by the time I got there, he was gone. I parked, climbed the fence, and found these on your step." He handed me my keys. "The lights were out in your apartment, so I told myself, 'screw it,' and hammered on your door: nothing. So I ran back to my car and chased after him. That's it. End of story."

"The hell it is," I said, angrily. "If you knew where I was, what the hell took you so long? Where are we, anyway?"

"Ah, well, I didn't...know, where you were, well, not exactly where. I knew where his car was: here, on Dodson Ave, in the parking lot of an old church. I knew you had to be in here somewhere, but there's a hell of a lot of it, the complex, outbuildings, and such. And I had to wait for backup, and then I had to find you... It was frickin' dark, everywhere, Kate. All I had was this." He held up his iPhone. "I couldn't see a damn thing. And, well, when I did...find you, I listened at the door for a couple of minutes. Hey, how long d'you think it was, anyway? It couldn't have been much more'n thirty minutes, well, forty-five at most."

I looked at him, aghast. I thought it had been hours. Then I realized I couldn't have been unconscious many minutes.

"You son of a bitch. You listened at the door. Why would you do that? He could have killed me."

"Are you kiddin'? I heard what he said. I'm your witness. You have what you need to close the case. Look, he wasn't going to kill you, not right then, anyway." He grinned at me, I looked away. I knew just what he was thinking. But he insisted on telling me anyway.

"He wanted to play with you first, Kate. Then kill you. Can't say's I blame him either—wanting to play with you, that is—I mean... Oh shit. I'm sorry."

"Yeah," I said, disgusted with him. "I know what you mean, you sick... And anyway, why in God's name were you following me in the first place?"

"Ah," he grinned. "You have Big Brother Henry Finkle to thank for that."

He noted my astonishment, grinned, and said, "You didn't think for one minute that he was going to stand by and let you screw with his career, did you? He's had me watching you since you interviewed him three weeks ago."

That was a serious waste of department money, and Finkle probably could have been fired for it, but he'd gotten lucky, and I made no complaints. In fact, I was damn grateful.

Tracy helped me to my feet, and then out to his car. I leaned against the passenger side door, my arms resting on the car roof, and looked around. The place was alive with flashing blue and red lights; dozens of cops were standing around everywhere. I felt terrible: my head was aching, my wrists were sore, and my pride had taken a direct hit. I'd been beyond stupid to allow myself to get taken like that and, well, I knew what Tracy would be thinking every time he looked at me from now on.

I looked to the building where I'd been held captive. I knew exactly where I was. The old church, long time vacant, had once been beautiful. Now, I couldn't help but wonder why they hadn't torn it down.

"You do get yourself into some scrapes, don't you, Lieutenant," a voice from behind me said.

I turned and was confronted by Henry Finkle.

"Hello, Chief," I said. "Fancy seeing you here." The sarcasm was lost on him.

"Yes, Detective Tracy called me. It seems he solved your case for you."

I was absolutely stunned.

"The hell he did. He saved my life, but I solved the case."

"Yes, of course you did," he replied. His sarcasm wasn't lost on me.

I grabbed his arm and pulled him to one side.

"I think you and I need to talk, Chief. We need to clear up a few things, not the least of which is you having Tracy follow me around for the last three weeks."

"I like that idea, Kate. How about I take you out to dinner one evening next week?"

I stared at him, open-mouthed, and shook my head in repulsion at his temerity. The nerve after what I'd just been through.

"Not one chance in hell," I said. "Damn it, Henry. Will you never change?"

He smiled benignly up at me. "Not one chance in hell, Kate; not one chance in hell. Seriously though, Lieutenant, you look like hell. How are you feeling?"

"Oh, I feel wonderful. How the hell d'you think I feel? I feel like shit."

He nodded. "Yes, I'm sure you do." He looked around, then said, "I see the ambulance is waiting. I suggest you go get checked out. Lewis is dead, so Detective Tracy is on automatic suspension while the shooting is being investigated. Internal Affairs is handling that. I'm sure they'll want to talk to you too. There's no hurry, though. I'll run interference for you until you're feeling better...and after you and I have talked on Monday. So, when you've finished at the hospital, I suggest you take the rest of the week off to recuperate." And then the son of a bitch turned and walked away.

Damn you, Henry Finkle!

I checked the time: it was just after one in the morning. *An hour.* I thought. *Only an hour... Seems like a lifetime.*

Chapter Thirty-Nine

Thursday, June 11, Early AM

No matter what Finkle said, there was no way I was going to take that much time off. I did, however, take his advice and let the doctors check me over. Apart from a few bruises, a raging headache—no, my skull wasn't cracked—and my badly wounded pride, I was none the worse for my final encounter with John Lewis. But what galled me most was that I knew I had both John Tracy, and yes, Henry Finkle to thank for that. Had it not been for them...well, let's not go there.

When I was done with the doctors, I called Lonnie to come and get me; bless him, he was already there, in the ER waiting room.

Lonnie is a strange cat. I found him in the waiting area leaning on the information desk; he looked like I felt.

He turned, spotted me, walked quickly to me and, without saying a word, wrapped his arms around me, squeezed, and didn't let go.

"Oh shit, Kate," he whispered in my ear. "I'm so frickin' sorry. I should have been there. I should have known that crazy son of a bitch would do something. I should have been watching you."

"Hey, *hey*," I said, gently pushing him away. "You couldn't have known; I didn't."

His eyes were watering.

"Stop it, Lonnie," I said. "I'm fine, well, except for a screaming headache."

He grabbed my hands, hesitated, then said, "He didn't..."

"No, Lonnie, he didn't, thanks to Tracy's timely arrival. Hey, look. I don't want to talk about it, okay? You want to get some breakfast? I need something in my stomach to calm it down. And about two gallons of coffee. Oh, but wait, I should call Harry."

"I already did," Lonnie said. "I told him what went down, and that you're okay. He went ballistic. Wow, was he upset. I guess you'd better call him. He's waiting to hear from you... Yeah, breakfast would be good."

I nodded. "Okay, just give me a minute."

And I made the call. I should have known better. Harry was —as Lonnie had said—upset. Upset? The word didn't even come close to describing it.

"*Where the hell are you?*" he shouted. "What the hell happened? Are you all right? Freakin' hell, Kate—"

"*Hey!* Stop it. I'm fine. I'm just leaving the ER with Lonnie. We're going to get breakfast."

"Lonnie? The hell you are. Stay where you are, I'm on my way." And before I could answer, he hung up; I called him right back.

"*What?*"

"I told you, I'm fine. There's no need for you—" He hung up again.

I looked at Lonnie.

"It's okay," he said. "Go have breakfast with Harry. I'll see you later." Then he grabbed my arms, leaned in close, pecked me on the cheek, and left me standing there.

I was mad as hell. *Damn you, Harry Starke!*

So I sat down and waited, and the longer I waited, the more pissed off I became.

I was seated there, twiddling my fingers, for fifteen minutes before he finally arrived, and I was ready to tear him a new one. But when he walked through the door...well, it was good to see him. And then he made an ass of himself.

The first thing he did was walk up to me, grab my face in both hands and kiss me, hard. Then he took a step back and proceeded to give me all kinds of hell.

"I should kick your fickin' backside," he said.

"Hello to you too, Harry. I'm fine thanks. Can we get out of here? I need coffee, and my gut aches."

And we did. Without bothering to ask me, he took me to his condo and, with the mood he was in, I knew better than to argue. The ride to Lakeshore Lane was a nightmare: he drove too fast and didn't stop nagging me until he parked the car. Then he stopped talking; I mean he didn't say another word until we were seated together at his kitchen table, coffee in hand and toasted bagels on the table.

"So, are you going to tell me about it?" he asked, finally calm.

Harry has a temper, but it's like a firework: it blazes hot for a short while, then fizzles away to nothing.

I really didn't want to talk about it, but I knew he wouldn't quit nagging me until I did, so I told him. He listened without speaking until I was done. Then he stood, grabbed my cup and his own, and made refills.

"Do you have any idea how lucky you are?" he asked as he sat down again.

I stared at him over the rim of the cup, the steam from the hot coffee shimmering in front of my eyes.

"Yes, Harry. I do."

He stared at me, shook his head, exasperated, then said as he stared into his coffee, "Frickin' hell, Kate. You should be dead, *right, frickin', now!* How could you do it? How could you let yourself get into such a frickin' mess? We, none of us, not even Lonnie, had any idea."

"Damn it, Harry. D'you think I did, for God's sake? I didn't know he was freakin' psycho. If I had—"

"You frickin' should have known. You've been a police officer for how many years, thirteen? You should have seen the signs. They were all there, for God's sake... Two missing wives? And you knew for sure he killed his first wife. You also knew he cut her up and put her into storage. That's a psycho, Kate. Sheesh!"

"You're right, Harry. I should have, but I didn't. I'm not you. He, he seemed harmless."

Harry opened his mouth to speak, but I stopped him.

"Yeah, yeah, I know. They're all harmless, until... Oh, screw it. I don't want to talk about it anymore. And I don't want to sleep with you, either, and probably not for a long time to come. I'll use the spare room."

I stood, left him sitting at the table, went to the guestroom in the basement, slammed the door behind me, stood for a moment with my back against it, my eyes closed, then collapsed on the bed and burst into tears.

And suddenly, Harry was there, holding me, rocking me...

Chapter Forty

❧

Thursday thru Friday, June 11 & 12

I DON'T KNOW WHEN HARRY LEFT ME. I DO KNOW IT was very early in the morning, and that I slept right on through until three in the afternoon. When I finally awoke, Harry wasn't there, but he'd left a note on the kitchen table. There was a frittata in the refrigerator and a bottle of Cabernet in the cooler.

I ate half the frittata but drank two cups of black coffee instead of the wine. Then, after a long hot shower, I put on a jogging suit—yes, I still kept a change of clothes there— and went for a short walk, much shorter than I intended. My mind was too full of the events of the past several days for me to even remember the walk, let alone enjoy it... And then there was Harry. He sure as hell hadn't made my life any easier when he called last night, or Lonnie's for that matter. The more I thought about it, the more I knew I had to do something, but what?

The answer was, of course, obvious, so I went back to the condo and spent the next half-hour packing my things. I stuffed everything that belonged to me in one of Harry's suitcases, called Uber, and went home, feeling better about myself than I had in a very long time.

I didn't speak to Harry again for several days, not until after I'd finally put the Lewis case to bed. Oh, he called me, several times, but I let the calls go to voicemail. I knew I had to end my on again, off again relationship with him once and for all. But I needed time, time to get over the trauma of the last twenty-four hours, and almost getting killed…

Look, Harry and I always had a special, but different kind of friendship, and I knew he loved me in his own way, but that way wasn't good for me.

THE NEXT DAY I WENT BACK TO WORK. IT WAS FRIDAY, June 12. Yeah, I know, I'd been told not to go in to work until Monday, but the hell with that. John Lewis might be dead, but I still had to wrap things up. Writing up the case notes took all day. Between writing about my ordeal, what I'd learned from Lewis, and the seemingly endless parade of people stopping by to gawk at the Lieutenant who'd managed to get herself kidnapped, I was drained. And then, to top it all, Chief Johnston insisted I speak with a counselor, so there was that too.

LONNIE STOPPED BY TO CHECK ON ME OVER THE weekend. I was pleased to see him, of course, but then he insisted that I needed to get out of the house. I really didn't feel like it, but he wouldn't give up so, reluctantly, I agreed to let him take me out to dinner that Saturday evening. We went to Blue Orleans downtown and, much to my surprise, I enjoyed it; even more surprising, so did Lonnie. The Shrimp Etouffee was to die for. The conversation...was a little strained, at first.

Right out of the gate he asked, "How are you doing, really doing, Kate?"

"Look, Lonnie..."

"It's okay," he said, soothingly when I couldn't continue. "I know what you've been through. What the hell it must have been like... Well, I dunno, but it might help if you were to talk about it."

I shook my head, laid down my fork, looked at him, and said, "No! Look, I'm fine." I picked up my fork, took a bite of my meal, and tears sprang to my eyes. I swallowed and looked at Lonnie. "I'm not fine. I do want to talk. But I just want you to listen, Lonnie. This isn't a problem that needs solving, all right?"

He nodded, looked relieved, and said, "Sure. Okay."

By the end of the evening, I had talked about it, and it did help. Lonnie had listened without interrupting or blaming. That's what partners do. They help each other.

Sheriff Drake's package arrived the following Monday morning. Sapphire's skull had been carefully and lovingly wrapped. *What a nice person you are, Gene Drake.*

I unwrapped the skull and compared it to Sapphire's photograph. It didn't help. In fact, I was suddenly overwhelmed with...first sadness and then with an all-consuming rage.

I rewrapped it and handed everything over to Mike Willis for analysis.

Henry Finkle called me into his office as promised for our "talk." The man is slippery. There's no doubt in my mind that he was consorting with—well, I'll just call them "professionals." He certainly stepped way over the line when he had me followed, but he got away with it because it saved my life. He was all sweetness and light. He claimed that, knowing what a "reckless cop" I was, he only had me followed for my own protection. When I asked him what prompted it, he simply smiled and said, "That will be all, Lieutenant."

There was still work to do. We hadn't yet found the bodies of Jennifer Lewis or Amber Watts. It was then that, for one fleeting moment, I regretted that Tracy had killed John Lewis. Although Lewis had confessed to the murders, he hadn't given away the location of their remains. Now, maybe we'd never know what happened to them. Still, I had to try.

On Tuesday, Lonnie and I were in my office trying to make sense of what we'd learned about John Lewis and his past. My thinking was that maybe if we talked it through, we'd come up with a fresh approach.

"What about his brother?" Lonnie asked. "He's an accomplice, right?"

"Yes, but we'd never be able to prove it. I recorded my interview with him and never once did he say anything to indicate he had anything to do with anything. I only have John's word for that, and he's dead."

"Maybe we should interview him again, then?"

I made a wry face and shook my head. "We could, but I don't think it would do any good. He knew exactly what he was doing when he spun that yarn for me. John Lewis said he was crazy. I think he is, crazy-smart."

"So what, then?"

I leaned back in my chair and stared up at the ceiling. In my head, I retraced the timeline from 1982 until the present... And then I had an idea.

"He had a storage unit in Highton," I said. "D'you suppose he had one here too?"

He stared at me, then jumped to his feet and said, "I'm on it. I'll make some calls." I smiled as he all but ran from my office.

He returned less than an hour later, grinning from ear to ear.

"I got one," he said. "It's not in his name though. It's under his company name, Lewis Realty."

"Okay. We need a warrant."

"I already arranged that. We can pick it up in thirty minutes."

"Great," I said, grabbing my phone. "Let's go."

The storage facility was located off Bonny Oaks Drive, some five blocks from Lewis' office.

Lonnie cut the hasp of the padlock with a pair of bolt cutters and hauled up the overhead door.

The first look inside was disappointing. The little room was packed with four-drawer file cabinets, all locked, some dated and labeled, some not. It was in one of the unlabeled cabinets that we found what we were looking for. Well, not exactly. There were no bodies stored in the unit, which was both a disappointment and also something of a relief.

What we did find, in one of the cabinet drawers, was a briefcase. It contained some papers, a Ziploc bag of what looked like several bone fragments, and some photographs. The photos included a very old one of Sapphire and John together; two old photographs, both of unidentified young women; a fairly recent photo of Jennifer Lewis; one of Amber Watts; and finally, one of...me. *Shit, that's one hell of a club to be a member of.*

I had Lonnie hand the Ziploc bag of bone fragments off to Mike Willis for analysis and send the two photos of the unidentified women to every law enforcement community in the United States. John Lewis was a serial killer, that much we now knew for certain, but what he'd done with the bodies...I had a horrible feeling we'd never know.

MIKE WILLIS CALLED ON FRIDAY. WE HAD AN ID: THE skull did indeed belong to Sapphire Williams Lewis.

With deep sadness, I called Ryan Williams and told him we had the location of his sister's remains. He took it well, better than I thought he would, but then again, she'd been gone a very long time. He thanked me and said he'd have her returned to Highton where she could rest in peace with her mother and father. Oh, how I hate making those phone calls.

Unfortunately, it wouldn't be the last such call I would make regarding the Lewis case. My call to Alice Booker was, if anything, more depressing than the one I made to Ryan Williams. I told her that Lewis had admitted that he'd killed Jennifer. She didn't take it so well. I could hear her sobbing. I felt like shit... *Well, at least she can stop searching.*

The bone fragments we found in the briefcase? Yes, they were human; small pieces of skull. They were also quite old,

ranging from between at least ten years and as much as twenty, and they belonged to four different women; none of them Sapphire Lewis, Jennifer Lewis or Amber Watts.

WHAT DO I THINK HAPPENED TO THE SIX MISSING bodies? I think Lewis learned from his experience of 1987, that nothing stays hidden forever, at least not in storage lockers. I think that at one time or another, years ago, he probably did have four bodies in storage, maybe more. And after his earlier debacle ending in Bolton County, he decided to get rid of them. But like all serial killers, he just had to hang on to something to remind him of "the good times," so he kept the bone fragments.

Finding Sapphire and finally putting her to rest was bittersweet.

Solving the Sullivan case, thanks to Lonnie's innovation, was very sweet. If you're wondering why Chief Johnston was so interested in solving that one, I can tell you, because I asked him. Rhonda Sullivan was the daughter of Georgia state senator Laughton J. Sullivan, Johnston's roommate at the University of Georgia.

And so it was over, all but for one final detail: I had a promise to keep. I'd promised to cook dinner for Detective Steve Wells. I was excited to surprise him with the news about closing the Sullivan case, one that he'd opened so many years earlier. And so, a week after we had the Lewis and Sullivan cases wrapped up, I called him, but he didn't answer. *Strange.*

I called him again thirty minutes later, still no answer, so I called the complex's admin office and was informed that Wells had passed away two days earlier. His funeral was to be held the following day, Saturday. I was devastated. I should have called him sooner, but with all that had happened over the—oh hell, there was no excuse. I...forgot...and I'll never forgive myself. He died, and I'd cheated him out of closure on the Sullivan case.

I thought of all the cold cases still in the morgue. The unsolved crimes, the unidentified bodies... Those victims and their families deserved closure, too. And that, I *could* do something about. So I pulled myself together, sat up straighter in my chair, and grabbed the next case file off my credenza.

The End

Thank you for reading *Sapphire* Book 4 in the Lt. Kate Gazzara series. I hope you enjoyed it, if you did and would like to read more of the story you can read Book 5, *Victoria*. Just CLICK HERE. Or you can copy and paste this link: https://readerlinks.com/l/683797

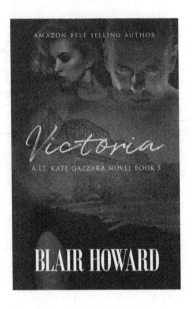

Acknowledgments

First, I'd like to thank my editor, Diane Shirk. Her suggestions were always thoughtful, insightful and helpful, and I am truly grateful. Thank you, Diane.

When an author needs help with forensics, he or she usually turns to the Internet for that help, but there's really nothing that can compare with the real thing. So, I'd like to offer a special thank you to Detective/CSI Laura Lane of the Bradley County TN Sheriff's Department. Many thanks for your help, Laura.

The people of Chattanooga: I love you folks. Thank you.

To all of my fans, and I can't believe how many there are of you, thank you for your loyalty and support. Without you, I couldn't do this.

Ron, Gene, David – you know who you are – thank you for your firearms expertise, and your friendship. I love you guys.

Finally, I'd like to thank my wonderful wife, Jo, for putting up with me and my obsession for almost forty years. I love you. You're the best.